THE BRIDE STONE

SALLY GARDNER

HEAD of ZEUS

An Apollo Book

First published in the United Kingdom in 2025 by Head of Zeus Ltd,
part of Bloomsbury Publishing Plc

9 7 5 3 1 2 4 6 8

A catalogue record for this book is available from the British Library.

ISBN (HB): 9781804541838
ISBN (XTPB): 9781804541845
ISBN (E): 9781804541814

Typeset by Siliconchips Services Ltd UK

Printed and bound in Great Britain by
CPI Group (UK) Ltd, Croydon, CR0 4YY

MIX
Paper | Supporting responsible forestry
FSC® C013604

Bloomsbury Publishing Plc
50 Bedford Square, London, WC1B 3DP, UK
Bloomsbury Publishing Ireland Limited,
29 Earlsfort Terrace, Dublin 2, D02 AY28, Ireland

HEAD OF ZEUS LTD
5–8 Hardwick Street
London, EC1R 4RG

To find out more about our authors and books
visit www.headofzeus.com
For product safety related questions contact productsafety@bloomsbury.com

To my wonderful sister Lucy,
who has patiently listened to me read this to her.
For her support and love.

The Return

February 1796

The sky at the break of dawn that day was a pale pink mingled with grey. Ice floated on the water, and the banks of the Thames were white. It was snowing, which gave the landscape a beauty that no other season could claim.

The brig, the *Mary Jane*, was full of émigrés, all of whom were grateful to put the brackish British Channel between themselves and France. Everyone on board had paid one guinea for a six-by-two-foot cubicle lined with straw – no light, just swaying shadows and the splash of waves, the neighing of the horses, the creaking of the ship's timbers, the dip and rise of the sea. Three days of hell in the darkness of the icy hold.

Only one passenger that bitter, frosty morning had the strength to brave the weather, emerging into the half-formed day as the *Mary Jane* nimbly manoeuvred her way up the Thames. The traveller, a good-looking young man, was unshaven, his curly dark hair long, his brown eyes tired. He appeared little bothered by the cold. He put his head back to taste the snow and wondered what awaited him in London. There had been no news from home since his imprisonment;

he wasn't sure if his family believed him dead or alive. At Rotterdam, while waiting for a passage to London, he had written to his father, his aunt, and his solicitor. By the time he had set sail, there had been no reply from any one of them.

At Limehouse Reach, the waters became congested with ships' masts. By mid-morning, London could be seen in the distance. Its bells rang out, seagulls shrieked above him, and he found himself laughing in the winter air, his breath frozen before him. The snow-covered city of spires was the most magical place he had ever seen.

'Is it what you imagined?' asked one of the crew. 'London, I mean?'

'Nothing is what one imagines,' said the traveller.

'Been away long?'

'Six years. I went away a young man with a head full of dreams; I return ancient with a head full of nightmares.'

The sailor laughed. 'You still look to be young,' he said.

'Looks can be deceiving,' said the traveller.

'What kept you away so long?'

'The Revolution. Prison.'

'Which prison?'

'La Force,' said the traveller.

'Bloody hell,' said the sailor, his interest piqued. 'And you survived?'

'I suppose I did.'

The brig docked at a wharf on Lower Thames Street, near the Tower of London. The passengers surfaced into the wintry day with smiles of relief and nervous excitement at what lay ahead. They disembarked and proceeded to the Customs House, a grand building with an imposing façade. The French Revolution meant there was no more ease in travel between the two nations. Suspicion of its neighbour's revolutionary zeal had made the British government fearful of spies and the Jacobean plots infiltrating England; the Aliens Act of 1793 had been brought in so that all émigrés would be accounted for.

The traveller waited in the large, noisy reception hall to have his passport checked. As he stood in line, he determined the first thing he would do once home would be to put to bed the argument he had had with his father before leaving London.

The Tall Hat

By the time the traveller emerged from the chaos of the Customs House, the day had taken hold. Despite the blanket of snow, he could hear the cacophony of the city. The wharf bustled with people and cargo; ships of all shapes and sizes were being made ready, rigging jangling, and coal-heavers were unloading the collier boats that brought the fuel to London. The February air was crisp, and the traveller thought, *This moment doesn't disappoint*. He hadn't imagined living long enough to hear the thunder of London again.

In among all the din, a boy was shouting the name of the traveller's father. Perhaps his lordship had come to meet him after all.

'Lord Harlington, Lord Harlington – is Lord Harlington here?'

He couldn't see who was shouting, neither could he see his father. But pushing his way through the crowd towards the traveller, red-faced and out of breath, was a young man in a tall hat. If he wasn't mistaken, it was the solicitor, Mr Gutteridge Jr.

'Mr Gutteridge,' called the traveller.

'Oh, Lord Harlington,' he said, stopping. 'Thank heaven, I have found you.'

The solicitor was saying his name, but the title he was using belonged to Duval's father. 'I didn't recognize you,' said Mr Gutteridge. 'It has been a while. I have a carriage waiting.'

'My father—' asked Duval, his voice steely.

'Did you not receive my letter?'

'No, sir.'

'Then… I'm sorry to tell you, Lord Harlington, but… your father has died.'

There were many things Duval had imagined occurring in the time he had been away, but his father's death was not one of them. He stood, not moving, and tried to catch his breath. *Dead – dead?*

'I am sorry. It is shocking news,' said Mr Gutteridge. 'And I will tell you all when we are in the carriage and out of this biting wind.'

But fear had been ignited in Duval. 'My aunt – Lady Harriet – is she still alive?'

'Yes, yes, Lady Haslet is in excellent health,' said Mr Gutteridge. 'And in high dudgeon over your father's will.'

Before Duval could ask any more questions, Mr Gutteridge turned on his heels and walked off determinedly towards Thames Street. There, a coachman was waiting, holding the carriage door open. Duval climbed in and sat down, stunned.

'St James's Square,' said Mr Gutteridge, tapping the roof of the carriage with his cane.

'Tell me, sir,' said Duval, 'when did my father die?'

'He died in his sleep, just two days and seven hours short of a year ago.' Mr Gutteridge paused, waiting for the new Lord Harlington to say something. Instead, he was met by Duval's silence. Mr Gutteridge hesitated, then continued. 'If you had arrived any later, my lord, I would have been obliged to inform you that you had been disinherited. I cannot tell you how relieved I am that you are back, but there are not as many hours as one would hope for.'

'I don't understand,' Duval said. 'Could you please explain what my father has done?'

The carriage set off with a jolt down Thames Street.

'I implore you, Gutteridge. Explain yourself.'

Mr Gutteridge cleared his throat. 'The argument you had with his late lordship, regarding your decision to study medicine in Paris, inclined him to instruct my father, Mr Gutteridge Sr., to alter his will. It now states that, unless you are married within a year to the day of his death, the estate in its entirety will go to your distant cousin, a gentleman by the name of Mr Ralph Carson.'

Duval paused for a few seconds, struggling to take in this new information. 'So, you are saying I am to lose everything if I am not wed in two days? This is insanity!'

'Two days, seven hours to be precise, my lord.' Mr Gutteridge paused. 'The alternative is that the will goes to probate. Thankfully, there is still time – albeit very little time – in which you can be married. I have done all in my power to make such a marriage possible, bar finding you a wife.'

Duval stared out of the window at the snow, which was falling heavily. In his mind's eye, he could imagine his father in the Sanctuary, planning the most lethal way to fire venom from beyond the grave at his only son.

The impossibility of the task ahead – marry, or lose everything he had been brought up to believe would one day be his – gradually began to dawn on him. In prison, the memory of Muchmore's tranquillity had kept him alive. He would imagine himself there and, for a while, escape the hell he was living through. For the estate had always been an oasis from the outside world; there was solace to be found in the beauty of the landscape, in the miles of rolling skies that led down to the sea, in the secrecy of the pond hidden in the woods with its island where, as a boy, he had fought the monstrous pirate. A place where Oberon and Titania might have lived. And though he had been hesitant to return to his neglectful, contrary father, he had found comfort in the thought that he would soon see his Aunt Harriet again. She had protected him against her tempestuous brother, had been his rock. If he had returned to hear of her death, that might well have been more than he could have borne.

On the ship he had told himself that, once he was home, he could recover quietly in the country, would stay there, at his father's estate, away from everyone, until he found his balance. (He recognized the irony in this plan – he who had once believed in the French Revolution, with its principles of liberty, equality, fraternity.)

Mr Gutteridge was now discussing the wedding arrangements, but Duval knew it was all pointless. Even if he had the inclination for it, there was not enough time.

'Gutteridge,' said Duval, 'the sum of it all is that without a suitable bride, I am stuck deep in river mud.'

The solicitor paused momentarily and gave a little cough. 'I suppose it depends on how you look at the problem.'

'I am looking at the problem, and it is insurmountable.'

'Please don't lose faith just yet, my lord… May I continue?'

'If you wish.'

'I have arranged a special licence for these exceptional circumstances. The Archbishop of Canterbury's office has agreed that there will be someone at Muchmore to make sure that your chosen bride—'

'Muchmore,' scoffed Duval incredulously. 'Muchmore!' He glanced out of the carriage window at the relentless snow. 'I might have stood a chance in London. But to travel to Suffolk in this weather is knuckleheaded.'

'The ceremony,' continued Mr Gutteridge, 'will be held in the private chapel at Muchmore House. It is imperative it takes place on Monday, the 22nd of February, before the final hour of seven o'clock, by your father's timepiece in the great hall. I will be there at the appointed time.'

'I never wanted to be married,' said Duval flatly, feeling the same ancient anger – that his father should have the conceit to try and control his life even from beyond the grave – rise within him. He remembered again their fearful row on the eve of his departure for Paris. Lord Harlington had told Duval exactly what he expected of his only son, which certainly did not equate to studying medicine in Paris. 'Your job is to find a bride from a rich, titled family. A bride with good, childbearing hips that will give the estate an heir or two. What you feel for her is of little consequence; it is her dowry that matters – and her inheritance.'

Duval, revolted by the notion, had responded, 'If that is all that is expected of me, then I have no intention of ever being married, and every intention to study in Paris.'

His father's last words to him had been bitter. 'You, sir, don't possess the brains or the intellect to be a physician.' These words, full of spite and fury, had stayed with Duval, and they came back to him now.

'Why wasn't I told of my father's will?' he asked Gutteridge.

'We received news shortly after his lordship's death that you were on the list of those who had been guillotined,' said Mr Gutteridge. 'It has been a time of much grieving. I informed the executrix, your aunt, Lady Harriet Haslet, that you were believed dead. She wanted to delay the reading of the will, but in light of your father's death and the tragic news of your, her nephew's, own demise, there was no other course of action.'

'Too many violins, Mr Gutteridge,' said Duval.

The solicitor straightened his back. He was uncertain what to make of the new Lord Harlington, but eager to keep his mind on the subject at hand. He continued, 'As long as you are married, the estate is yours. I should add, my lord, that all those who work at Muchmore have been praying that you are successful.'

The Viper – that was what Duval used to call his father. It had been the servants' nickname for their troublesome master. To Duval, the word had perfectly represented the coldness and distance between the two. The late Lord Harlington had always been thought eccentric; there was no doubt he was difficult, with an exaggerated sense of his self-importance and an arrogant demeanour.

Duval felt no grief at his father's death, just relief. Theirs had been a miserable relationship, with little affection, and his father had become more a figure of tempests and fogs as he aged.

Now Duval wondered what his mother would have said if she were still alive. He smiled to himself. When life became painful, he always thought of the mother he had never known, certain that she had taken a bit of his soul with her. She had died only hours after he was born, and it was her death that had sprained the Viper's brain. His grief had been so morbidly extreme that he exiled himself from London society. He bought land in Suffolk, built a house in the grand neoclassical design, and moved there. Named it Muchmore, because his life would have been much more had Lady Harlington lived. He left his numerous clubs and friends behind and became a hermit, occupying a wing he called the Sanctuary. His groceries, though, were still sent to him from Fortnum & Mason. Relishes and condiments couldn't be trusted outside London.

'How long until we arrive?' Duval asked, impatient as they came to a halt. The traffic was bad in Fleet Street and they had hardly moved for the past half-hour.

'Another hour, I reckon,' said the coachman.

'If I am going to undertake this challenge, I will be faster on my feet,' Duval said.

'Would you like me to accompany you, my lord?' said Mr Gutteridge.

'Thank you, sir, but no. I will see you at Muchmore – with or without a bride.'

Mr Gutteridge handed him a valise. 'This contains a copy of Lord Harlington's will, plus all the information I have gathered about Mr Carson, which I thought may be of use.

'There is one more thing to mention, a stipulation in the will that you must be aware of. You cannot marry anyone who has anything to do with the Muchmore Estate.'

Duval laughed. 'This is a farce that only my idiotic father could have thought up.'

'And finally,' said Mr Gutteridge, 'here are sufficient funds for—'

'Two days and seven hours?' said Duval, opening the carriage door. He set off towards St James's Square. This world of the ton, that fed off gossips and scandal, the who-will-marry-who and the meat market of it all, repulsed him. Had he really been in prison for all that time, in solitary confinement for nearly thirty days, to come out to this mess of a fantasy?

Wallpaper

Duval knocked on the front door of his father's grand London house, only then thinking he must be an unprepossessing sight: unshaven, long-haired and dirty.

The door was opened by a footman he didn't recognize.

'This is not the tradesman's entrance,' said the footman pompously.

'It never was the tradesman's entrance,' said Duval.

He tried to pass the footman, who was wearing the most ridiculous of wigs, but found his way barred.

'I am Lord Harlington,' Duval said. 'And I intend to enter my own house.'

The footman looked uncertain, but wisely decided to let him pass.

The house had been impeccably decorated by one of the most prominent interior designers of the day. The late Lord Harlington had, after all, been a connoisseur of beauty and art.

But the hall was in an uproar of ladders and planks, and a small army of workmen with paint pots and wallpaper. Duval was convinced his world was growing madder by the minute.

'Where's Granger, my late father's butler?' Duval asked the footman. 'He has been in charge of this house for as long as I can remember.'

'Mr Carson told him he was no longer wanted, my lord,' said the footman.

Duval stopped at this information. The man could have at least had the courtesy to wait. There was something so greedy and destructive in Carson's approach. It made Duval think of a dog marking its territory.

The unknown footman was slinking away when Duval said, 'Stop right there. You and anyone else attached to Mr Carson will leave my house immediately. I will not have it butchered. You will remove all of Mr Carson's belongings and he will wait the allotted time before moving in.'

Duval heard a voice from the landing. 'Oh, my lord, I'm so very glad to see you.' It was Jameson, his father's valet.

'Jameson! Jameson!' exclaimed Duval. 'The world hasn't gone completely mad after all! Thank God you're here. Now, I need a bath, clean clothes and a barber. And if you can find Granger, reinstate him.'

'Yes, my lord.'

Duval had intended to take a quick bath, but he fell asleep in the hot water. He felt he could sleep forever. He was roused by Jameson, who informed him that Mr Carson had ordered all the carriages and horses be taken to Muchmore House.

'The minute he heard you were on your way home,' added Jameson.

Duval felt an invisible gauntlet had been thrown down. 'Damn the man.'

The mention of Carson turned his mind once again to the matter of a bride. He wondered about Arabella Collins, if she was married. She had been his mistress before he left to study in Paris.

Jameson came to help him dress. 'That lady married about five years ago, my lord,' he said. 'And she has a daughter. I am sorry, my lord.'

'Who did she marry?'

'Mr Gosling, a banker.'

A thought came to him in the near-forgotten form of Jocasta Beale, the youngest daughter of a Suffolk neighbour who had fallen on hard times. Mr Beale's eldest daughter had married poorly, and the second had married into trade. That left Jocasta, a very young, pretty girl whom Duval had danced with at two assemblies before he left. Mrs Beale had hoped the dances would lead to something more; she had already had them married.

'No, not the Beale girl,' the Viper had said at the time. 'She's no more than fluff on the skirting board of society.'

He supposed his father's opinion was of little consequence now. She might still be available, and by now the right age.

A good barber can make you feel years younger. Duval's face tingled, clean-shaven, his thick hair, with its natural curl, elegantly cut.

'Powder, my lord?' asked the barber.

'No,' said Duval. 'Hair powder was in part responsible for the French Revolution.'

'Surely not,' said the barber, anxiously touching his wig.

Hair powder was made from flour, which had meant there wasn't enough left to make bread. But Duval wasn't going to tell the barber this – he was enjoying the look of confusion that rippled across the man's powdered features.

Duval almost recognized himself in the mirror now. His clothes, though, were definitely out of fashion. Neither did they fit him properly – he was too lean. There was nothing he could do about it, and the clock was not on his side.

Perhaps he should be sensible and find lodgings in London, instead of running around after impossibilities. This idea was attractive, and if he hadn't felt so enraged by the wallpaper and the sacking of the butler, he might have been able to think more clearly. He had never been able to tolerate injustice. It lit the fire in his blood and led him into all sorts of trouble – including, ultimately, prison.

Jameson helped him into his frock coat. 'We all pray you will be wed, my lord. For Mr Carson to inherit,' he added with passion, 'would be a tragedy.'

While the valet tied his cravat, Duval inquired if he had any information regarding the Beales, specifically the marital status of Miss Jocasta. Regretfully, Jameson did not.

On a good day, the journey to Suffolk would take seven to ten hours. If the weather was bad, it could take up to two days to travel from London to Longfield Manor, which was near the border with Norfolk, and where the Beales resided. That would leave hardly any time at all to negotiate a marriage settlement.

A pot of hot chocolate and a plate of biscuits were brought up and a decision was made.

'But it's a gamble,' said Duval. He had never thought of himself as a gambler. That way lay the kingdom of fools.

Duval took with him Jameson and William, the only groom who had refused to go to Muchmore without instructions from his master.

For a long time, there had been little or no comfort to Duval's days and nights; he'd travelled in farmers' carts or walked, and was used to sleeping where he could. The post-chaise surprised him – it was as comfortable as a vehicle that was in constant motion could be. Jameson had packed fur rugs, a basket of food, and wine-warm bricks for his master's feet. Duval had insisted Jameson travelled inside the carriage too.

Jameson had an easy, reassuring manner. 'This,' he said proudly, as they set off, 'is one of the best and fastest teams in the business.'

It was a journey of roughly eighty miles, and the horses needed to be changed every ten miles or so. The snow turned to rain, and Duval felt they were making good headway.

They reached the county of Essex. It was a dark, moonless night. The weather worsened, the temperature dropped. Much as he would have preferred to keep going, Duval knew it would be cruel to the horses and postilions to do so in these conditions. At the next inn, Jameson took rooms, and Duval fell into a dreamless sleep as soon as his head touched the pillow.

At daybreak, Duval looked out of the window and found snowflakes falling in endlessly varying motion. It seemed nothing could be living in such a world. Everything was a dazzling white, exquisite in its beauty. Every bough and branch was cloaked in snow.

After breakfast, they were on the road again, a road that could hardly be seen under its winter coat, the sky and the land almost merging, punctuated only by black rooks flying up from the trees.

The day and the miles slowly passed. They became stuck

once, but the light powdery snow was easier to travel on than an icy surface. Duval slept or watched the changing countryside. What he didn't allow himself to do was think too deeply about what the future held – a future he had never wanted, with a wife he didn't want to wed. Perhaps he should have asked himself, *Why did I expect anything different from the Viper?* Even from a young age, he had understood that his father's decisions were often beartraps.

'Eton is where you will go to school,' his father had told him when he was twelve.

Clothes were bought, his trunk packed, the carriage called for. Then an hour before he was due to leave, the Viper had summoned him to the Sanctuary and told him he wasn't to go after all. Duval, an isolated and lonely boy, felt tears sting his eyes.

'Why not, sir?'

'That is not a question I have any interest in answering,' replied his father. 'It is foolish, like all your questions.'

'Then what made you change your mind, sir?'

His father held up an essay Duval had written for his tutor. 'You have even spelled your name wrong. You don't have enough brains for my old school.'

From that heartbreak, Duval had learned to believe the opposite of what his father said. So, why was he now obeying the terms of his father's will? He remembered what his friend, the famous artist Etienne Bouchet, had said before he was taken to the guillotine: 'The Revolution is a painting with a false perspective.' Duval knew the painter was right. Was he, too, failing to see the vanishing point?

One thing he knew: he would be pleased when they stopped moving. Still, time was ticking away.

Dregs of Hope

Nothing much happened in Witchling Village from one day to another, from one season to another, from one year to another – history and time seemed uninterested in the goings-on of its small community. So, when a post-chaise hurtled down the main street at nine o'clock, even those about to turn in for the night rushed to see who it could be. The carriage, with its lamps shining, was heading in the direction of the only grand house of which Witchling could boast. What drama could have brought it to this small, near-forgotten part of Suffolk on a night like this?

Longfield Manor, too, was stirred into action as the chaise made a loud entrance into the sea of untouched snow surrounding the house.

Duval knew it was too late to pay a courtesy call. Turning up like this would take some explanation. He had contemplated waiting until the morning, but that would leave so little time for the onward journey. He had no option other than to ask for Jocasta Beale's hand tonight.

He hesitated on the doorstep before pulling the bell. He had a sinking feeling this was a fool's errand.

The door was opened by a butler. He was shown into the drawing room, where the maid sleepily rekindled the fire and lit the candles. Duval was left to wait while the grandfather clock in the hall ticked away the minutes.

Finally, Mr Beale appeared in a dressing gown and boudoir cap. 'Lord Harlington, this is a most unexpected visit, if I may say so.' He was followed into the room by his wife, who reminded Duval of a hen with ruffled feathers, plucking at her husband.

'Indeed, sir, it is,' said Duval. 'I apologize for the lateness of the hour, but it is a matter of some urgency.'

'We are most sorry for the loss of your father, my lord,' said Mr Beale.

As he spoke, Mrs Beale sniffed pointedly, then sniffed again. These sniffs were directed at her husband.

'We heard about your late father's will from your relative, Mr Ralph Carson.' Mr Beale paused, much to his wife's obvious irritation. 'Have you come to inquire about Jocasta?'

Duval was surprised that they knew Mr Carson at all. Slightly wrong-footed, he confirmed that he had indeed come to inquire about their daughter.

'Jocasta is married,' said Mrs Beale abruptly.

Her words fell like a china plate onto flagstones. Duval looked down, expecting to see there the shattered pieces of his hopes.

This, he thought, *was a bad idea, pulled from the dregs of a disturbed mind*. What on earth was he thinking, coming here? His gamble had failed, his last card played.

Mrs Beale was more than delighted to elaborate. 'Our darling Jocasta was married a month ago. I am afraid that you are too late in more ways than one. The admirable Mr Carson will soon, I believe, be the new owner of Muchmore.'

A manservant returned with the brandy decanter. Mr Beale

poured some for himself and Duval. 'This must be a most terrible blow for you, my lord,' he said.

Before Duval had a chance to answer, Mrs Beale said, 'Jocasta is married to Colonel Fitzwilliam, a serving officer with Prince Frederick, Duke of York and Albany.'

Duval remembered the colonel well – they had briefly shared a cell together in La Force. He said nothing.

Mr Beale was more sympathetic than his wife. 'I heard the terms of the late Lord Harlington's will were somewhat... er... unwise – if you'll forgive my presumption. Unfortunate for you, my lord, given the circumstances. I doubt now that there is time enough for you to find a wife.'

Mrs Beale interrupted. 'Your lordship had the opportunity to propose to our daughter some years ago. She was quite taken with you,' she added vindictively.

'I didn't realize.'

'But she had the sense to recover herself, and has married for love. It is all the rage, I'm told.'

'He is a very lucky man,' said Duval.

At least the horses hadn't been standing out in the snow too long. The chaise was turned round, and with all haste, they made their way back through Witchling.

It was nearly eleven when they arrived at the Tollgate Hotel in Thetford, just across the county border in Norfolk, only to find the hotel full.

'Because tomorrow is market day,' said the landlord jovially to Duval, who was too tired and too hungry to argue.

When Jameson told the landlord quietly that his master was Lord Harlington, the landlord said, 'Why did you not say so, my lord?'

Because, thought Duval, *I'm not used to the name.*

'It's an honour, my lord,' said the landlord. 'If you would care to wait in the snug, rooms will be prepared for you.'

Duval was tempted to ask how rooms had magically been found, when a moment ago there were none. Instead, he said, 'Is any food available?'

'A meal, of course, my lord,' said the landlord. 'I'm proud to say I have one of the finest kitchens in Norfolk, and the best wine cellar.'

Duval was served an excellent meal in front of a blazing fire in the snug, rounding it off with stilton and a very good port. As he ate, he read through the document on Mr Ralph Carson that Mr Gutteridge had given him in London. Duval was certain he hadn't heard of this distant cousin; his father had never once mentioned him. The port went some way towards softening the blow.

The family was descended from your paternal grandfather's side of the family. Your great-great-uncle, to be precise. His son, after a failed business venture, went to try his luck in India, which is where Mr Ralph and his sister, Miss Sarah Carson, were born.

This was most definitely the first he had heard about any such branch of the ancestral tree.

The families grew apart, continued Mr Gutteridge. *Your father wanted nothing more to do with them.*

Duval, interested to know what this black sheep of the family died of, read on. *Malaria in Delhi*, he discovered. Duval continued reading.

I wish I could say that Mr Carson and his sister Miss Sarah

Carson – who lives with him – were gentlefolk. But they have a narrow disposition, the result of growing up in an enclosed British community in Delhi. The word 'provincial' might have been designed with them in mind. Mr Carson, who at first was full of disbelief at his unexpected good fortune, now sees Muchmore House and the property in London as his by right. To this end, he has rented Monkton Manor, a house that far exceeds his means, its merit being that it is a grand enough residence for his presence in the neighbourhood to be noticed. Your father, as I am sure you are aware, was not liked by much of the local gentry. But now Mrs Beale, the wife of the magistrate, has taken Mr Carson under her wing and busied herself introducing him at Woodbridge assembles as the rightful heir of Muchmore. I fear he will not relinquish that idea. He wrote to tell me as much this morning, knowing your ship was due in. He is confident that you stand no hope of finding a bride in the allotted time.

Left alone to think in that witching hour before the clock struck midnight, Duval concluded he was no different from the many French aristocrats who had had their lands confiscated by the Revolutionary Tribunal. He had, to begin with, supported the Revolution and believed passionately in its principles – was he going to be like those men who thought different rules should apply to them? The Carsons hadn't been born into wealth as he had, so perhaps there was some justice in that, despite Ralph Carson's arrogant behaviour and dreadful taste in wallpaper.

The thought of the Revolution once again brought his old friend Etienne to mind. Etienne had been a portrait-painter, the darling of the countesses. They had met on the Rue du Ballet at the beginning of the September massacres, when roughly one hundred and fifty men, far from becoming heroes of Paris, became murderers. Among them were butchers, fruiters, tailors, boot-makers, watchmakers, jewellers, hatters, haberdashers; they terrorized the city for a whole week, while the rest of the population became mere spectators. Among the murderers could be found a few brave men determined to save as many victims as they could from their clutches. Duval had met, in this bloodthirsty crowd, Etienne, who, like himself, was risking his life. He first saw Etienne standing on a box, a tall man with long dark hair and fiery eyes, waving his elegant finger about his head as if swatting flies. But it was his words that stopped the murderous crowd. 'You are nothing but a lot of miserable bullies; you are armed. I am not, and neither is this innocent young woman.'

Duval had gone to their rescue, for he had recognized the young woman. She was the wife of a doctor he knew. 'She is pregnant with a son of France,' he bellowed. The crowd broke into a cheer of, '*Vive la Révolution*!'

She was far from the last they saved from the slaughter that week. Both he and Etienne had been arrested a year later, at the start of the terror, and sent – ironically – to La Force prison, which stood not far from where they had first met.

When Etienne found out that he was on the morning list for the tumbril, he had laughed.

Duval had said, 'There is nothing humorous about this. You are to be guillotined.'

Etienne had responded, 'Oh, English, you are wrong. There is much wit indeed in it. I can assure you that laughter is the only way to deal with the follies of life. After all, this is just a comedy written by the gods, not to be taken too seriously. Mankind is too given to wallowing in regret. Laugh, laugh, laugh, and regret becomes a feeble creature that is hardly able to draw breath enough to become a tragedy.'

Now, Duval raised his glass to the ghost of his best friend and smiled. 'You're right,' he said to the crackling fire. 'I have kept my life. I have freedom. And I will not be tied down to a foolish will.' With that – and another glass of port – he began to resign himself to the loss of his estate.

Tomorrow, he would buy a horse and ride over to see his beloved Aunt Harriet – he had to ensure that she was provided for. Seeing her would be his reward for travelling this far. He would be as gracious as he could be in handing over such a treasure as Muchmore to this unknown Mr Carson. Mr Gutteridge had said he would be there, no doubt to express his condolences. Then Duval would return to London and start life afresh. With a horse, the road was his and he had the freedom to go where he wanted. Tomorrow, he would stop dancing to a dead man's tune, once and for all, and become plain Doctor Duval Harlington.

Jameson was waiting in the bedchamber. The room was better than Duval had expected, and the valet was determined to be enthusiastic about the chances of his master finding a bride. He had become downcast when Duval told him the outcome of his conversation with the Beales, and now became even more so when Duval told him of his plan to ride with William straight to Muchmore.

'You can follow in the chaise,' Duval said.

'But what about a wife?' asked Jameson. The look of disappointment on his face was heartrending. 'Surely you're not giving up, my lord?' he said pleadingly.

'I am, Jameson,' said Duval, resolute. And with that, he watched the admirable man make an exit worthy of Hamlet after seeing his father's ghost on the battlements.

Now well fed and warm, Duval remembered how much he had once enjoyed his bachelor life. The one thing he had no wish to do, the one thing he had never done, was fall in love.

When he thought about it, he held the heart responsible for the madness of his father. If the Viper had not allowed love to ruin his days, Duval was certain he wouldn't have left such a foolish will. Yes, Duval would be perfectly happy if love never came near the door to his soul. He considered it an emotion for fools, an empty treasure chest, a ring of deceit, a lifelong prison sentence.

Jameson was up before the cock crowed the next morning and was delighted to find that Duval was still fast asleep. He went downstairs to where the fires were being laid and the hotel badgered into life. The landlord was in the kitchen.

'Breakfast won't be served for another hour,' he said.

'No,' said Jameson, 'it's not breakfast I am after. I wonder if I might have a word.'

'Certainly. How can I help?'

'I want to know if you could answer my question about the… sale—'

The landlord interrupted him. 'Ah, you want to know about the horse fair, the one that takes place in the market?'

'No, not that,' said Jameson. Dropping his voice to no more than a whisper, he told him just which sale he was interested in.

'Is this for yourself, Mr Jameson?' asked the landlord.

'Might be,' said Jameson. 'But am I right in thinking it is happening today?'

'Yes,' said the landlord, 'always on this day.'

'Most fortuitous,' said Jameson, 'otherwise this would've been a wasted journey.'

The landlord looked him over. 'You know it goes against the law?' He laughed. 'But then again, the law is senseless. The sale starts at roughly ten thirty, stops about twelve thirty for lunch, then starts again at two o'clock until four – depending how many there are for sale.'

'Where does it take place?'

'The King's Head,' said the landlord. He chuckled. 'It costs to get in. What would your master say if he knew what you were up to?'

'What indeed,' said Jameson.

Duval woke refreshed, with a philosophical view on the outcome of this day.

'My lord, if I may speak?' said Jameson.

'Of course you may speak,' said Duval. 'But I know what you're going to say.'

'No, my lord, you don't,' said Jameson. 'I was merely going to suggest that you take a look round the town, then attend the horse fair, which is to happen today. I have arranged for William to meet you by the entrance to the King's Head at ten o'clock, after you have had breakfast. If I may be so bold as to request that I may visit the tailors' shop, recommended by the landlord, and buy you a greatcoat that would be more appropriate than the one you are wearing…'

'A great greatcoat?' said Duval, who could see nothing wrong with the coat he had on, other than it was out of fashion.

'Yes, my lord.'

'Yes, by all means buy the greatcoat, and I will buy a horse.'

The town of Thetford had been jostled awake by the clutter of carts and carriages, their occupants eager to see what was on offer.

It had begun to snow again as Duval went in search of his breakfast. It was a novel experience to stroll in the open without fear of arrest, and he enjoyed observing the activities of the market holders and street sellers. You could buy oysters, hot eels, pea soup, pies, puddings, and baked potatoes to warm one's hands. The sound of the hurdy-gurdy completed the scene.

He passed the King's Head and briefly wondered why a group of men was waiting there. It was too early to meet William. He settled on a coffee house whose bow window allowed him to see the comings and goings of the marketplace. As he watched, a soldier in a faded red coat stopped outside the window and put down the box he was carrying. He had with him a woman, poorly dressed in widow's mourning black, with a lace cap and a bonnet that hid her face, so it was impossible to gauge her age. There was some disagreement between the two of them.

The woman turned away from the soldier and walked across the street to a market stall selling ribbons and lace. Two young maidservants, their baskets full, were busy examining what bargains there were to be found. Duval noticed the soldier was pointedly studying his boots as if embarrassed by his companion. Duval was about to turn to order more coffee, when he saw the widow take something from one of the maidservants' baskets. She returned to the soldier while the maidservants, unaware of the robbery, disappeared among the street sellers.

The soldier picked up the box, and the bell on the door of the coffee house jangled as he and the widow came in. For the first time, Duval caught a glimpse of the woman's face. It was he who looked away first. Her skin was a vivid, bruised canvas of purples, blues and pinks. All he could make out was the outline of a heart-shaped face. She possessed a good figure and wasn't as old as he had first thought.

Duval had survived much of his childhood – and his time

in prison – by making up stories. Here was a thought to entertain him while eating his breakfast, to take his mind off the loss of his estate. He decided the soldier was either her lover or her husband, a cruel, thoughtless man given to drink and violence. She, being dressed in mourning, must have lost a child, and the soldier had made her steal the money. Yes, that was how it went. Or so he thought, until the soldier asked her, 'Do we have enough for a full breakfast?'

'Of course,' she said, and with those two words, Duval suspected her of being French. He thought it made the intrigue more interesting. He started again. The young widow had escaped France, been brought to Norfolk and had sought protection from the soldier. After being beaten for…

Stop it, he thought. *You will never know.*

He looked up at the clock on the wall. It was coming up to ten. In just over nine hours, it would all be over: he would have lost the Muchmore Estate.

He realized he was absent-mindedly staring at the young woman. In turn, she looked straight at him. For some reason her gaze unsettled him. He paid and left.

William met Duval at the King's Head.

'Are all these men queuing for the horse sale?' Duval asked.

'It's a wife sale, my lord,' said William.

'A wife sale?' said Duval, 'that sounds positively medieval.'

'Do you remember the head groom, Mr Brown, my lord?'

'Yes, vaguely,' said Duval. 'Why?'

'He sold his wife for a fair penny at the sale here. They were not suited, and there was no way he could afford to divorce her. Even if he had worked all his life, he wouldn't have had the money. The wife sale was his only hope.'

'So he sold her,' said Duval.

'Yes, my lord. A wife is chattel; put a scarf around her or a rope, and you can take her to market just as you would a sheep or a cow. The law on divorce is an ass, and we know just where to put the ass's tail.' He paused. 'Shall we go and find a horse?'

'Yes,' said Duval, walking briskly away.

Among the many potential buyers at the horse auction were military men, farmers, and breeders looking for an undiscovered champion to race. William had gone earlier to look over the horses and had seen one he fancied.

'The owner tells me it has a good temperament, my lord, and a bright and gentle nature.'

What Duval was thinking about had nothing to do with the horse in question, and everything to do with the wife sale. A man walked past with a hen tucked under his arm, and Mrs Beale's words came back to him. 'The admirable Mr Carson will soon, I believe, be the new owner of Muchmore.'

No, he told himself, *you can't. It would never work.*

William was still looking at Duval expectantly. 'Ask to see it walked and trotted up,' he said to William. 'Then, if you think it's sound, we'll buy it.'

As he stood in the crowd, waiting for the auction to begin, Duval overheard a conversation. 'A widow, you say? I haven't heard of a widow being brought to the wife sale – not for a while.'

'Gilbert Hyde has brought her,' said his companion. 'She should fetch ten shillings or more.'

'I don't know. I heard that bastard of a parson cut her hair off and beat her in a fit of righteous rage.'

'He was a man for fire and brimstone.'

Duval turned to the men standing beside him. 'Excuse me, gentlemen,' he said, 'when does the wife sale start?'

One man took out his fob watch. 'Starts at ten thirty, which is any minute now,' replied that man.

'That's why we're here for the horses,' said the other. 'There are bound to be bargain prices for them, with so many men distracted by the women up for sale.'

The first asked, 'Are you in need of a wife, sir?'

William, emerging through the crowd, came over and interrupted them. 'Quick, my lord,' he said. 'It's the next horse.'

'You settle it,' said Duval, before hastily making his way to the King's Head. Maybe, just maybe, he still had a joker to play.

There were now even more men gathered outside the inn than before. A farmer was having an argument about the entrance fee with the man on the door.

'Two and six it was last summer, two and six it is this new year,' said the man on the door. 'If you don't have it, you can't come in.'

Duval put down his money.

'You have to buy a drink, sir,' said the man on the door. 'That's the deal.'

Inside the inn, Duval ordered a beer, and since all the chairs were taken, he stood against the wall, drink in hand, like the rest of the men. There was a carnival feeling about the gathering.

A large gentleman in an ill-fitting riding jacket strode into the middle of the room; the jacket was red, his face was red, and his nose was redder. The only things detracting from the redness of his features were his ample whiskers. He carried with him a wooden half-barrel that he upended and placed in the centre of the floor, then, with some difficulty, he stepped up onto it. This was the ringmaster.

'Gentlemen, we are here today so harassed husbands and wretched wives might, through consensual dissolving of their marriage, have the chance to bring about a happier union. We have five husbands and one son: the son is here to sell the recently widowed wife of his late father.'

Duval saw several soldiers and an officer from the horse sale among the men lining the walls.

A drunken man led a woman into the centre of the room by a neck scarf. 'Mr Alderley,' he said to the red-faced man on the barrel. 'Mr Alderley, I am here'—he hiccupped—'to sell this woman, my spare rib.'

'Sir, the floor is yours.'

The man was careful to stay upright, lest the floor knock him unconscious. He leaned on his wife, who was much taller, broader, and altogether more furious-looking than her husband.

'Get on with it, man,' said Mr Alderley.

The husband, straightening himself, said, 'She can cook and clean better than many…' Here he was lost for words, which produced gales of laughter. 'But I do not need her now, preferring my own company to that of this moon-eyed hen whose tongue refuses to lie still. She is a woman with two stomachs and sharp teeth, and anyone who wants her is…' He stopped, remembering one thing that might help with the sale. 'She has a hunger for the bed and wants a child that she hasn't yet had—'

'Do I have a bidder?' interrupted Mr Alderley. 'Yes, sir? Four shillings. Any advance on four shillings? No? Going, going, gone.'

She was sold to a man she knew, who was delighted with

his purchase, as was she, and the three went off to settle the matter.

Duval thought this had more brutal honesty to it than the assembly rooms of Almack's or Bath. No dillying, no dallying. Take your pick, choose your poison.

A man of about forty, in shabby but genteel dress, stepped forward, leading a smart-looking woman by a handkerchief round her neck.

'Who will buy my wife?' he shouted loudly.

A young good-looking gentleman offered four shillings and was immediately outbid by an older gentleman, offering five. In the end, she was sold for five pounds. The money was paid and the husband handed over the handkerchief to the purchaser, before declaring he'd got rid of a troublesome, noisy wife. This caused much merriment in the room.

Three more wives were sold, the atmosphere had grown more lively, and there was a sense of excitement at the prospect of the last sale of the morning.

From his place on the barrel, Mr Alderley said, 'We come now to the *pièce de résistance*. We rarely have a bona fide widow for sale. This widow is brought here by her late husband's son. Mr Gilbert Hyde, the floor is yours, sir.'

Duval was surprised to see the soldier from the coffee shop and the thieving widow emerge through the crowd. The soldier reluctantly took off his scarf and put it round the widow's neck, then led her to the centre of the room.

Of all the endings Duval might have invented for the story of the widow and the soldier, this he would never have imagined. He wondered if she was truly a widow, or whether they were both a couple of fairground rogues. If they were, he had to admit they were worthy actors.

'You have to say something,' the widow muttered, head bowed beneath her bonnet.

This brought more laughter.

Yes, he thought, *definitely both actors.*

'Um… this lady is the widow of my father…'

'Speak up!' shouted a man at the back. 'We can't hear you!'

'This lady is the widow of my father, Samuel Hyde. Being French, she is lost here, now my father is dead.' The soldier stopped, unsure where his words were marching. 'Um… I will be returning to my regiment if I can, and therefore can't look after her.'

Someone said, 'Are you talking about Samuel Hyde, the parson at Witchling? He was a drunk.'

Duval saw the eyes of the officer from the horse auction were fixed on the widow. Though the soldier clearly found the circumstances uncomfortable, there was something genuine about his performance. Duval began to revise his opinion of the couple, as a thought came to him. *No*, said his inner voice, *don't be ridiculous. But if it's ridiculous…* his inner self retorted, *why am I still here? Only out of interest*, he told himself, *that's all.*

The ringmaster asked, 'What are her good qualities, Mr Hyde?'

Gilbert Hyde floundered as he searched for something to say.

'Let's see her,' shouted a man in the audience. 'Take off her bonnet, so we can have a better look at her face. We need to know what we're bidding for.'

Humiliating, thought Duval. The widow took off her bonnet. Her face was indeed bruised and swollen – there was no make-up involved in what he saw – her hair had been brutally cut; it was jagged and stood up in tuffs. He didn't doubt for a moment that her appearance was genuine. She stood there, defiant. There was courage in her quiet dignity. An image of Saint Joan of Thetford crossed Duval's mind.

'I'm not responsible for any of it,' said Gilbert Hyde. 'My

father was a bastard. He did that to her, before he died.' There were murmurs in the crowd.

Duval edged forward, as had the officer. The widow shivered, moved closer to Gilbert.

'What are her virtues, sir?' prompted Mr Alderley.

The widow whispered in Gilbert Hyde's ear. He almost jumped back. He said aloud, 'You can't say that!'

'Say what?' said Mr Alderley. 'Come, you are here to proclaim her virtues and sell her.'

The soldier looked at the widow. Her expression remained stoic. 'She is still a virgin,' he said.

There were shouts. 'I can well believe that – married to Samuel Hyde,' a voice called.

'Ten shillings,' said a wiry man at the front, his voice cutting through the noise of the crowd.

'One guinea,' said the officer.

Duval saw the widow look frightened. *No*, he told himself. Whatever thoughts he had had about this wife sale, now was the time to leave. He moved towards the door and hesitated when he heard the wiry man bid. 'Two pounds, ten shillings.'

'Five pounds,' said the officer. 'I would say it's a fair price, considering the marks on her.'

'Five pounds it is,' said Mr Alderley. 'Going once, going twice, going—'

Duval felt the words rise up in this throat and escape unbidden from his mouth. 'Seven guineas.' Now you could hear a pin drop. The look on Gilbert Hyde's face was one of incredulity.

'Eight pounds,' said the officer.

That's that, said Duval to himself, until he saw the widow look straight at him. He had a flash of disconnected memory. He was near the Abbey prison. In that moment, the widow represented all the women he had seen murdered in the days of the September Massacres. He watched as she closed her eyes.

There were whispers around the hall – where will these gentlemen find money like this?

At eight pounds, Duval was certain the officer had reached his limit.

'Are we all done?' said Mr Alderley. 'Good. Then... going, going—'

'Ten guineas,' said Duval.

'Gone!'

Cold Vittles

Duval asked Gilbert Hyde to bring the widow to his rooms at the Tollgate Hotel. Best to meet her there, away from curious eyes. As he walked back, a memory came to him, of Etienne in prison. His friend had said, 'If you ever decide to marry, my dear Duval, choose a woman whom, if she were a man, you would want as a friend.' He had laughed. 'I doubt I will live long enough to find a wife.' At that, a small, almost forgotten voice inside Duval said, *This is madness*.

What was extraordinary – nearly as extraordinary as having bought himself a bride – was that Jameson already seemed to know about it. A table was laid out with cold pies, bread, cheese, apples and a bottle of brandy.

'What's this for?' asked Duval.

'It is the custom in a wife sale, my lord, for you and the first husband – in this case, the husband's son – to seal the sale with drinks. You must take on full responsibility for your new wife, and the husband – in this case, the husband's son – hands over the documents concerning her previous marriage – in this case, to his deceased father.' Jameson struggled to refrain from smiling. 'As you will want to leave as soon as possible, I thought cold vittles would be easier for the soldier to take in his knapsack.'

'Did William buy the horse?'

'Yes. And I bought you a great coat, and took the liberty of buying a burgundy red fur-lined ladies' cloak, just on the off chance, my lord.'

There was a knock on the door. Jameson opened it and Gilbert Hyde came in carrying the box, followed by the widow. He seemed surprised to find a servant there.

'Brandy, Mr Hyde?' said Jameson.

'A small glass,' said the soldier. 'I need to keep my wits about me.'

'And you, Mrs Hyde?' asked Jameson. 'Would you care for a glass?'

She was studying Duval. 'Yes – no,' she said. 'No, thank you, sir.'

Duval noticed her eyes were a green-grey, and again he felt unsettled by them. He couldn't make out the features of her face, probably a result of the bruising.

Gilbert Hyde took the glass of brandy and asked if he might help himself to some food.

'It's here for you,' said Duval.

'Thank you kindly, sir.' The soldier looked again at Jameson and turned to Duval. 'It is you she's marrying, not him?'

'It is me,' said Duval.

'Good,' said Gilbert Hyde. 'Good.' And remembering where he was, he wiped his mouth on the back of his sleeve and said, 'I feel I should be honest with you, sir.'

The sky had clouded over, the room had grown dark, and it had started to snow again. To Duval, this man and woman appeared as cut-outs, as silhouettes.

'I'm not a thinking man, sir,' said the soldier. 'But I should tell you I've known Mrs Hyde less than the hours of a day and a night. She is a fighter, brave, I give you that, and no complainer. But who she is, or why she should have married my brute of a father, I couldn't say.' He helped himself to more bread, then, with his mouth still full, he took from his knapsack some letters and a collection of papers tied with a ribbon. He waited until he had finished chewing before he said, 'Here's my father's record of the marriage, sir. Here' – he tapped a middle finger on the documents – 'are her papers under the Aliens Act.'

'You can take the food and the brandy with you,' said Duval, as Jameson handed over the payment.

'I thank you, sir.'

Gilbert Hyde counted out the ten gold coins and handed half to the widow. He pushed towards her the box he'd been carrying, then carefully put the food and brandy into his knapsack.

'That's it, then,' he said to the widow. 'Do you want to say anything about the cat?'

'No,' she said firmly.

'Good.' And without a word of farewell, he was gone.

Duval did not know what to make of this strange parting, but the awkwardness of the situation stopped him from asking. The silence between him and his new bride seemed to thicken. She stood before him, a slight figure. Duval spoke to her – in French this time – 'Are you from Paris?'

Now sunshine danced in the green-grey eyes that were as still as pond water.

'Yes,' she responded. 'Your French is excellent.'

'It should be,' said Duval.

'You have a Parisian accent.' She paused to study his face, then proceeded with the question that was clearly on her mind. 'Can I ask – why did you need to buy a wife? Is it because you like men more?'

Never had Duval been stumped by a woman before. He had been about to ask how the hell she came to be sold off by her stepson, but her directness wrong-footed him. Instead, he said, rather formally, 'No, madame, I can assure you I like women. But I am in a predicament. I will lose my inheritance if I don't marry before seven o'clock today. After we are wed, I will give you enough money to live on while you decide what you want to do.'

Again, she studied him carefully, taking in his clothes, his hair. 'You are a good-looking man,' she said. 'I would imagine it would not be hard to find a wife. You must be desperate, if you are buying me at a wife sale. Your clothes are out of fashion. You speak French too well, as if you have just arrived from Paris. I wager, therefore…' She paused. 'You have been in prison.'

Duval marvelled. How the hell did she know that? 'Yes, you are quite right. And I returned to find I had two days and seven hours to find a wife.' Duval hesitated, then said, 'The marriage will be dissolved in due course, and you will have your freedom.'

'I don't want my freedom; it's no good to me.'

'Why not?' he asked. 'I would be generous. You could live where you wanted.'

She shook her head.

'Then what do you want?'

'I need your name to protect me.'

She doesn't know my name, he thought. 'From what? From whom?' he asked.

She didn't answer. Instead, she said, 'You need to marry to keep your money?'

'Yes, to fulfil the terms of my father's will.'

'I need a husband,' she said. 'And you need a wife.'

They stared at one another, her gaze still unblinking.

A thought came to him. What would it be like to make love to her? *No, no*, he told himself, *that will never happen*. This marriage would be dissolved, they would go their separate ways... And at this, he remembered the question he should have asked when she first came into the room.

'What's your name?'

'Edmée,' she said, not asking for his in return. 'How far do we have to go?'

'If the roads are clear, then the journey will take two to three hours, but if the weather worsens' – he looked out of the window – 'which it has, then... who knows? And I would be too late.' He corrected himself. '*We* would be too late.'

'Then we must make haste,' said Edmée.

'Don't you want to ask any questions about me?'

'No, I want to leave here and marry you. You paid ten guineas for me. A wife sale is a wife sale. It is not a perhaps-you-will-marry-me-if-there-is-enough-time sale. It is a wife sale.'

Yesterday, all out of other options, he had contemplated abandoning the idea of inheriting his father's estate, buying a horse, and going to London to be a physician. He had been certain that he had run out of cards to play. Yet, this unknown woman represented an optimism he hadn't felt since setting out on his father's ridiculous challenge.

It was past two o'clock when the new horse was secured to the back of the chaise.

'A new horse?' she said as they set off. 'Did you come to buy a horse or a wife?'

'Both,' he said and smiled.

They sat apart from one another, she in a new fur-lined coat, a look of relief on her face at finally being warm. Duval, in his new greatcoat, waited for an onslaught of questions. He had one of his own. 'From whom are you seeking protection?'

She smiled a crooked smile that stretched the bruising on

her face and made her wince. 'From all the hungry animals that were at the wife sale.' Then she leaned back in the corner, pulled her fur-lined cloak tight about her, and fell fast asleep.

The snow whitened everything out before them. The landscape was monotonous, and it was impossible to gauge if they were making good progress. Left alone with no company, Duval had time to contemplate who this mysterious woman might be. If he was honest with himself, she intrigued him, and he hadn't been intrigued by anyone for a long, long time. She seemed guarded, unwilling to lay bare the mystery surrounding her circumstances, so maybe he would never know. Then again, maybe it didn't matter. At least he stood a chance – weather permitting – of keeping his inheritance.

When Edmée woke, the light was fading and the gentleman who had bought her had his eyes closed. Discreetly, so as not to disturb him, she studied her husband-to-be. He was handsome, had well-defined features and a generous mouth. At the wife sale, she had initially sought him out for having a kind face. But now, in the sobering twilight of a late February afternoon, her bold confidence – rather like the light itself – was beginning to vanish. Since her marriage to Samuel Hyde, she had ceased to trust in her own judgement. She felt a panic rise in her at a sudden thought. *What if he is just a better-looking version?* Even handsome men can be monsters. *No*, she reassured herself. He was wealthy. He offered her freedom. He had a manservant, a groom, and enough money to buy her and a horse. Maybe this time – *Please, this time* – it would be alright. If it had been anyone else, she would have reminded Gilbert to feed the cat. That would have been his cue to get them both out of the King's Head as fast as he could manage it.

The one thing she regretted was lying at the wife sale. It

wasn't the best way to start a marriage, but how else was she to get his attention in that cattle market other than by saying what she did? She knew how to flatter a man, and the word 'virgin' made even the most hard-hearted pay attention. To be the first at anything was something men valued. But he looked intelligent, too intelligent to be so easily persuaded of her innocence.

The next two posting inns were not as efficient as those on the main roads; there were tolls to pay at turnpikes and everything seemed to take longer.

Duval opened and shut his fob watch, opened and shut it, and still time was running against him. In prison, time had no meaning – there was nothing you could hang upon it except fear. You marked its passing with the loss of friends. But here, time continually gathered speed. It was now four thirty.

They had passed the Suffolk border when Edmée said, 'How much further is it?'

The horses were being changed, legs were being stretched and refreshments taken, but the overriding truth was, as the postilion pointed out, the weather had taken a turn for the worse. It was unlikely they would reach Muchmore House before seven o'clock.

'What time must we be there?' asked Edmée, who was waiting in the carriage.

'By six, if we are to be wed by seven.'

The snow was now falling heavily.

'Can you ride?' Duval asked her.

'Yes,' she said. 'But not side-saddle.'

His boxes were taken down, and Jameson took out his lordship's warmest clothes and gave them to Edmée.

'Change into them,' said Duval.

'It's a good thing you bought that horse, my lord,' said William, once Edmée had gone into the inn. 'A fast one, I reckon.' He went to see what other horses might be hired.

Duval looked again at his watch.

William managed to hire two horses, and finally they were saddled and ready. Edmée had cut her gown – underneath her cloak, she was wearing breeches. She had a scarf at her neck and a hat over her lace cap.

A true daughter of the Revolution, Duval thought, as he helped her into the saddle. He and William mounted their horses, and they were ready.

'Wait,' she said. 'My box. I can't leave it.'

'Madam,' said Jameson, 'I will guard it with my life.'

She hesitated. 'No. I must take it with me. There might be highwaymen...'

Duval, seeing she wasn't going to move, ordered the postilions to show her their pistols. 'They are first-rate shots,' Jameson assured her. 'I promise it will be quite safe.'

They set off slowly, until Duval had the measure of the horse he had bought, and both he and William had an idea of Edmée's riding skills.

'She's good enough,' said William,

Yes, thought Duval, *she is*, as he kicked his horse into a canter.

The wind was bitter, the light was gone – but this was a part of the world Duval could travel with his eyes closed. It was a route he used to take as a boy, knowing he could get home fast. Still, it took nearly two hours. Just after six. The horses were spent, as were their riders.

'Not far now,' he said to Edmée, impressed she had not lagged behind.

'You ride on,' said Duval to William. 'Tell them we are on our way.' William needed no encouragement, and spurred his horse on.

A Husband-to-Be

A long drive led through a beech wood to Muchmore House. It looked majestic to Edmée, with candles alight in all the windows, seated in a sea of snow – the home of some fairy king. She rode close to Duval. 'Whose house is that?' she asked.

'Mine, as long as you marry me, madam.'

'That is your house?'

'Yes.'

'All of it?'

'Yes.'

'No! Who are you?'

The front door opened and Watkins, the butler, said, 'Welcome home, my lord.'

Duval helped Edmée from her horse and the stableboys ran to take the horses away.

'Lord?' she repeated. 'You are a lord?'

'An earl,' said Duval.

'That might alter everything,' she said with a half-smile.

'Are you jesting?' he asked.

'Of course,' she said.

In the house, they were greeted by the sound of a cello.

Duval stopped. 'What is this?' he asked.

'Your father's request, my lord,' said Mr Gutteridge, appearing, with a look of relief, from the drawing room. He glanced quickly at Edmée. 'I take it you have a bride.'

Duval took Edmée's arm and started towards the chapel. It was now twenty past six.

'My lord,' said Mr Gutteridge. 'You must change.'

'Change?' said Duval incredulously. 'Surely it's enough that we are here in time.'

'Your mode of dress is another of the late earl's stipulations,' said Mr Gutteridge.

Duval said, more to himself than to Mr Gutteridge, 'What else should I have expected from him but further folly?'

Two housemaids and an abigail hurried Edmée up the stairs. Duval went to his old bedchamber, where he found clothes laid out. They had been altered to suit the fashion of the day. He washed and dressed faster than anyone could have imagined.

Outside the chapel, Mr Gutteridge was waiting. Duval handed the solicitor the papers Gilbert Hyde had given him.

'Where is she?' Duval asked a footman.

'She will be here, my lord,' he said.

The cello played on, and Duval's beloved aunt emerged. 'I knew in my heart you would be here in time,' she said, 'and that those awful Carsons would not inherit. Nevertheless, I confess I have been worried, especially when young Mr Gutteridge told me you were dead. That state of affairs was quite unacceptable.'

'I'm very glad to see you, Aunt Harriet.'

'I wish it wasn't under such ridiculous circumstances. My brother was an ass.' She waved at the interior of the chapel, bedecked with medieval figures. It had become a sanctuary for Catholic carvings of Christ and the Madonna. 'He preferred rescued icons from France to people,' she added, before taking her seat in a pew.

'The papers are all in order, sir,' said Mr Gutteridge to the priest.

The awful Carsons were seated near the front. Both looked as if they had emerged from a fashion plate, taking the style of the day to extremes. Mr Ralph Carson wore a wig, as did his sister, and both had painted faces. They grudgingly rose to greet Duval. Mr Carson briefly bowed, holding a handkerchief to his nose as if warding off an unpleasant smell. His sister made a deep curtsey, and he waved his handkerchief at her as if she were a lapdog.

'Enough, Sarah,' Ralph snarled. 'Sit.'

Duval looked at his watch. Five minutes passed. He felt the minutes as though they were hours. If he'd had any doubts about the wedding, all he now wanted was to be married.

'By my watch,' said Carson, 'it is fifteen minutes to seven, which is becoming too late for—'

The chapel door opened.

What magic the maids had worked in the little time available! Edmée was dressed in a simple front-fastening pelisse with long sleeves and a high waist, and a bonnet with a lace veil that covered her face. She held a posy of winter flowers.

With her head held high, she took her place beside Duval for the ceremony.

*

In the hall, the cellist continued to play, while the entire staff of Muchmore House waited anxiously, all eyes fixed on the grandfather clock. It was exactly seven o'clock, and as the clock struck the hour, the doors of the chapel opened to reveal the newly married Lord and Lady Harlington.

The Codicil

Champagne was served, the bride and groom congratulated, and for a heartbeat, all seemed to be as it should. But Duval had no idea who he had married, for better or worse. She was the widow of a parson, yes. Her papers stated she was French; the Alien Office confirmed it. She could ride, yes; she had spirit, yes. She was, perhaps, a thief. All she knew about him was this house and the madness of a demanding dead father.

'The Sanctuary is ready, my lord,' said a footman.

'Why is the Sanctuary ready?' asked Duval.

'It is where your father requested the codicil be read,' said Mr Gutteridge. 'The terms of his late lordship's will simply stated that you were to marry within a year to the day of his death. This is the codicil to be read *after* you married within the time stated.'

Duval shook his head incredulously. So, his father had not finished with his poison darts. He had been played for a fool. 'I do not wish to go to the Sanctuary,' he said.

There was an awkward silence. Then Mr Gutteridge said,

'I see no objection, my lord, to the letter being read in the library.'

'Is it necessary that you read it out loud at all?' asked Duval.

'I'm afraid it is, my lord,' said Mr Gutteridge. 'Please know it gives me no pleasure to do so.'

All the time he had been driving helter-skelter across England to find a bride, Duval had allowed himself to believe it was the final move in the game. Now he could hear the Viper's voice: *Did you think I would give you all this so easily?* And for the first time in a long while, the old frustration and rage at his father rose, primeval and raw. An estate such as this would not, even in death, be relinquished easily from his father's bony grip. All Duval's learning, all his philosophy and his determination to live a happy life, were distorted by the Viper rattling his chains of misery.

In the library, Edmée stood quietly, watching as chairs were set out by the servants.

'We don't need so many,' said Duval.

Mr Carson sidled up to Edmée, bowed, and introduced himself. 'Lady Harlington, may I ask, where did you meet Lord Harlington?'

Edmée pretended not to understand a word this unpleasant little man was saying. She had, in her life, been around greedy men – they had a certain perfume, one she couldn't stand. Survival had given her an instinct for those you could not trust, and here, in all the folly of fashion, stood such a man.

Duval answered for her. 'What concern is it of yours, Mr Carson?'

'I heard you returned to London—'

'Yes,' said Duval.

'So you brought your bride from France?'

'Excuse me, Mr Carson,' said Duval. He took Edmée's arm

and led her away. 'What's the delay?' he asked briskly of a footman.

'It seems your mother and father's chairs must be at the front, my lord.'

The late Lord Harlington's wing-back chair was brought in by two footmen. There was no special chair for his mother. Both chairs remained empty. Mr and Miss Carson hovered, uncertain where to sit, and were guided by a footman to the back of the room.

Lady Harriet sat to Duval's left, the unknown woman who was now his wife to his right.

Mr Gutteridge took the letter from his valise and held it up for inspection. He opened it with a paper knife, read it through once, and then again – the Viper's writing was always illegible – before reading aloud:

My dear Duval,

I knew you would not fail me. Now you have married, you no doubt feel it is only right and proper that you inherit the estate.

But I place one more caveat on such entitlements – as you have surely come to expect. For the first year of your marriage you will own the Muchmore Estate, retaining it thereafter on condition that twelve months from the date of your wedding, it can be proven that you love your wife, and that she is worthy of your name.

Once I was a man, and as a man, I loved your mother. On her death, I wondered if I trusted the depths of the love I felt for her. Was it remorse for not understanding the power of that emotion she had kindled in me? Your mother loved me, she forgave me my follies, and that broke me. I became a babbling infant, and with no knowledge of the path I should take to become a man again, grief made me a fool.

Mr Gutteridge paused briefly, glanced at Duval, and resumed reading.

How do we judge this liquid emotion that, when it is so light, is everything, and weighs so heavy when it is nothing? Your wife could say she loves you and lie, but true love can't be hidden. The most powerful force in nature is passion. I want to be sure you love the woman you chose to marry with a passion that only the grave, and perhaps not even the grave, can rob you of. This time next year, Mr Gutteridge will make his decision. It cannot be counted by the birth of a child, for that has no effect on what I am talking about. You told me you would never love, never marry. Well, sir, you are married. Let us see about the rest.

I trust that in these humble requests you will not fail. If you do, you will not inherit the Muchmore Estate. It will pass to Mr Carson, a man who is, I can guarantee, a spendthrift and, like his father before him, has not an ounce of financial sense.

I am, etc., your father,

Harlington

Carson sprang up, clapped his hands and, turning to Miss Carson, exclaimed, 'We are not to give up hope, my sister!' Quickly realizing it was ill-mannered to have spoken so, he sat down once again.

With all eyes on Carson, no one had seen Duval rise to his feet and leave the room; it was the slamming of the door that alerted them. An air of gloom settled over those he had left behind. His bride was abandoned. The cellist put away his instrument.

*

Duval's rage changed the colour of everything he saw. What an idiotic knucklehead he had been, manipulated like a puppet, even though the puppet master was in his grave. His footsteps echoed in the hall. A year, another year. More games. To hell with it all.

A footman came to tell him the wedding supper was served.

'I want my best horse saddled and ready.'

'Yes, my lord.'

Mr Gutteridge was standing in the doorway. 'You must be exhausted after your journey, my lord.'

'My horse,' repeated Duval to the footman.

Mr Gutteridge was wise enough to say no more.

'And ask my aunt if she would kindly join me,' said Duval, as the footman was leaving.

'I know you are upset,' said Lady Harriet, sweeping into his bedchamber a few minutes later. 'Harold's behaviour is appalling, even in death.'

'My father thought me lacking in intelligence,' said Duval. 'A person's intellect, money and social status were all that mattered to him. Love meant nothing. And don't tell me he cared for me – he didn't.'

'He... he wasn't a good father, that much I know,' said Lady Harriet.

'That, my dear aunt, is a polite way of admitting he was a bastard.'

'You cannot leave now. What about your new wife? She has feelings.'

'Does she? I don't even know who she is,' said Duval. 'I bought her for ten guineas at a wife sale in Thetford.'

Lady Harriet sank into a chair.

'Oh, my word. Duval, I beg of you – tell me it's not true.'

'Aunt, how else was I to secure the estate? I arrived in London a little over two days ago. My ridiculous father left me no choice. I intended to have the marriage annulled, but now that's impossible if I have any hope of keeping Muchmore. To hell with it all.'

'But this is beyond...' She stopped. 'To buy a wife at a sale... It will not take long for this to be the talk of the neighbourhood, and then of London society. What will the bon ton make of this? We will be ostracized; no one will invite you to any of the season's balls, dinners, routs or assembles. She might be a Jacobin for all we know – a spy! You must stay, you must.'

Duval laughed. 'Too many novels, my dear aunt.'

'How did her husband die? How long ago?'

'Ten days ago.'

'That's indecent! Think of the gossip. Heavens, you will be ruined. Who was her husband?'

'A parson by the name of Hyde.'

'My dear, let's think about this quietly, not when your mind is on fire. We must... we must...' His aunt was on the point of tears. 'I've hardly seen you. You could have an accident, Duval. Please wait until tomorrow morning if you must go, but not tonight.'

Duval tore off his cravat. 'I have been in prison for three years,' he said. 'I thought when I came home I would be able to rest, but no. This house that I loved. All the years I thought of it as home, and now, to have the Carsons hanging around me like scavengers... No, I cannot stay.'

'And what shall I do with your bride?' asked Lady Harriet.

'Do with her what you want. I will give her an allowance for pin money. Go shopping, do whatever ladies do to while away days of boredom. I don't care.'

'What if she runs away?'

'Let her run.'

'Duval, this isn't like you. You are just wed. Surely you should try to get to know your wife?'

'No,' said Duval. 'Now, Aunt, if you will excuse me, I must change.'

Half an hour later, Duval descended the stairs. A footman opened the front door, and without a word to his new bride, Duval mounted his favourite horse and set off once more. Tonight, his way was lit by a full moon.

A Ghost from the Past

London was grey and wet, its streets filled with mud, and Duval felt he was dragging behind him the miserable ghost of his father who, like the mud, clung to his ankles. He could hear him above the roar of street criers. *You can't escape me, you never could, you never will, you'll end up just like me, just like me.*

In an attempt to free himself from the weight of the past, Duval spent his time visiting his tailor. If only fitting into his old life was as simple as fitting into his clothes. He was tormented by memories of friends and lovers lost. London society appeared so frivolous now.

The news that he had recently returned from a Paris prison lent him a certain notoriety. Many who knew him, or professed to know him, were anxious to learn what part he had played in the Revolution. Duval was invited to parties and dinners, and at the end of three weeks in London, he felt his spirits beginning to fail him.

Finally, on a wet and windy day near the end of March Mr Gutteridge summoned Duval to his chambers in Lincoln's Inn. There, on the steps, Duval found a sign painter erasing the name *G. Gutteridge Esq., Solicitor* and replacing it with *R. Gutteridge Esq., Solicitor*. With a brushstroke, a life was written out and forgotten. Once again Duval's thoughts were rudely interrupted by the ghost of his father, now in a judge's wig. 'No paint will eradicate my name,' said the late unlamented Viper.

Duval had never before visited the chambers. They were cold and damp. The fire in the clerk's room gave out little heat, though the chamber Mr Gutteridge occupied at least had the merit of a roaring fire. On the mantelpiece above it was an impressive clock, but otherwise the room was lined with books standing in brooding judgement on their shelves. The room had the musty smell of accumulated knowledge, legal and otherwise, being left to go mouldy in glass-fronted, mahogany bookcases.

The solicitor rose from behind his desk and bowed. 'My father, my lord,' he said, waving an elegant long-fingered hand around the chamber as if that was enough to explain everything.

'I was sorry to hear of your father's death,' said Duval.

'I think, on the whole, there is little to be sorry about,' said Mr Gutteridge.

'Did you not get along with him?'

'He thought me too tall,' said Mr Gutteridge. 'In our family, no one is tall.'

Duval smiled. 'Would it be presumptuous of me to assume he doubted you were his son?'

'Very. But you would be correct,' said Mr Gutteridge.

'And your mother?' asked Duval with genuine interest. He could tell the solicitor was rarely asked about himself.

'You, my lord, know all about difficult fathers.' Mr Gutteridge was finding these questions as unsettling as they were interesting. He coughed in the manner of a full stop, hoping that they might now return to the matter at hand.

'Your mother?' repeated Duval.

'Perhaps you should have become a lawyer, rather than a physician,' said Mr Gutteridge and, seeing that Duval had no intention of letting go of the question, added, 'she was an opera singer, and no, she was not tall either.' Mr Gutteridge tried again, with a clearing of his throat, to move the conversation away from such a personal subject. Failing, he closed his eyes, then said, 'She died in childbirth, along with my newborn sister, when I was four. It is a terrible thing, childbed fever.'

'It happens,' said Duval, When I had my own practice, I knew many physicians who refused to update their medical knowledge. Often it is not in their financial interests to do so.'

Mr Gutteridge, clearing his throat, now said firmly, 'I have asked you here today to discuss your father's will, my lord. And your marriage.'

'Yes, sir,' said Duval. 'I want to contest the will. I think we have good grounds to do so. The codicil was a ridiculous piece of play-acting. I was married on the dot of the day requested; that has to be enough.'

'May I ask, have you seen Lady Harlington since the wedding?'

'I have every intention of returning to Muchmore soon,' said Duval.

'That doesn't answer the question, my lord.'

'I was married – surely that was the main request of my father's will, and it has been achieved.'

'Unfortunately,' said Mr Gutteridge, 'if the marriage has not been consummated, the request will be regarded as incomplete or invalid in both legal and religious contexts. Consummation is seen as an essential act of finalizing a marriage, even more so when the wife in question has been bought at a wife sale. Without it, grounds for annulment could be pursued. And in that case, the terms of the will would not have been satisfied.'

Duval clenched his fist.

'Mr Carson is prepared to take the matter to court,' continued Mr Gutteridge. 'His lawyer is arguing that since you didn't know the woman you married, left the house straight after the marriage ceremony, and have lived apart since the wedding, that means the marriage is not legally binding in the eyes of the law. I will write back to Carson's solicitor and argue that you have, by your father's codicil, a year to sort the problem out. I've gone over all the documents again, and there is nothing to say you couldn't marry a widow, but if the marriage is not made legal—'

'I am back at the beginning,' interrupted Duval.

'I am afraid so. Even if this marriage was annulled,' said Mr Gutteridge, 'and you were to remarry, that would be against the terms of your father's will. If your wife was to die before you returned to Muchmore...'

'I understand perfectly,' said Duval.

Mr Gutteridge saw him to the door, by which time the sign painter was packing up his brushes. The new words stood out in white: *R. Gutteridge Esq., Solicitor*, though the ghost of his father's name could still be seen, judging his too-tall son.

Duval went alone to Brooks one evening and was sat in a darkened corner, drinking his wine, when Arnold Prescott, with whom he had been at Oxford, asked if he might join. Duval nodded. Arnold looked even more scruffy than usual, though his clothes were made by the finest tailors. He had a charmed air of fog about him, but this only concealed his razor-blade of a mind that missed nothing.

'Suppose you've been inundated with questions about being in prison and the death of Marie Antoinette, etcetera, etcetera. All too boring and too violent for my liking, but are you alright?'

'No. Thank you for asking,' said Duval. The one thing he didn't want to do was talk about La Force.

'Quite understand, old man,' said Arnold, sitting down with a sigh. 'Do you know, for all my first-rate buggery of an education, I have ended up not writing the great English satire. That dream went to hell in a hay cart. Instead, I write for scandal rags. And the unsettling thing about it is I rather enjoy what I do. But it's been a bit of a dull season. So many desperate young girls, all with long faces and ancestral noses that look better in portraits than they do silhouette to silhouette.'

Duval smiled.

'But you look, as always, effortlessly elegant. Dashingly handsome, though not very happy. Whereas I, on the other hand... I'm in fine fettle and wear a corset. My better half tells me to leave off the puddings.'

'You're married?' said Duval.

'No, don't be ridiculous,' said Arnold. 'You know me too well.'

Duval smiled again. Changing the subject, Arnold said, 'But I heard that you were—'

'Were what?' interrupted Duval.

'Married.'

'And who did you hear that from?' asked Duval.

'Well, that's the thing. From a rather unpleasant little shit called Mr Carson.'

'Mr Carson,' repeated Duval. 'Wherever I go, there seems to be Mr Carson.'

'He claims to be your cousin,' said Arnold, 'and the rightful heritor of your family seat.'

'Where did you meet him?'

'There is a particular den of iniquity for gamblers, which is usually good for cheap gossip, off The Strand. That's where I found the little toe-rag. It's amazing what people tell you when they are on the brink of losing. Carson tried to sell me his story; he was accompanied by a man, a bit on the rough side, turned out to be a good gambler, far better than Carson. Mr Veldt was his name. I made some inquiries about him; he reminded me of a ferret, with small eyes that didn't miss a trick. Told me he owned a pub. Unlike Carson, he knew when to stop gambling. I couldn't quite work out why or how those two knew one another and thought maybe you could enlighten me.'

'No,' said Duval.

'Not like you – you're always one step ahead of everybody. Poor Duval, you're in a bad way – the black dog pulling you down?'

'It shouldn't,' said Duval. 'But it has. I wish I could laugh at it all, but it just doesn't seem to be in my nature to do so.'

'Mr Carson rather takes the humour out of things, I suppose.'

'How long ago did you see him?'

'About a week ago.'

Duval stood up.

'My dear boy,' said Arnold, 'a word of warning. Unfortunately everyone has had enough of the war – the wife sale is a story that people are hungry for. Not that I am going to say a word or write a word about it, honour bound.'

'Thank you,' said Duval.

The following morning, Duval finally decided to read the letter that had been waiting unopened since it arrived a couple of weeks ago. It wasn't his aunt's handwriting – he hadn't heard from her since he'd come to London, though he had written often. He took his coffee and sat by the fire in the sitting room.

My dear Duval,

I would like to know that you arrived safely in London, and that your mind is calmer.

I thank you for the protection of your name. A great name, I have discovered.

I understand your vexation and will not in any way impinge on your life or make scenes, if you decide to annul the marriage.

Perhaps this is a foolish thing to say, and of little consequence, but I had a feeling when I saw you in the coffee house that I would know you for a long time. I hope very much that will be the case, whatever the outcome.

I am, my lord, your obedient wife,
Edmée

Duval wrote back.

London
30th March, 1796

To an unknown woman, my wife.

You intrigue me.

He signed it, sealed it, left it to be sent up to Muchmore, then went out and promptly forgot all about it.

Duval decided that walking was the best way to soothe his troubled soul. Three days later, he found himself – consciously or unconsciously – in Soho. He came to a house in Greek Street he once knew well, which had had the impertinence to elbow its way between two taller buildings. The façade was painted dark red. He looked up at the house that had once been his refuge, the place where he'd learned the art of love. He wondered if the door still had a lady's hand for a knocker. He had stopped for a moment near the railings, when the door opened and light spilled onto the pavement.

A stick-thin maid came down the steps with a veiled lady and helped her into her carriage. 'Goodnight to you, madam,' she said.

He could almost see the young man he once was, eagerly running up those steps into the hall, longing to spend the night with Minnie Floss, a voluptuous beauty in her day. Very few had been chosen by her; he had been one of the lucky ones. He had forgotten that once he had been considered a lucky man.

Duval had turned to go when the maid called, 'Wait, sir – is that you? Is that Viscount Harlington?'

He turned back. 'Scrap,' he said. 'You haven't forgotten me.'

''Course I haven't. I don't forget anyone. You'd better come in, my lord.'

He remembered this house as having once seen grander days, but to his surprise it had a smell of new paint and had been freshly decorated *à la mode*.

'Minnie is doing well,' he observed.

'Better than ever,' said Scrap. 'My mistress has a head for money. She doesn't have to do a thing, except when the mood takes her.'

'Who is it?' came a voice from upstairs.

'A ghost from the past,' said Scrap. 'Shall I send him up?'

Duval stayed where he was. At the top of the stairs appeared a woman wearing a dressing gown. Gold glittered at her wrists and at her neck. Her face was heavily painted, yet Duval thought she looked more glorious than he remembered.

'Come,' she said in a deep, gravelly voice. 'Let me see you.'

He mounted the stairs towards her. 'Duval Harlington – what a delightful surprise.' She dropped a low, mocking curtsey.

'Minnie. You are as beautiful as ever,' he said.

'Candlelight, my love, and gold – that's the secret of staying young.' She chuckled. 'Champagne,' she called down to Scrap and ushered him into the salon that had once been full of her girls and a few gaming tables. Now, all was elegance, the room decorated in the French manner. 'I'm doing better than ever.'

'How?' asked Duval.

'Ladies,' she said. 'In my opinion, they don't have their fair share of fun. As well as private sessions, I do shows, *Two Naughty Ladies* – me and another girl. This one prefers the men, which is a shame. I'm still looking for someone perfect.'

Scrap brought the champagne, and Minnie sat on a chaise-longue and poured two glasses. Duval hovered.

'You've been in the wars, I hear.'

'In prison,' he said.

'And by the looks of things, you're still there. That old bastard of a father took the key to the house to his grave, did he?'

'Yes.'

'You were one of my favourites,' said Minnie. 'I believe I took your virginity.'

'You did. And you taught me well.' He sat down. 'Did you always like women?'

She smiled and took a sip of her champagne. 'I liked you a lot more than many. But ladies pay better than gentlemen, I have to say. Tell me,' she said, 'is it true you had to marry by a certain date or lose your estate?'

'How do you know that?' he asked. 'Did you hear from Arnold Prescott?'

'Surprisingly, no. I heard it from a frightened little bird who told me you'd found a wife in the nick of time.'

'Who was that little bird?'

'I'm speaking out of turn.' She flashed him a wicked smile, then said, 'Shall we go upstairs? I don't think I ever showed you my living quarters. Bring the bottle.'

On the top landing was the door to her inner sanctum. In all the hungry years of his youth, he had not once been allowed in there.

Minnie's chamber was decorated in the French style, with painted walls depicting exotic scenes. It was a salon given over to comfort, and beyond was a chamber dominated by a huge bed. The fires were lit; the whole room smelled of roses and spoke of all kinds of delights.

Minnie let her dressing gown fall open. He had never known a woman who was better dressed with nothing on.

'Isn't this why you came to see your Minnie?' she asked.

He hadn't thought that was the reason, but now he could think of nothing else.

He kissed her.

'You look ravishing,' he said, kissing her neck.

'And you look too well dressed, my lord,' she said, undoing his waistcoat, button by button.

Later, lying in her bed, staring up at a ceiling painted with cherubs doing what cherubs didn't usually do, he said, 'It's been a long time.'

'You have been through a lot,' she said quietly. 'And you've married.'

He turned to look at her. 'Yes,' he said, kissing her neck. 'Now tell me how you know.'

'A new client came about a week ago for a private session. She was shy and embarrassed about her needs. It took a while to reassure her she was safe here. I'm treading carefully, you understand. Predictably, she gave her name as Miss Smith. She told me that when she was eighteen she'd met a young lady, and by all accounts, they'd had a very passionate love affair. But her brother discovered them and threatened to have her locked away. She never saw her love again. She hates her brother, but has no means of escaping him, having no money of her own. She was hoping her brother might make a settlement on her, once he had inherited. But now, she said, there was another delay. I didn't quite get the gist of her story, and when I questioned her as to what inheritance and whose son, she looked like a startled deer. She kept saying sorry and she shouldn't have said anything, and she didn't mean anything by it. She left in a terrible fluster and forgot to take her reticule with her.' Minnie took hold of his hand and kissed it. 'I would like seconds,' she said. 'The first course was surprisingly divine.'

'By all means. But first – who was she?'

Minnie looked at him. 'You're going to get cross and waste this moment.'

'I will try not to.'

'Scrap looked inside the reticule and found a bill made out to Mr Ralph Carson. Am I right in thinking that's the same man who is hoping to inherit your estate?'

'Yes,' said Duval and lay back on the pillows. To hell with it all, he thought – this Carson was infiltrating every part of his life. Still, there was some consolation to be had in knowing his sister was no more fond of her brother than Duval. Her sapphic persuasion had garnered his respect as well as his intrigue.

'Now give me your hand, my lord,' said Minnie, 'and let me read this palm of yours.'

Minnie studied it for a long time. 'You have a creative soul,' she said at last. 'Imagination and loyalty. And you will love once and love long.'

'Stop it,' he said, snatching his hand away. 'I have never been in love and have no wish to be. I don't trust that emotion. Rubbish. Hocus-pocus. The lines on my hand mean nothing.'

'Come here.'

He kissed her again, delighting in the softness of her skin. She giggled and wrapped her arms around him. He relished the pleasure that came from making her back arch, and he kissed the part of her that drove her wild.

Duval woke to find Minnie gone, and a bath and breakfast waiting for him.

As he was about to leave, Scrap handed him a note. For a moment, he thought it was a bill for his night of pleasure. Instead, written boldly in Minnie's hand, he read:

The lines on your hand don't lie. You have already met the woman you will love.

No Reply

Edmée had woken up with a start that first day at Muchmore after the wedding. She had thought she heard Mr Hyde in the room and sat up in such a fright that she could hardly breathe or make sense of her surroundings. Perhaps she screamed. Yes, she must have screamed, for the poor maids, as silent as ghosts, had rushed from the room without touching the fires they had been sent to light. Edmée was aware that her behaviour would be reported back to the housekeeper, who would immediately report back to Lady Harriet, no doubt believing the new Lady Harlington to be insane.

Edmée knew this to be the case, for last night, after the wedding, she had trailed the furious Duval upstairs and stayed in the shadows, unsure of what to do or where to go. She had no desire to spy on her new husband. All she wanted was to avoid the Carsons and their endless questions.

She heard Duval say, 'I don't even know who she is; I bought her for ten guineas at a wife sale in Thetford.' There was a quieter voice with him in the room – she supposed it must be Lady Harriet. The last thing she heard before

Jameson hurriedly ushered her away was, 'I intended to have the marriage annulled.'

Left alone in her chamber, feeling sure she had been forgotten, she once again heard a voice – Lady Harriet, she was certain this time. The voice had sounded some way off. Edmée had left her room and tiptoed down a corridor. At the end was the grand staircase, leading to the great hall. She listened as Lady Harriet addressed the servants in a commanding voice, making it quite clear that not a word was to be said about the new bride or the circumstances surrounding the marriage, if those working there wished to keep their jobs. If Lady Harlington was to visit any other chamber in the house, then it was imperative that a footman accompany her, and the room inspected after she had left for any missing items. All unusual behaviour was to be reported to Lady Harriet right away.

Edmée, exhausted in mind and body, had returned to her chamber. Still in her wedding robe, she had lain down on the bed and fallen asleep – that was, until her screaming had woken her up.

After the maids had left, Edmée tried to find her old clothes to change into, certain that she would be asked to leave that morning. She looked around the chamber but couldn't see them anywhere – all she could find was her box. It had been left by Jameson who, true to his word, had delivered it safe and unopened. Edmée was thrilled to see it, for it contained all she possessed – the most important item among them her father's precious book.

She was about to bend down to the box when there was a knock on the door.

'Yes?' she said, standing bolt upright.

There stood a young maid, face washed clean, her nose and cheeks red from her journey. 'My name is Hannah,' she said. 'I am here, my lady, to look after you.'

'Look after me?' Edmée repeated.

'I arrived from Woodbridge this morning. Now, would you like a bath?'

'Yes. Yes, I would.'

Edmée stood by as a procession of footmen brought in a bath and then pails of piping-hot water.

Finally alone, Edmée climbed into the bath and let the water soothe her bruised and battered body. She put her heavy head under the water and opened her eyes, to see Hannah looking down at her. Edmée rose up, gasping for air. Hannah said, in a calm, measured voice, 'Are you in pain, my lady?'

Edmée nodded. 'It is getting better.'

'You stay there.' Hannah rang the bell and orders were given. Arnica poultices and camphor and chamomile lotion were to be brought up, along with a breakfast tray and a freshly ironed nightgown. With no judgement, no questions asked, Hannah attended to the scratch marks on Edmée's body – it looked as if a wild animal had attacked her – while speaking as she might to a terrified child, soft and gentle.

Edmée listened and the tears that, like a warrior, she had refused to give into broke against Hannah's persistent kindness. She wept until every part of her felt as if it had been shaken and rearranged.

Utterly exhausted, she was helped back into bed. Lying back on the soft pillows, she said, 'I don't think there is enough water to clean me,' and fell into a deep sleep.

It took Edmée until February passed into March to go further than the bedchamber. She relished her days of rest in that sweet heaven. An island of peace free from fear and tempest. The walls were wallpapered in exotic birds from another land, flying in the golden richness of a sunset that bore no resemblance to the grey skies of the first day of March outside her own window.

Along with the breakfast tray that morning, boxes and boxes arrived. Hannah, looking pleased with herself, said, 'I took the liberty to have some gowns bought for you. I wrote to the housekeeper at St James's Square. She knew the right emporium in London for gowns and chemises.'

Edmée looked at the three gowns – a morning gown, a tea gown and an evening gown. They were slightly dull, but she could, she supposed, alter them. Hannah said, 'I explained that you had come from Paris, and I was sure you would not relish a corset or padding. Lady Haslet has asked if you would dine with her tonight, you see, and she will expect you to be dressed accordingly. I asked Mrs Appleby to make you another robe from her designs, just in case the ones the housekeeper sent were not to your liking.'

'Thank you. You have chosen well,' said Edmée. She held up one of the evening gowns. 'This one is exquisite.'

'There's hardly anything of it,' said Hannah. 'It was made in Woodbridge by Mrs Appleby. She is a French émigré, like you, my lady.'

Edmée looked at the dress again, examining it carefully.

'Tom, her husband – a sailor – rescued her from drowning. He was a catch. Many a young lady in Woodbridge wept bitter tears when he married the dressmaker.'

Edmée was still staring fixedly at the gown. *Madame Dupont*, she thought, and felt her stomach to be filled with lead. It couldn't be the same woman, could it? But there was no mistaking her signature – a little embroidered bee – sewn into the lining. This woman had the power to have Edmée cast out of this enchantment once and for all. With one word, all this would disappear.

'Let's get you outside, my lady. Just a little walk to stretch your limbs,' said Hannah.

'Could I have some writing paper and ink?'

'Why the sudden urgency? It will be here when you get back, my lady. Don't look so worried, it's only a bit of fresh air.'

There was no way to refuse without arousing suspicion. She would write to Madame Dupont as a matter of urgency when she got back, and pray to the Supreme Being that the modist would not unpick the stitches of her well-concealed past.

Her new boots sounded loudly on the gravel outside. Spring was still being held tight in winter's bony hand, and Edmée's breath was icy before her. The air smelled sweet. Rooks rose, charcoal black, their wings smudging a grey sky.

A little way off was a gardener on a ladder. He climbed down on seeing her and bowed.

'My lady, can I be of any help?' he asked, his face as wrinkled as an old conker. 'Would you like me to show you the garden, your ladyship?'

'Yes,' Edmée said with relief, certain she was being watched from behind the long windows of the house.

The lawns rolled down to the lake. Beyond that, there was a walkway through a path of silver beech trees, ending in a fountain. At the centre was a sculpture of Neptune.

'How long have you known Lord Harlington?' Edmée asked.

'I have known him since he first brought his wooden horse out into the garden. He was such a sweet little fellow, just like his mother. I always say, show me a gentle boy and I will show you a gentleman.' He sighed. 'It's a long time since we have had people down here,' said the gardener. 'The late Lord Harlington didn't like visitors.'

⋆

That evening, Edmée was dressed by Hannah, who had magic fingers. When Hannah finished, she had managed to make Edmée's short hair look as if it had been done by design, not rage. When the mirror was turned round for Edmée to see herself, she wondered if she had metamorphosed back into someone she used to be, because now she could only vaguely see the ghost of Mrs Hyde staring quizzically at her.

'You look perfect,' Hannah said encouragingly. Edmée took a deep breath and went down to supper with more confidence than she had felt for a long time.

The dining room was large and the lady sitting at the end of the long table looked formidable. She was dressed in a gown that was out of date, belonging to a time before the Revolution. Whalebone corset, padding – clothes that were meant to put you in your place, to show who the true aristocrat was. Lady Harriet did not rise on seeing Edmée, but waited for her to be seated as far away from her as possible, where there was little hope of any conversation. And true to the distance between them, Lady Harriet showed no interest in talking.

The first course came and went. The silence grew more awkward.

Edmée jumped when, finally, Lady Harriet spoke. 'I'm sure you are aware that my nephew was in prison in Paris.'

'Yes,' said Edmée.

'This marriage to you was his only way of securing the estate.'

'I know.'

'My nephew has written and told me that he intends to take legal advice as to his father's ridiculous will. He hopes that it might be sorted out and this marriage will be annulled in due course. Lord Harlington is a generous man and will provide for you. But you must understand that such a marriage is unacceptable, and the idea that a country parson's widow – a widow of just ten days – could marry a man of Lord

Duval's standing is ludicrous. When this is over, and let's hope it does not take too long, I will be asking you to leave. Do I make myself quite clear? For you to have any expectations of staying here would be folly.' The candlelight caught a steely look in Lady Harriet's face as she stared at Edmée. Edmée said nothing.

Lady Harriet rose and announced that she would be taking her evening tea in the sitting room. 'There is no need for you to join me. I wish you goodnight.'

Edmée too stood up and curtseyed, then – rather unexpectedly – responded, 'I quite understand your feelings, Lady Harriet. I am sure if I was in your position I would be equally angry to find a stranger foisted upon me, especially after having grieved for a nephew I believed dead. I can well sympathize with the disappointment you must have felt. You perceive me as being beneath him in both class and in education, and think that a marriage between your nephew and me is nothing short of scandalous. I have no wish to dispel the impression you have of me, but I will say that I survived the September Massacres and a dreadful marriage to a truly monstrous man. This has been a safe harbour, and I thank you for it. I am sure, in time, your nephew will be free to find a suitable bride and I will be gone. I wish you goodnight.'

Upstairs again, Hannah helped undress Edmée. Before she left, Edmée requested a new notebook. Finally left alone, she sat down to write her second letter of the day to that unknown husband of hers.

Edmée was surprised when, the following day, Hannah began laying out her one and only evening gown, wondering aloud how to alter it for the evening ahead.

'Why?' asked Edmée.

'Because Lady Harriet sent word that you were to dine with her again tonight. She will think it strange that you only have one gown.' Edmée tried to conceal her surprise at this, and instead asked for a needle and thread. She knew how to make the dress look different. She took out the heavy lining and let the cotton cling to her figure.

That evening, Lady Harriet met her in the drawing room. She was seated upright in a wing-back chair, the fire ablaze. A glass of sherry was poured.

'Your English is good,' said Lady Harriet, 'and my French is bad. Last night, I was unforgivably rude to you. I detest rudeness in others. It is not your fault that you found yourself at a wife sale and it is not Duval's fault that he bought you. I have no idea how long it will take to untangle this mess, but while you are here, I think we should both make an effort to get on in a civil manner.'

'Thank you,' said Edmée with a curtsey.

'Do you read?'

'Yes, novels, but I have not mastered reading as fast in English.'

'A pity. My eyes are not what they used to be, and at night, even with mirrored candlelight, I cannot see the print.'

'I could tell you fairy stories,' Edmée suggested.

'No, I am not a child.'

'Neither was the countess who told them,' said Edmée. 'These are not suitable for innocent ears, for they talk of unspeakable acts.'

'Well,' Lady Harriet said, 'that sounds entertaining.'

Edmée felt relief wash over her, and after dinner, she told the first of the many fairy stories that she knew.

At the end, Lady Harriet said, 'That, my dear, has been the most entertaining evening I have had for quite some time. Until tomorrow, then?'

I'd better get some more dresses, thought Edmée.

*

March passed faster than Edmée had thought possible. The snow turned to rain and the earth turned to mud. Story by story, she and Lady Harriet began to get to know one another, though Edmée's husband remained a mystery. She had no idea who he was, but she knew he was greatly loved by his aunt and by all the household staff who had put up with his terrible father, and that he, like her, had been in prison. All of this led Edmée to believe the two of them had more in common than not.

Towards the end of the month, she finally received a letter from Duval.

To an unknown woman, my wife.

You intrigue me.

Never had so few lines given her so much hope. She felt irrationally excited, and wrote back, hoping this would be the beginning of a correspondence.

There I was, thinking you hadn't read my letter. Is being intrigued enough, or are those the only words you had time to write? I suppose your inkwell and your pen must have fallen into some profound disagreement with one another, and their quarrel is the reason for your lack of sentences. On the other hand, my pen, in the quiet of this room, seems too full of the words I want to write to you. Would to heaven you were my friend, in that we might find a starting point. Is it too much to ask to be friends with a three-word writer?

Now a dark thought has come to me: I am being dismissed by you. My intrigue is tiresome, perhaps. But as I have nothing to lose, I have nothing but hope that the quarrel between pen and ink resolves itself and you may write again.

Edmée finished the letter and sent it, hoping it was playful enough to catch Duval's attention.

April arrived and spring felt ready to burst through. But Edmée's spirits were low. There had been no message, no letter, not a word from Duval. Lady Harriet would often ask her to read out the letters Duval had sent to his aunt. He spoke to her of the parties he had attended, the folly of London society. Never once did he ask about his wife, or mention when he planned to return.

Edmée was beginning to see the tenuous piece of string that attached her to him growing thinner, ready to break away.

Tiredness returned, and she put it down to her disappointment that Duval hadn't written. Perhaps she was a little put out, too, by the dresses in the boxes marked *Arabella* brought down from the attic. Lady Harriet had been so impressed with Edmée's ability to give her evening gown so many variations that she had requested Edmée's help to make her look, as she put it, less staid in her appearance. Mrs Appleby the dressmaker was sent for, to see if any of the fabric in Arabella's gowns could be put to good use. She had replied to Edmée's letter, saying that she believed the young woman her ladyship was referring to was long dead, that there was no need for Edmée to be at all concerned about the matter, and that she looked forward to meeting the new Lady Harlington. The letter had been signed by a Madame Dupont, and had filled Edmée with a relief too great to measure.

Arabella's robes had been aired, hung up and left for inspection in Lady Harriet's dressing chamber.

'Well,' said Lady Harriet, 'Arabella is no longer spending time at Muchmore, so I think we could make use of these dresses. I so despise waste.' She waved an indifferent hand to all the gowns hanging there and said, 'Arabella did have style when it came to dressing. The fabrics were, I remember, heavenly in both touch and quality.'

'Who is Arabella?' Edmée asked, knowing her suspicions would be confirmed.

'She was Duval's mistress.'

Seeing Edmée looking downcast, Lady Harriet said, 'My dear girl, Arabella was, in my humble opinion, a rather frightful woman. She only appealed to my brother, who knew how to tease her with false promises. And when she realized that Duval would not get a penny until Lord Harlington was dead, her devotion to Duval disappeared. You needn't worry, though – she is now married to a banker, I believe.'

After supper, they were playing cards when Lady Harriet said, with a slight edge to her voice, 'The housekeeper tells me that you haven't had your monthly, and you have been here long enough. Is everything as it should be?'

'Yes,' Edmée replied. 'I think that all the upheaval has affected me.'

'Quite,' said Lady Harriet.

Edmée told herself that she wasn't to worry. She was just late. Another week and no letter from Duval. Another week and she knew then that she was in trouble. *No, no*, she said to herself. *Mr Hyde cannot ruin all this. Not now. Please. Please not now.*

Such a Scandal

Duval was in his library that sunny April morning, wondering why he hated the smell of hyacinths so much, before remembering that it was a flower his father had particularly loved. There was a knock on the door and a footman came in to inform him that a Mrs Philip Gosling was in the drawing room.

'Who?' asked Duval.

The footman cleared his throat. 'Mrs *Arabella* Gosling.'

Duval had been meaning to call on Arabella, but the thought of her drawing room, cluttered with gossips, had put him off.

She had always been a diamond that men flocked to, but today she was alone, standing by the window, looking – as she always did – expensively dressed. She wore an open ochre netted cotton robe trimmed with matching satin ribbon. Her headdress was extravagant.

'My dear Duval,' she said, as he took her hand to kiss it. 'The reports are correct. You are much better looking than you were. You have more gravitas than you had in your youth.'

'Champagne, Mrs Gosling?'

'What else is there?'

She strolled round the room, studying some of the ornaments, draping her gloved hands over the backs of chairs, as if thinking how best this conversation might go. After the champagne had been poured into fluted crystal glasses, she seemed to conclude that there was no good way to start, and sat down.

'News – no,' she said, 'not news – gossip, of, let's say, an… interesting nature has reached me, and I thought I would ask if it was correct.' Duval sat opposite her, his legs crossed, his face still. 'I think you know what I'm about to say.'

Duval said nothing.

'Tra-la-la. You are not going to talk. So let me start. A rather unpleasant gentleman, returned from a sojourn in the countryside not far from Muchmore House, brought with him news so scandalous that he hopes it will have you thrown out of all society drawing rooms and gentlemen's clubs. He values the scandal that highly.'

Duval still hadn't moved. He took a sip of his drink and a slow smile spread across his lips. 'You look content with life,' he said.

'Yes,' she said, laughing cheerfully. 'Who would have thought it? My husband is ten years older than me and resembles a small bear. We have a daughter… But that is not why I am here. As I was saying, this little man—'

'I take it you mean Mr Ralph Carson.'

'Yes. I met him at the Wallington's and he said he was only doing his civic duty—'

'Then, I suppose, you have come to ask me if I bought my wife at a wife sale, to which the answer is yes. I have no idea who she is, and no doubt he found that out from someone at Muchmore.' Duval laughed.

'It isn't funny,' Arabella said, doing her best to conceal a smile.

'Oh, but it is. A farce.'

'Duval, you are incorrigible. You must dine with us on the 23rd, and no more hiding away.'

'I am not.'

'Oh tra-la-la. I insist. And tomorrow you must join our party at the theatre where you will meet my husband. *The Beggar's Opera*. I insist. Look, this scandal has the potential to ruin you, but I am prepared to help. A scandal in the right hands can be the making of one. I, of all people, should know that, and fortunately I am a past mistress of turning misfortune into gold.'

After she had gone, Duval sat remembering Arabella's irritating whims from the time when she was his mistress. He would be lying if he said that the notion of putting an end to the affair hadn't been one of the reasons for him going to study in Paris in the first place. Being married to her would have been unbearable. So what was he doing now? After all, he knew the sticky threads of guilt that she could stitch around one.

Duval sat there for some time, until the light had begun to disappear, the bottle of champagne was drunk and the sounds of London were distant – the noise of the carriages, the horses clip-clopping by. There was a door opening. A window shutting.

Left with little else to distract him, Duval found himself travelling back to the darkest of places in the twilight of his memory. He remembered the days of promise after the fall of the Bastille, when the clocks had been stopped and restarted, the revolutionary fever high in his blood. At last, it had seemed, there would be an equality in the classes, a uniformity in fashion. The aristocracy would no longer be riddled with etiquette and guilds that told them what they could wear and where they stood in the great hierarchy of France.

He saw his friend Etienne once more, seated opposite

him. He dared not look at his face. Instead, he studied his shoes, his friend's filthy stockings. *You want to talk about scandal – what luxury is that? Does any of this folly amount to anything? Do you remember how we, among all our fellow prisoners, commanded affection?* Etienne said.

'Go away, Etienne,' said Duval, but he had gone too far. He had already arrived back in that dark place. He saw his friend's bare knees, the buckles of his breeches undone.

Remember, said the ghost. *There was not a breeze. Above us, in the immense halls of the Palais de la Cité, fashionable citizens of Paris shopped and admired the superb galleries filled with perfumes and elegant refinements. But below, no further away than the thickness of the vault, were bolts, gratings, groans, rags, and an insupportable stench. That is where we were. And she wants to talk of a scandal?*

The mention of scandal brought Duval's mind back to Edmée. He thought about the way she had stood there at the wife sale, the way she walked, the grace of her limbs, the perfect shape of her neck. Finally, he understood what he had failed to notice that February day, though it had been there when he first saw her in the coffee shop. She had a grace, a glimmer to her that Arabella, for all her expensive clothes and contrived manners, never possessed.

At last, sighed Etienne, *at last you see. C'est des conneries. So, what does this scandal matter?*

The story originally appeared in the scurrilous pamphlet that the bon ton loved to read, the *Courteous Reader*. It had been picked up by the heftier papers of the day, and for the past week, Lord Harlington and the wife sale had been a story that the nation couldn't get enough of.

An image came to Duval of the chattering ladies of

London, faint with romantic notions of what that might mean; gentlemen at their breakfast tables wishing their own marriages had been so easy to arrange.

Duval read an article in the *Comet* that posed the question: what is a peer of the realm to do when given two days and seven hours to find a bride?

'The scandal,' it continued, 'if there is a scandal, rests firmly with the late earl, who knew of his son's imprisonment in Paris, but still arrogantly went ahead with a last will and testament that put in jeopardy one of England's finest estates.' The *Morning Post* used the word 'émigré' to describe Edmée. *The Times* proclaimed that the practice of wife sales was shocking and surely must be outlawed, going as it did against Christianity and a sense of common decency.

By the morning of the Gosling dinner, the scandal had been somewhat overshadowed by the Battle of Mondovì and Napoleon's advance across Europe. As Duval drank his coffee, a Shakespeare quote came back to him – *All the world's a stage, and all the men and women merely players. They have their exits and their entrances; and one man in his time plays many parts*. He had survived the Terror, prison and the guillotine. He was not going to be defeated by this ridiculous thing. It was nobody's business but his own and no one had the right to judge him. He was pleased, nonetheless, that interest in the story seemed to be fading.

As he got up from his desk, he saw the letter Edmée had written to him. He had forgotten all about it. He smiled when he read, *Is it too much to ask to be friends with a three-word writer?* and remembered the three words he had sent her: *You intrigue me*. Perhaps the time had come to find out who this unknown wife of his was. He had looked at death; now he would start to examine living, and he wondered if that might not be harder.

Chitter Chatter

'This is much better than we feared, my lord,' said Jameson, dressing Duval that evening for the Gosling dinner. 'Lady Harriet will be pleased.'

Duval studied the waistcoat that Jameson had chosen, elegant in its simplicity, then said, 'What exactly are you referring to?'

'I meant the coverage in the newspapers is rather sympathetic.'

'Ah,' said Duval, 'not one mention of your role in the affair, which must be most satisfying.'

'My lord, I don't know what you mean,' said Jameson, going red. 'I would never talk to the press; neither would William.'

'I know you wouldn't, but you can't tell me that William, and you in all your innocence, had no idea there was such a thing as a wife sale at Thetford. It was just one of those convenient coincidences, nothing to do with Mr Brown, the head groom at Muchmore, who bought himself a wife there.'

'It was a desperate moment,' said Jameson. 'Mr Brown is very happy, has two daughters and another on the way.'

Duval smiled. 'I agree, a desperate moment,' he said.

*

Granger the butler came to tell Duval that Sir Arnold Prescott was waiting for him in the drawing room.

'There you are,' said Arnold when Duval entered. 'The very picture of a dashing man about town, the connoisseur of wife sales.'

'Good to see you too, Arnold.'

'I wonder if I could accompany you to the Goslings'? I am in desperate need of champagne.' He began to walk back and forth across the drawing room. 'This is perhaps the handsomest drawing room I've ever been in,' he said at last, sitting down. 'Your wretched father did have good taste.'

A footman brought the champagne in, poured it and left. The first glass Arnold drank in one go; the second he slowed down on.

'I just want you to know,' he said, 'that I didn't write this... my dear love, I never would. Someone seems to be on a mission to inform all and sundry that your marriage will be annulled, so Cecilia Cartwright has written in the *Courteous Reader*. Here, look for yourself.'

Duval read it.

> He would have married a horse to save his estate. It was fortunate that his lordship found an obliging widow at the wife sale. But ladies, do not despair, I have heard from a reliable source that the dashing Lord Harlington will soon be back on the marriage market.

'Who is the source for this?' Duval asked. 'Do you know?'

'I have no proof, but I know that Arabella has been chattering away. I was at Almack's the other night. Quite frankly, the audience Arabella had around her would have made Covent Garden blush, and the subject that had brought so much attention was you, my dear love.'

'This is the last thing I want to have happen,' said Duval, screwing up the pamphlet. He went and stood by the window. Down below, the carriage was waiting.

'What are you going to do?' asked Arnold.

'I'm going tomorrow, back to Muchmore. As for the scandal – God's blood.'

In the carriage, Arnold talked. Duval wasn't listening. He was thinking of Edmée. Perhaps she would understand the loneliness buried deep within his soul, for he had begun to suspect that they weren't so different.

'Yes,' he said out loud.

'Good,' said Arnold. 'Just remember, when we leave, if Arabella tries to question you, you are to say Monty is expecting us. That should silence her. She can't stand the man – my dear love could eat her for breakfast.'

Yes, Duval thought, *it's time to return to Muchmore*.

Hanover Square was one of the quintessential squares of the England of George I, built on graceful lines that reflected a country in control of its destiny. But now, the chaos of the rest of London, with its growing population, was beginning to infringe upon the square.

Mr Philip Gosling's house was elegant in the simplicity of its Parisian decoration, and was as grand as a house could be. Arabella had done well for herself. Duval and Arnold were shown up to a drawing room. Duval was announced first by the footman.

Arabella greeted him, wearing a muslin gown that showed off her figure to perfection. She clapped her hands with delight when she saw Duval, then, as if not knowing he and Arnold had arrived together, introduced Arnold to Duval as one of London's most notorious gossips.

Arnold immediately annoyed her by saying, 'Duval and I were at Oxford together and, more recently, we shared the carriage here.'

Arabella pretended she hadn't heard a word and said, 'Arnold is now responsible for a column called "Titbits". These days, his brutal pen is dipped in the blood of the best bits of gossip and scandal on the butcher's slab.'

'I don't know if that's true,' said Arnold, 'it seems I have a rival.'

'Who?' asked Arabella.

'You, my dear,' he said.

'Oh, foe fiddle,' she said, blushing. 'It has been such a dull season, apart from that foolish girl who drowned in the Serpentine. Quite honestly, I believe she did it purposely.'

'And I believe,' said Arnold, 'you expressed that view in front of her betrothed.'

'No, never. You mean that twig was her intended? All I can say is it's hard to know which one was more spared. Excuse me.' And she took Duval purposely by the arm and moved him away. 'I must tell,' she said, a wicked smile on her lips, 'I have invited the most conceited of all the émigré community, and the richest: the Marquis de Soule. You will see straight away why the French Revolution caught on.'

'I know why the French Revolution caught on – I was there,' said Duval. 'I thought the marquis would have been guillotined. He is the personification of the *ancien régime*.'

'Tra-la-la. To tell the truth and shame the devil, I didn't think for a moment he would accept. But I mentioned your name in my note, and he agreed. I would imagine he is fascinated to meet an Englishman who has survived La Force. It is, I believe, a horrid little place with lots of nasty dogs.'

'Don't allow yourself to be complimented, Lord Harlington,' said Philip Gosling. 'The marquis is a famous roué who can never resist a beautiful woman. I also happen to be his banker.'

Arabella's description of her husband had been cruel and inaccurate. He was a man with great charisma – and yet, for all his charm, Duval could tell he found his wife irritating. If this was a supposed happy marriage, he wanted none of it. To live in a loveless relationship interested him little: in that one thing, he did agree with his father.

'The Marquis de Soule,' said Mr Gosling to Duval, 'unlike some of his fellow émigrés, is in a fortunate position. I encouraged him early on to transfer his money to my bank. He has wealth beyond the dreams of many English aristocrats, and he lives in one of the grandest houses in Marylebone.'

'I can't imagine that you were solely responsible for his good fortune,' Arabella retorted.

Next to arrive was the politician, Sir Wilfrid Fairly, who heaved his majestic frame up the stairs, exclaiming with wheezy breaths, 'I believe there are more of these damnable stairs tonight than there were last time we were here.' In his wake came Lady Anne, his wife, a plain woman who hardly ever spoke and wore upon her lips a smile that never altered.

They were followed by Lord Sutton, who turned out to be a cheerful gentleman, accompanied by Mrs Cora Dent. Only then did Duval remember reading about Lord Sutton's mistress, a woman well known for her charitable work. It had been Lord Sutton who had invested in Mrs Dent's passion, which was a small revolution of her own making – that of saving servants, slaves and women who were victims of abuse. She had caused many a scandal by telling the perpetrators exactly what she thought of their behaviours; she had also been known to knock a man unconscious if he was fool enough to stand in her way. Her plumage was as bright as a parrot, and she spoke with a strong cockney accent. She was not a woman given to ceremony, and going up to Duval, she curtsied briefly and said, 'May I congratulate you, my lord. I do love a man who finds his way round a problem. "A wife sale?" I said to Lord Sutton. "That is a man of initiative."'

Duval said, 'Thank you, I would be too dry in the boot if I was to take all the credit. I think I owe my valet his fair share of the accolade.'

Lord Sutton introduced himself, then said, 'Many men would do better in a wife sale than they do in the marriage market – a brutal affair at the best of times.'

Duval, finding himself in a corner of a room with Arabella, asked her about the gossip in the *Courteous Reader*. Arabella was having none of it. Instead, she said, loud enough for Mr Gosling to hear, 'Don't be such an outrageous flirt, my lord.'

Duval stepped quickly away from her.

Mrs Dent came to Duval's rescue. 'Are you enjoying being back in London, Lord Harlington?'

'No,' he said, 'I seem to have lost my ability to swim with the tide.'

The last to arrive was the Marquis Reynaud de Soule, wearing a tall wig, an embroidered frock coat, satin breeches, and red-heeled shoes with diamond buckles. His cravat was tied most elegantly, in the style known as the waterfall. His age was almost impossible to guess.

'Monsieur le Marquis,' said Arabella. He bowed and, with all the etiquette and manners that belonged to the *ancien regime*, kissed her hand. 'May I introduce Lord Harlington,' said Arabella triumphantly.

The two men bowed and murmured politely. The marquis regarded Duval through his quizzing glass.

*

The conversation round the dining table that night flowed as freely as the wine, and when Sir Wilfrid Fairly warmed up for one of his political speeches on the subject of the Revolution, he was stopped immediately by Mr Gosling. 'You are not in Parliament now, Sir Wilfrid.'

'The question still demands an answer,' said the politician. 'Mrs Dent asked me if I thought we had been too lenient with the number of émigrés we have allowed into the country, and my answer is yes, far too lenient.'

'Do you imagine for a moment, Sir Wilfrid,' said the marquis, 'that any Frenchman or Frenchwoman wants to be an émigré? To be forced to leave their lands, their houses, to start again in a country that doesn't possess their humour or their language and is frightened of their religion?'

'But Monsieur le Marquis—' said Sir Wilfrid.

However, de Soule was not to be interrupted. 'And to cross La Manche in a small, unseaworthy boat, to discover they have paid a fortune, only to be at the mercy of sailors threatening to throw them overboard unless they pay double?'

Lady Anne Fairly, who spoke so rarely that, when she did, she was listened to intently, said, 'It is tragic, the poverty that is suffered by so many who come here from France.'

The plates were cleared away and the second course was served: roast beef, roast pork, chicken and vegetables, accompanied by sauces of various kinds.

Arabella, who clearly felt inspired to feel empathy for the Marquis de Soule, all of a sudden, said, 'Oh, Monsieur le Marquis, what you suffered. Was everything taken from you?'

The marquis didn't answer.

It was Lady Anne Fairly who asked, 'They didn't steal your gemstones, I hope?'

There was a pause, and then, without an ounce of modesty, the marquis replied, 'No, they wouldn't have known where to find them.' He paused. 'Jewels,' he said to Duval, as if he might not understand, 'were easier to bring to London than art.'

'And the most valuable of yours?' interrupted Arnold. 'Which stone was that?'

'An emerald without flaw, perfect.'

'Is such a gem possible?' asked Arabella.

'Yes, of course, and I own it.'

'And how much would the emerald cost?' inquired Arabella. 'If it was ever for sale?'

The marquis, ignoring Arabella, said, 'There is a curse on this emerald – maybe because such perfection needs to be protected.'

'And its price?' persisted Arabella, giddy with the thought.

'More money than anyone in this room possesses.'

There was a silence while this piece of information was digested and found not to have a bone in it to be argued with.

The third course was served: fruit pies, jellies, a selection of cheeses, and small cakes.

Lord Sutton said, 'I must compliment you on your cook, Philip.'

'Hear, hear!' said Sir Wilfrid. 'One of the best tables in London.'

Better make the most of it,' said Mrs Dent cheekily, 'before the Revolution starts here.'

'My dear lady, it won't,' said Sir Wilfrid, 'not when we have a parliament that can speak fearlessly to the upper house.' Turning to the banker, he said, 'Philip, you were one person who saw the French Revolution coming.'

'I wasn't alone,' said Mr Gosling.

'But not many of us,' said Lord Sutton, 'had the wit to go every week to Paris, before the storming of the Bastille, in order to persuade the aristocracy to move their money to

London. One could argue that you, sir, are responsible for what happened to the unfortunate king. If his subjects hadn't abandoned Paris to come here and be near their bank, he might have held on to his head.'

'I doubt it,' said the marquis. 'He was a foolish man, with little understanding of his people or their suffering, always searching for someone else to make decisions for him. Even if we had all stayed at Versailles, I am in no doubt the outcome for him and the queen would have been the same.'

'Is it likely you will ever be given back your châteaux and lands?' asked Lord Sutton.

The marquis said, 'If I was a fool, I might hope for that, but I am not. I think we have been permanently disinherited. There are too many émigrés living here who are banking on their property being returned to them one day. But no one in France has any interest in that. No one wants us back.'

'Monsieur,' said Arabella, 'I heard a story that when the Bastille fell—'

He smiled. 'My dear Mrs Gosling, there were many fantastical stories about me. There is no accounting for them, but I do so admire people's imagination.' He turned to Duval. 'You supported the Revolution, did you not, my lord?'

'I did, Monsieur le Marquis.'

'Are you one of those Jacobins, Lord Harlington?'

'No, monsieur,' said Duval. 'The Revolution is one of the most extraordinarily radical ideas of our time, perhaps of all time. But it has taken too much blood from the body of France.'

'As for the role of women having equal rights with men,' said Sir Wilfrid, 'that was, in my view, folly.'

'In my view,' said Duval, 'it was one of the most exciting ideas to come out of the Revolution, but unfortunately, far too ahead of its time.'

'In the end, it will all be the same,' said the marquis indifferently. 'Revolution or no revolution, nothing will change – or rather, everything will change, and no one will know the difference.'

Duval looked into de Soule's eyes and found he was reminded of his father. *Here*, he thought, *is a man just like him: arrogant and convinced of his own infallibility*. He pictured both of them as enormous slugs, leaving a silver trail of slime behind them.

The fourth course provided a temporary respite. A sugar sculpture was placed on the table, a replica of the house in Hanover Square. Plates of marzipan and sugared almonds accompanied it.

'It's absolutely delightful,' said Mrs Dent.

Arabella, waving the decoration aside as if every day such follies of sugar were placed before her, said, in a slightly aggrieved manner, that the marquis had not told his famous story about the lion. She tried again to coax him, with equal lack of success.

'Your wife' – the marquis turned to Duval, waving Arabella away as you would a wasp – 'is English?'

Duval, having no desire to talk about Edmée to this insolent man, hoped he might get away with a straightforward 'no'.

But the marquis was having none of it. 'Is she French?'

'Yes,' said Duval.

'What was her family name?'

'Where in France is she from?' asked Lord Sutton.

'From what I read in the papers, I understand she was a widow,' said Mrs Dent.

'A widow of a French gentleman?' asked the marquis.

'Oh no, he was an English parson,' said Lady Wilfrid, to everyone's surprise. 'His parish was in Suffolk, I believe. Is that right, Lord Harlington?'

'So, she has never been to London?' asked the marquis.

Duval wasn't sure where she had been. He was certain that he had had enough – more than enough – of the questions.

'You must bring her here immediately,' said Arabella.

The marquis interrupted her. 'I try and keep a record of all those who arrive in London. It hadn't occurred to me there would be more coming to England at different ports.'

Arabella, now on a topic she enjoyed, said, 'You positively have to introduce us to her. The perfect time would be a ball, let's say, next month – remember you promised? And which dressmakers has she visited? I mean, she can't come here and look like some country bumpkin, that would never do. Her eyes – what colour are her eyes?'

'Green,' said Duval.

'Just green? I mean, there are many shades of green,' said Arabella.

'They are the green of a pond when sunshine dances on its surface.'

'Sounds rather unpleasant,' said Arabella, 'but perhaps, when you look at them, they are more enchanting than that. Are they?'

Arnold, sensing Duval's discomfort, chose that moment to announce that the pair were leaving; the gentlemen could have their port without them, and the ladies, 'I've no doubt, have more than enough to discuss.'

'You can't leave,' said Arabella, with a sharpness to her voice. 'After all, I went to considerable—'

Arnold interrupted, 'I know it is unforgivably rude of us to leave so soon but...'

It was Mrs Dent who said, 'I would imagine, Lord Harlington, that after being incarcerated for so long, the foolish etiquettes around table manners must appear monstrously silly.'

Duval nodded his head, and thanked his host and hostess. He heard the marquis say, 'Prison, I have been told, does remarkable damage to the soul – that is if you manage not to lose your head.'

Duval's carriage was brought round to the front, where Arnold gave the driver an address in Berkeley Square.

Duval leaned back on the upholstered seats. 'Thank you for rescuing me.'

'Delighted,' said Arnold. 'Hopefully, Arabella will never forgive you, which I think you should be eternally grateful for.' Sitting upright in the carriage, he looked out of the window. His voice serious, he said, 'Be aware of Arabella. What I saw tonight of her behaviour makes me think she has designs on you, my dear love. As we know, she has always wanted to be a lady, not a plain Mrs. Now you are the Second Earl of Harlington, she will be after that title. I would suggest giving the vengeful spider a wide berth.'

The carriage drew up outside a house that looked as if it rarely saw a party. 'Perfect. I'll get out here,' said Arnold.

'So will I,' said Duval. The carriage drove off.

'Do you want to come in?'

'No,' said Duval. 'Are you going to write about that? Arabella, I mean?'

'No,' said Arnold. 'I am going to write about the marquis and the lion.'

'That,' said Duval, 'is an old story.'

'You know it?'

'Of course I do. It has become a part of the myth surrounding the French Revolution.'

'Oh damn,' said Arnold.

'Never mind,' said Duval. 'You can always embellish it. And only the marquis knows the truth of the tale.'

Duval was about to walk away when Arnold said, 'Your wife sounds mysterious. This scandal will pass, my dear love. Everything does.'

The Lion

The marquis had spoken English all evening. The language sounded harsh in his mouth; it lacked the poetry of his native tongue.

Perhaps that was the reason he so rarely went out. Overall, he preferred his own company, his memories of the time before the Revolution, when he had his house in Paris.

He thought about Arabella, her desperation to hear the story about the mythical lion, which, according to fable, had roamed his garden. It was, of course, a fantastical story without a grain of truth in it, and tonight he had refused to be the performing monkey for Arabella's guests and regale the story once again. Now alone, he sat in his study, the candles all lit, and relished the memory.

The marquis had been in his dressing gown that morning; the day had already gathered to it a remorseless heat that clung to everything and everybody, and perspiration ran down his forehead. He felt as if the walls themselves were sweating. The windows onto the garden were open, which was how he saw a child of eleven or twelve tiptoeing barefoot around his topiary.

He stood up, or perhaps he had remained seated. It was not the weather for moving. Irritating how these details are so easily abandoned in the graveyard of lost memory. But he remembered the boy. He would never forget the boy.

'I threw my shoes over the wall so the lion would know I was about to climb over.'

'The lion?'

'The old marquis has one, and I've never seen a lion.'

'Are you not frightened it would tear you to pieces?'

'Not the lion. The old marquis might.' The boy picked up his shoes. 'Do you work here?' he asked.

'I do.'

'What's your name?'

'Reynaud. And yours?'

Before this interesting conversation could continue, several of the marquis's servants ran into the garden to drag the boy out.

'What?' he said, leading them a merry dance. 'Am I to be thrown into the Bastille?'

The marquis waved his servants away. 'I am the old marquis, Reynaud de Soule,' he said.

'No, you're not,' the boy said.

At this, the marquis laughed. Not many people made him laugh, or spoke to him with such lack of respect. He invited the boy in, who walked barefoot on the marquis's parquet floor, leaving dusty footprints as he followed the marquis to his study.

He told the boy to wait while he dressed. When he returned, the boy was nowhere to be seen.

'How many books do you have?' a voice said. Looking up, the marquis saw the boy sitting on the top of his bookcase. 'My father is a bookbinder.'

'And who is your father?'

'Bernard Simoneau.'

This boy was unruly as well as wild, and an idea came to Reynaud, who was bored and looking for entertainment. He would change the course of this boy's life. For everything was for sale, if the price was right – even this free-spirited child.

He went to his safe, where, in those days, all his gems were laid out. Beside each one of them was the replica, a fake gemstone made to look like the real thing, almost indistinguishable from the accompanying priceless gem. They had been made for him in Switzerland, and were some of the finest things he owned, these stones from the Rhine turned into emeralds, turned into diamonds – the craftsmanship involved in making a stone into a gem took true wizardry. It was always the fake stones he would wear these days, for the real ones were too valuable to risk ever seeing daylight.

The gem that fascinated him the most out of all his collection was an emerald known as the Eye of Envy. There was a story that went along with it which said the gem was cursed. Whoever owned it was sent mad with envy, certain that their lover will be unfaithful. But the marquis was not a man given to superstition, and as far as he was concerned the gem was perfect in every way.

That day, the day the boy climbed into his garden, he had picked it up along with its replica stone, placed them both in a velvet bag, then closed his eyes and asked the fates to choose which, real or counterfeit, he should use to buy the boy. He selected one, held it up to the sunlight. It sent beams of green light about the chamber as only a gem so priceless could. He hesitated, then took the boy back home.

The boy's father had been shocked to see his child return in a carriage so grand it blocked the street. The marquis took the father into his small, untidy office at the bookbinders', and told him what he wanted. The bookbinder was lost for words when shown the gemstone that the marquis was prepared to give in payment.

But just when the marquis thought the deal was done, the bookbinder had sealed it with his own request.

The past was the only country the Marquis de Soule wished to live in, the future of little interest to him. Alone in this chamber, the closest resemblance to the one he owned in Paris, he could see the boy in the candlelight, sparkling like an emerald.

'Where are you?' he called out, as might a wolf howling at time itself. His servants knew better than to ask their master what he wanted, for what he wanted not even the gods could give him. Tears ran down the marquis's white-painted face.

'A Pierrot,' he said with a sob. 'Sometimes a fake can outshine the original.'

A Letter

Duval had walked home, regardless of being dangerously well dressed – which, according to his valet, meant he was a target for any villain. *Evening clothes be damned*, he thought, and arrived to find Jameson in the hall. 'Thank goodness you are back, my lord. A messenger has arrived from Muchmore House and is waiting for a reply to this. It is from Lady Harriet.' Duval looked at the clock. It was nearing eleven.

Jameson handed him the letter. Duval broke the seal and read:

Duval,

I am writing because I am afraid the scandal is far from over. I have discovered more about Edmée's past. Samuel Hyde, an Englishman, took Edmée from Paris to Suffolk, where he said she would be safe, promising her it would be a marriage of minds. But he was a cruel man with a harsh temper.

Her maid Hannah, employed by me to look after Edmée, informed me yesterday that upon her arrival at Muchmore, the day after the wedding, she saw her mistress in the bath. There were bruises on Edmée's face and scratch marks over her belly, her bosom and thighs. Hannah said it looked as if a wild dog had attacked her.

Recently I noticed that Edmée was paler, and though I encouraged her to come with me on outings, I could see that she was not up to these little expeditions. I asked her how she was feeling every day, and she would only reply that she was well.

Two days ago, Edmée went out for her afternoon walk and she was found collapsed by the garden wall. We called the physician, Doctor Merritt, in preference to your father's doctor, Doctor Brewer, who is too old and forgetful to be of much use.

Oh, Duval, we find ourselves in a dark place indeed.

Edmée is seriously ill. I must tell you, I am not sure whether she is going to live. I cannot write more.

I beg you to come home.

Duval changed into his riding jacket, breeches and leather boots. Jameson handed him his gloves, hat and riding crop. 'Good luck, my lord, and a speedy journey.'

Before leaving London, Duval woke up an apothecary he knew and purchased what he thought he might need. He left shortly afterwards, on one of his favourite Arabian horses known for his speed. Duval was a good rider, and all his horses were kept in excellent condition for just such an emergency. It was a clear night with a spring moon to guide him, and once he was out of London, the road was his.

In all, he stopped three times at the designated coaching inns where his horses were kept, so the minute one horse was exhausted, another could be used. It meant the journey was fast and smooth. He went over and over what he suspected was the cause of such a sudden and serious illness.

The day broke, the sun rose pastel pink in the sky, and he knew where he was. He took a path away from the post road through the woods, where the bluebells were beginning to appear among the tenderest of green leaves. Muchmore House had candles burning in the windows and he wondered if, like himself, the inhabitants had not slept. At a gallop, he went down the long drive. Watkins came out immediately to greet him.

'How is her ladyship?' Duval asked as he dismounted, handing the reins to a groom.

'Seriously ill, my lord. We sent to Woodbridge again for Dr Merritt and he's here now. But he doesn't agree with the midwife's methods, and my lord, heated words are being exchanged between him and Lady Harriet.'

Duval was not listening. 'The midwife?'

'Lady Harlington miscarried three days ago.'

Not Worth the Fight

Inside the great hall, it was dark, but the morning sun was sending shafts of light across the polished surface of the wooden floor. From the drawing room, Dr Merritt could be heard berating Lady Harriet.

'...And I do not know if her ladyship will now be capable of giving Lord Harlington the heir the estate needs.'

'Oh, at last,' said Lady Harriet with relief, as Duval entered the drawing room.

'Dr Merritt,' said Duval.

The physician was plainly in a state of much agitation and relieved to see Duval. *Finally*, he thought, *here is a man of reason*. 'It was a hard birth. It often is, when a fruit is not ripe, and if she lives...' He hesitated.

'How many weeks?' Duval asked.

'She was in her sixteenth week,' said the physician. 'I fear she has childbed fever.'

'Then why are you not with her?'

'Because,' said the physician, the rage in him rekindled, 'the midwife claims only she knows how the patient should be treated, an opinion Lady Harriet shares.'

'Mrs Southey has been the midwife on this estate for the past thirty years and has delivered countless babies,' said Lady Harriet. 'The truth of childbed fever is tragic – I am afraid hardly any woman survives it.'

Duval turned on his heels and ran up the stairs. On the landing, a chambermaid was carrying bedding. She curtsied and blushed. 'Which is her ladyship's chamber?' he asked.

The maid was too tongue-tied to speak, and only pointed.

Duval heard a scream. He knocked on the door and tried the handle, finding the door locked. He demanded it be opened.

A muffled voice reached him. 'All is in hand, my lord, just as I told the doctor.'

'You will open this door, Mrs Southey.'

'This is women's work, my lord,' came the reply. 'Best leave it to me.'

Duval gave the door a furious shove and it flew open. He was hit by a wall of heat and the smell of sickness, sticky and thick. Every window was covered in drapes, the fire stacked high and Edmée was buried under covers. He started to pull down the drapes.

'No, no, my lord,' shouted Mrs Southey, 'it will be the death of her to let in the fresh air.'

He opened a window. A lady's maid, Hannah, he presumed, was standing white-faced in the doorway. 'I need hot water brought up here now,' Duval said to her.

'What are you doing, my lord?' said Mrs Southey. 'You'll make matters worse.'

Duval went to the bed and felt Edmée's forehead and pulse. It was fast.

'Ice,' he called to a footman. 'Buckets of it.'

'Ice? Have you lost your reason, my lord?' said Mrs Southey.

'Quiet,' said Duval. 'That's enough.'

Edmée spoke in a rasping voice. 'Why are you here?'

He lifted the covers from her. 'To see you.'

'I'm not looking my best,' she said. She started to shiver violently.

'Mrs Southey, why has Lady Harlington's soiled nightgown and bedding not been changed?'

'And risk the cold air getting to her?' said the midwife.

Hannah returned with hot water. 'More,' said Duval. He took Edmée's hand.

'I didn't want Lady Harriet to send for you. I told her not to... I did tell her not to,' she said in a whisper.

'It's alright,' he said gently.

Lady Harriet opened the door and immediately put a handkerchief to her nose. 'Duval,' she said, 'this is most—'

'Aunt,' Duval interrupted, 'go and rest. You are exhausted.'

'Her ladyship should be bled,' the physician announced.

'No, sir, her ladyship will not be bled. It would only quicken the fever. Thank you for your concerns, but I will care for her now. Have you heard of the physician, Mr Charles White?'

'No...' said Dr Merritt.

'He is a surgeon in Manchester,' said Duval, 'and one of the first physicians to have his work published. In his treatise on the care of women in childbirth, he calls for hygienic practices, warns against heavy blankets and argues in favour of fresh air. Lady Harlington must be washed and given clean linen, not be stifled by this filthy bedding.'

'With respect, my lord, what do you know of medical practice?'

'I trained in Paris, qualified as a physician. And, sir, I had a thriving practice in Saint-Germain-des-Prés.' Duval took off his coat and rolled up his shirtsleeves. 'I bid you good day, Dr Merritt.'

'A gentleman should not be in this room, watching a lady in all her nakedness,' said Mrs Southey. 'I've never seen such a thing. Good day to you too, my lord.' She bobbed a curtsey and was gone.

The sharp slam of the door roused Edmée from her sleep. 'Am I dreaming?' she asked.

'No,' he said. 'You must get better.'

'How often does one die before one is dead?'

Duval drew up a chair and sat with her. Her eyes were wide, staring at him, her breath shallow, her temperature stubbornly refusing to go down, her pulse still too fast. She lay writhing in pain. Ice wrapped in cloth was placed on her head; she was still burning with fever. He tried willow bark – an antipyretic medication – to lower her temperature, quinine to treat the fever, laudanum for the pain, and was frustrated at being able to do so little to ease her suffering.

Most of the time, he sat and talked to Edmée, for fear that, if she didn't hear his voice, she might think herself alone and slip away. She shouldn't have been given this chamber – it was the one Arabella used to stay in. *Though*, he thought, *it does look different, plainer, stripped of all its fussiness*. The paintings of the of hunting scenes were gone and, surprisingly, a portrait of himself hung over the fireplace. There was a desk by the window, which was laden with books.

In the midst of all her pain, Edmée's courage was remarkable. He had seen many a man, less ill than she, give up the ghost and slip away. In those quiet hours, he had time to reflect in a way he hadn't allowed himself to do since he had first arrived back in London. He had, for a long time, been a man without gravity – numb, disconnected from others.

Slowly, as he nursed her, he felt something inside him changing. The thought of losing this unknown woman became more unbearable every day. He realized that since his arrest he had been trailing ghosts, and a revelation of sorts came to him. None of it mattered – not the will, not his bitter father, not the even the estate. Perhaps it never had. What mattered was this unknown woman's survival.

'I'm not worth the fight,' she said one day. 'Let go of me.'

'I will not,' he said. She closed her eyes, and when he was certain she was asleep and his words would float over her, he said, 'I want to know you, to heal you and' – he kissed her hand – 'to love you better.'

Pea Soup

Seven days had passed. Duval had no wish to leave Edmée, but he knew he could no longer ignore his aunt.

'Oh, Duval,' said Lady Harriet, as he entered the dining room, 'have you come to tell me that—'

'That I am joining you for dinner? Yes,' said Duval. 'And Edmée is sleeping.'

'I cannot bear it,' said Lady Harriet. 'I cannot bear the thought of there being no Edmée. It's too upsetting to contemplate. And you have missed knowing her.'

'I hope not.'

'So do I.' She toyed with her soup for a moment and then said, 'I should warn you about Carson.'

'No, not now, Aunt.'

'Yes, now. I am afraid there is no avoiding this.'

'If you insist. But I am exhausted,' said Duval.

'That unbearable man. Having failed to create sufficient scandal for you in London, he has now employed a horrid little man by the name of Veldt, whose business it is to pry into other people's affairs. And this man, Veldt, has been to a place called Witchling Village.'

'What has that to do with us, my dear aunt?'

'Everything. Witchling, as you know all too well, is where that wretched Mrs Beale, the wife of the magistrate, lives, the mother of that girl – Jocasta. But it is also where the late Mr Hyde was parson. This Veldt has been going round asking all sorts of questions – loaded questions, I must add – and apparently, it wasn't hard to find parishioners to tell him there had been strange goings-on at the parsonage.'

'Why is this relevant?' asked Duval.

'Let me finish. Mrs Beale recently paid a special call to tell me villagers were gossiping about Edmée. They are saying she was responsible for Mr Hyde's drinking, because he had been as sober as a nun before he married her.'

Duval smiled. 'Sober as a nun?'

'Oh, you know what I am trying to say.'

'Must we really talk about this?'

'Yes, we must. I also think it is imperative that we send for the lawyer, Mr Gutteridge, straight away.'

'What on earth for?'

She paused. 'This is very shocking. I thought I might not have to say it out loud. That you would by now have understood what I am trying to say without me saying it...'

'Honestly, I am not up for riddles. I would be grateful if you could just tell me what this is about.'

'Edmée is suspected of the murder of Mr Hyde. Apparently her being sold at a wife sale acts as proof of her guilt.'

Duval put down his soup spoon. 'And did this man, Veldt, find any evidence to back up the gossip?'

'No,' said Lady Harriet. 'Not that I've heard.'

'Has anyone been here asking questions?'

'No.'

'Then this is nonsense,' he said. 'Aunt Harriet, the best way forward is to forget about it.'

'But it won't go away,' said Lady Harriet.

Desperate to change the subject, Duval said, 'I'll be damned if Carson will inherit this estate.'

'Well, thank goodness for that,' said his aunt. 'And if Edmée does recover, will you return to London?'

'I don't know. I will have to see Gutteridge again. But I'm not going anywhere yet.'

Duval stayed at Edmée's bedside that night. She didn't wake until about three in the morning, when the arrival of a terrible thunderstorm rattled the windows.

Edmée put her arms over her head. 'Don't hit me,' she cried. 'No, no more, please no more.'

Duval lit the candles, as lightning illuminated the room.

She sat up. 'Where am I?' He heard something fall from the bed onto the floor with a thud.

'You are here, at Muchmore House.'

'*Où est ma puce*?' she said, and with that, fell back into a deep sleep. Duval repeated what she had just said – 'Where is my flea?' It was a term of endearment. Who, he wondered, could she mean? He doubted she was referring to Mr Hyde.

That night, as he sat down to keep his watch over Edmée, he recounted the day that had passed. There had been nothing of note – except, he now remembered, the thing that had earlier thudded to the floor. He could see nothing, until he looked under the bed and pulled out a leather-bound notebook with marbled endpapers. It had been bought in Woodbridge. It must have been hidden under the mattresses and become dislodged. A letter had fallen out. He picked it up. It was the only letter he had ever written to Edmée. As Duval went to put it back, his eye was caught by the title page. It was written in French.

Shells From the Shallow Shoreline of the Soul

He hesitated, then thought that if this was a journal she might have mentioned a relative, someone he could write to, for he knew hardly anything about her. He started to read.

15th March 1796

It is pointless. Lady Harriet told me I am to be annulled, the scandal of the wife sale put an end to, that such a noble estate as this cannot be associated with the disgraceful act of buying a wife. It was quite inconceivable to think that my portrait would ever be hung next to that of the first Lord Harlington.

But when I think about it, aren't all wives bought? A few through love, most through want of money and noble birth. I suppose you could argue that ten guineas was an honourable transaction – far more honourable than my marriage to Mr Hyde.

30th March 1796

I have this brand-new book with lined pages that smell fresh and clean, bound in leather, a book hungry for words. Not to mention a jar of quills. And a desk. My desk, with a view, a view I could look at for the rest of my life.

Alas, I think this might just be the interval and I will soon be asked to leave. But it's no good worrying about next Monday when it's just turned Tuesday.

Two letters I have sent him. He sent back three words: 'You intrigue me'. I pressed his three words in the middle of this book, waited in hope he would write again and through letters we might become better acquainted, but it's not to be. So I will write out all the letters I would have sent him, though what a three-word writer might have replied I cannot answer for.

Duval read pages of her unsent letters to him. They were witty and insightful, and had the effect of making him feel ashamed of his arrogant behaviour – for it was true, he had not given her any consideration on their wedding day.

'Forgive me,' he said aloud, 'for I have proved myself as selfish as my father and given no credit to your feelings.' He wished that his words would bring her up from the depth of sleep.

Only when he was alone, and the house was quiet, did he pick up the book again. With every page, he grew to know Edmée better.

Alongside her entries about Muchmore, Edmée had also transcribed some entries from what he could only assume was an earlier diary. The more of the snatches he read, the more mysterious she became.

2nd September 1792

I think I would have married the devil himself to get out of Paris. Samuel Hyde is a small, insignificant man. The only merit to him was he had papers that guaranteed he and his wife safe passage out of Paris. He assured me that if I helped him escape France it would be a marriage of minds.

We were hastily wed, everything being in such chaos, but his papers were good.

It was a hard journey to the coast and never was I more grateful than when at last, after waiting in Rotterdam, we had a passage bound for England. I thought we would go to London, but we landed at a place I had never heard of and I could not pronounce. I know it now as Lowestoft, a busy port. Up to this point, Mr Hyde had been so terrified that I had no idea as to his character, apart from his bad breath and a vague unpleasant smell of onions about him. But the minute we were in a carriage bound for Witchling, something in him changed. I asked him where London was. He told me sharply that he would never take me there. It was a city of sin.

The parsonage was cold, a miserable dwelling filled with overbearing, pompous furniture. The housekeeper Nellie Moore looked furious when Mr Hyde introduced me as his wife. Tears of rage glinted in her eyes.

4th October 1792

The thought of me, an alien, in the village when England was at war with France was a shock to its residents. This place had not been shaken since the Normans – or do I mean Romans – had first trudged through the mud to get here, and I have no doubt they regretted it as much as I did.

Mrs Beale, the wife of a magistrate, who must have a nose so long that she can sniff out other people's business without leaving the comfort of her own home, declared that poor, unworldly Samuel Hyde had been duped into marriage by a wicked Frenchwoman. This was confirmed when I was first taken to church by Samuel. The women of the village looked at me with scorn and the men with lust.

Mrs Beale suggested that it would be better for the souls of the community if I was not seen in church on Sundays.

Duval smiled. *Yes, Edmée, you are a very good judge of character.*

15th December 1792

Samuel collapsed into a morbid depression and agreed that he had made a terrible mistake in marrying me – conveniently forgetting the circumstances of the marriage – and took to the bottle. I had, he said, ruined his life. By that I think he meant he wasn't invited anymore to dine with the Beales, or anyone else of standing in the village. He told me that he had often been asked out, five times a week or more, to various houses. But that was before he was married.

My suggestion to invite people to dine here was greeted with an unintelligible moan. 'I don't possess a cook,' he said. This was true. When I suggested we hired one, Nellie Moore went into a fit of rage at the idea. Samuel agreed that he didn't have the income for such luxuries.

24th January 1793

I asked Samuel many times for my band box. Finally it was returned, yet there were no books inside. I asked for them back, but he refused, saying that all I owned was now his. I tried to talk reason to him. 'Why do you want the books?' he asked.

'Because they are mine.'

The study was barred from me. According to the Bible of Samuel Hyde, reading corrupted women's minds and gave them ideas that their intellect did not know what to do with. Nevertheless, I was determined to find what belonged to me. Those books were all I had left. And one, in particular, was more important to me than I can say.

12th March 1794

I don't quite know how things have become as bad as they are. I suppose, like all evil, it started gradually – a few hits, one black eye, a grovelling apology – then it became steadily worse. Over time I have become more and more invisible. He hardly ever allows me out of the house. Samuel claimed that he wasn't like this – it was only since he had married me; it was under the guidance of the bottle that he was finally able to assert himself as a man and claim what every married man should be able to claim. One would hope, you might say, the love of a good wife, but that's not what he meant. This, he told me, was no longer a marriage of minds, and that I should therefore fulfil my wifely duties.

Duval was furious. It was a good thing that Samuel Hyde was dead, otherwise he would have killed him. How could he have done this to Edmée and still claim to be a man of God?

23rd June 1795

Nellie has talked to anyone in the village who will listen to her. It seems I am the topic of much gossip.

'What could you expect?' I heard Nellie ask our neighbour's servant. 'I mean she's just strange, with foreign ways.'

Time has lost all meaning. I feel this will never end.

Duval knew well what that felt like. He read on.

It is one thing to escape danger, quite another to live with the consequences. What did I think would happen when I married a man I didn't like, didn't trust, who didn't even have the decency to give me back what was mine?

Survival is a thin cloth, and demands you make the best of it without complaint. I had not realized that I would end up being a prisoner in the parson's house. But that's what I have become. And I have been kept mostly... in a bare room, save the bed, the shutters nailed down. I escaped once and asked to see the magistrate. Mrs Beale sniffed me out and had me taken home.

After that, I felt the village had forgotten that the parson even had a wife. Nellie told me that everyone thought I had run away.

He knew he had been a fool only to have written to Edmée once. *Three words...* he thought. If he had only three words for her now, they would be: *Just wake up*.

1st February 1796

Mr Hyde stopped drinking when he heard the news that Mrs Beale's daughter had become engaged, certain that he would be asked to perform the service.

But Mrs Beale wanted no less person than a bishop to bind those two for good. Samuel's mood became murderous.

Only Miss Weeks, who lived next door, ever came to inquire after me. She had a small dog that Nellie hated because of its barking. I heard the little dog had died.

The next day Mr Hyde and Nellie were out. Samuel had forgotten to lock my door. The house being empty,

I was determined to escape, but first I had to find the most valuable of my books. It was meaningless to Hyde, but of great significance to me; hidden there was my only chance of survival.

I couldn't find it in his study. I found there a number of books, but not mine, and in my search, I had left it too late. I heard the door. The minute Samuel saw me in his study, he shouted, 'Which book is it?' as he came towards me.

I won't say what he did then, but I doubt I would have survived another attack like it. He cut off all my hair… forced the wine down me… and more. Miss Weeks, our neighbour, could see into the study, and I saw her looking on in horror. I stood up and walked out past Nellie Moore, then collapsed in the bedroom. I could hear Nellie downstairs, shouting, 'You bloody bastard! That's no way to get the devil out of a woman.'

I think I would have preferred the guillotine to this. How far I have fallen. He murdered me, yet still I have a heart that beats.

He told me he burned the books. I don't believe him.

Duval had hardly slept. He had taken to watching pigeons fly past the window, wondering how on earth such ridiculously plump birds managed to stay in the air. He put these thoughts down to exhaustion.

Edmée's notebook was the closest he could come to knowing this sleeping beauty. All he had read unsettled him greatly. He felt the same impotent anger that he had done in prison at the wanton cruelty of man, and wondered about the nature of survival. How does one recover from such brutal mistreatment? It was a question he had battled with since his return. To know this had happened to Edmée filled him with a profound sadness. There was so much left out of her account; he thought that perhaps this journal was her way of making sense of the senseless. He dreaded what he would read next and was pleased to see, didn't start with Mr Hyde.

12th February 1796

Nellie's attitude towards me changed after that. She brought me food as well as a small kitchen knife, so the next time Samuel came for me, I would be able to protect myself. I hid the knife under the floorboards. Then she revealed something to me. She was once his wife too, without a ring to show the truth of it. Now, she said, she knew he was the devil.

When will it stop? When will women stop being used like this?

I was thinking how cold I was that morning, when I heard a knock on the front door. Cursing, Nellie went to answer it.

I heard Samuel shouting for something to eat and a whisky. The back door opened again; the kitchen door shut, the study door opened, and then all was silent. I knew something had happened, but what, I had no idea – until Nellie came running up the stairs. 'You've got to come tell me if he's dead... 'cause I think the devil's dead...' We went downstairs together. He was lying face down in the plate of muffins (he'd eaten the lot), his eyes wide open. Dead as dead might be.

I watched Nellie pack her bag, saying, 'I am not staying here with him dead in this house. He was a vengeful man and Satan will make him a vengeful ghost.'

I lit a candle and started to look for my books. They had to be here, but I couldn't find them. A doctor came; he stank of drink and hardly looked at the body, just told me Mr Hyde was dead. That couldn't have been more plain.

22nd February 1796

Mr Samuel Hyde was buried on the 20th of February. It snowed quite heavily; a few of the villagers turned out, but many stayed away. Mrs Beale wasn't there. It was a very long and dull service. Someone had left a parcel of clothes and a meat pie on the step for me when I returned home.

I received a letter the next day. The Church would like me to be gone in two days' time.

I would leave when I found my books, not before. The only room I hadn't searched was Hyde's. I had tried, but it made me vomit every time I opened the door. The smell of him was enough to make me retch.

The following day, I finally told myself I had to. I looked through all the drawers, nothing. The shelves, nothing. I saw the chamber pot under the bed and bent down, *and there found them. Two had been ruined, but by a miracle, the one I wanted was still intact. I hurried downstairs. In the kitchen, I stepped back, bumped into the table. Through the glass, the face of Samuel Hyde stared back at me.*

The ghost tapped on the window, demanding to be let in. The next tap on the window was more urgent.

'I'm Samuel Hyde's son, Gilbert Hyde. I have a right to come in.'

I didn't know Samuel had a son.

'Who are you?' he asked abruptly when I opened the door, snow whirling round him. 'And where is my mother, Nellie?'

I told him I didn't know where she had gone, but I was his father's widow. 'You?' he said, and looked curiously at my bruised, swollen face, my chopped hair. He nodded, as if he understood, but he didn't comment.

Gilbert Hyde wore the uniform of a regular foot soldier, and like the man himself, it looked worn out.

'My father married.' It was more an accusation than a question. 'He never said. You're French? An émigré? You must have been desperate to have married that clunch.' He spoke slowly. I could almost hear his feet marching to the beat of his words.

There was an awkward silence. Then he pushed past me into the drawing room, his breathing wheezy. He took off his knapsack and leaned it against the wall, resting his hat on top, then scratched his head, glancing at the fire, and a room bare of furniture.

I said there was no coal, no firewood, no food.

'I take it, from the box in the hall, you're on the point of leaving.'

I told him I had nowhere to go.

'So you chopped up the furniture?'

'Yes,' I said. 'It belonged to the Church.'

'Good,' he said.

I found his bluntness odd. Without a word, he started to add more chair legs to the flames. It was liberating to see ugly furniture being put to good use.

I asked what 'clunch' meant – the word wasn't known to me.

He didn't look up from the job in hand. 'An awkward, clownish fellow. But actually, my father was worse, much worse than that. And no one found him funny.'

That was true.

The fire blazed; the parlour was warm and it felt as if the house was being released from a great burden.

'No food?' he asked.

I shook my head.

'And I haven't a penny,' said Gilbert. 'We both must hope the solicitor has a surprise for us.'

I must have looked puzzled, for he explained that, while he was in hospital, a letter had come from Samuel's solicitor, requesting he call on him in Thetford to discuss his late father's will. 'Didn't he write to you?'

When I said no, he said there must have been a mistake and his father would surely have left me something. I thought it best to remain silent.

He said, 'Thetford's a bloody long way if you've just been discharged from hospital.'

When I asked where he'd been when he was wounded, he didn't answer, just said, 'Hungry,' put on his hat, buttoned up his coat and left the house.

I thought he would return drunk, full of stories he'd been told about me being a witch. At least there was a fire. I curled up in front of it like a cat.

Some hours passed, and I had determined to give the past no more thought when the kitchen door creaked open.

'It seems no one liked my father,' said Samuel's son. 'They were ashamed when I told them you hadn't any food. And that he had beaten you. They all said they had heard as much.'

He was carrying a bottle of port and had a loaf of bread under his arm. From his pocket, he produced a lump of cheese and two apples.

It was a feast. I fetched plates, glasses and cutlery from the kitchen. We sat on the floor near the fire and spread the picnic out before us.

'I nearly forgot,' said Gilbert, reaching into his pocket. 'Two boiled eggs. They're still warm.' He peeled one of the eggs, throwing the shells on the fire. 'The butcher offered

us a lift to Thetford tomorrow. I thought you might want to hear what the solicitor has to say. I never imagined my father marrying, let alone marrying a Frenchwoman. He used to call France "our natural enemy".'

'Do you think we are?'

'I don't think. I gave up thinking when I joined the army at sixteen. Thinking – I leave that to men who are well educated. I march to order, and when told to fight, I fight. Just now, I'm awaiting orders. I'm a foot soldier, plain and simple. What clothes have you got in that box of yours?'

I showed him my thin black coat and my boots.

He said they were completely unsuitable for such harsh weather, and from Samuel's bedchamber brought down stockings, boots and an overcoat. They revolted me – everything Samuel owned had such a prevailing smell of onions that for a moment I thought I might lose my supper.

He said simply that it was going to be very cold at five o'clock in the morning. 'And your coat wouldn't keep a squirrel warm.'

He stuffed Samuel's boots with paper from the study and selected stockings for me to wear. 'And his hat will be far warmer than that flimsy bonnet. You can change when we're there if you wish.'

I decided I would take my trunk with me; it would be better to be in Thetford than here in this small village. Where I would go from there, I had no idea.

Gilbert went outside and found four stones, which he put in the fire. He slept on the floor. I slept on my bed, fully dressed, and still, it was freezing.

At five, we waited at the village green for the butcher. Gilbert held up a lantern and examined me. For the first time, he smiled. 'French,' he said. He handed me two warm stones and picked up my box, as we heard the butcher's cart approaching.

Duval thought, *If it had been one day later that Gilbert had arrived, I would never have met Edmée.* His life would have taken a different path and been all the poorer for it in so many ways. 'Please,' he whispered to her, 'wake up.'

Despite the stones, I was chilled to the bone by the time we arrived at the market town. The butcher said a brisk goodbye and, blowing into his gloves, set off to find himself a handsome breakfast. We watched him go as if he were a plate of ham and eggs.

We found the solicitor's office, down a narrow side street away from the market.

The solicitor himself looked as if one of his feet was already in his grave and he merely snorted when Gilbert introduced me. I waited in the outer office on a wooden bench under the window, my box beside me. The place was colder than a lead-lined coffin. I picked up a flyer advertising a wife sale from the bench and was reading with interest when Gilbert, red with rage, stormed out of the solicitor's room, letting the inner door slam behind him. The glass panes rattled in the window. I picked up my box and followed him into the street.

'Nothing,' he said. 'He has left a total of nothing.' He hit the wall of the building. 'And I thought he might have remembered me... Nothing. The fucking bastard didn't even leave enough to pay his debts. I could kill him.'

'If he wasn't already dead.'

He looked unamused. 'He didn't mention you.'

In a doorway, I started to change into my black coat and bonnet. Gilbert asked me what I was doing.

I told him, 'There is a wife sale.'

He said, 'There is also a moon – what difference does that make?'

'You could sell your father's widow.'

'Well... I suppose I could. You are my property – well, my father's – so I have inherited you. About all I have bloody inherited.'

'Sell me,' I said, and we will divide the profits.' I could see Gilbert was thinking. 'But if I don't like him, then you must help me out of the puddle.'

He said it was a risk. I said, so was breathing.

After a cold minute, he said, 'No offence, but we'd only get about five shillings, because of your face and hair. Half of that would be more than enough to get me back to the barracks, but I don't know how I could help you out of the puddle.'

'If I say to you, when the sale is done, "Don't forget the cat," you must help me escape.'

'Damn it,' he said.

We had a deal.

Finally, thought Duval, *I understand what the cat had to do with it all*, and he smiled. As much as he should sleep, he read on.

I heard Gilbert's stomach rumble. 'I hate being hungry,' I said. We stopped outside a coffee house, and I told him to wait there and not let anyone take my box.

You see, ma puce, *you cannot take the thief from within me. It is still there. Two maids, giggling together, their baskets filled with purchases. They didn't feel a thing as I stole their pennies.*

Inside the coffee house, Gilbert asked me what we were going to pay with.

'The king's coin,' I said and put the money on the table.

He looked at me. 'Who are you?' he asked, marvelling.

'A daughter of the Revolution.'

Yes, thought Duval, *who are you indeed?* He looked at her, sleeping on the edge of the living world. There was just one more entry.

30th March 1796

A troubling thought has come to me. I have not bled for some time. No, I tell myself, surely nothing could be created in such a violent manner. What kind of creature would it be? My bruises are better, though the ones on my stomach are still painful. I have started to see spots of blood. I don't know if that is bad. I think it is. Oh, little one, this isn't your fault. I still have nightmares about the monster, that bed. The hatred on his face, the enjoyment he took in causing me pain. I often wake up with a vision of him. How do I wash away all memories? I need to rest and recover.

Lady Harriet has been more than kind to me, kinder than I deserve or could have imagined. Sometimes I think there is a God.

Now I know I will be told to leave, and I will never see Duval's portrait again. Neither will I be able to talk to him at night, as I do now, and find consolation there. We will never know the truth of each other; perhaps it is better that way.

Duval was overwhelmed by all he had read, a journal of a journey that no woman should ever have been subjected to. If she did wake, the physical scars would mend, but how long the ones in her mind would take to heal – that was unknowable. He put the journal back where he had found it, went to his bedroom and fell into a deep, dreamless sleep.

At four in the afternoon, he heard Watkins say, 'My lord, wake up, you must come now.'

Blurry-eyed, Duval ran down the corridor fearing the worst, certain that she was dead, cursing that he had left her room for so long.

To his surprise, the housemaid and other servants were gathered in the corridor. They parted as he approached. The door of Edmée's chamber stood wide open, and for a moment, he could make no sense of what he was seeing. His aunt, who never cried, was in tears, while Hannah had her back towards him, blocking his view of the bed.

It wasn't until Hannah moved away that a stream of sunshine broke into the room. Duval stared in bewilderment as Edmée, propped up on the pillows, said, 'You're here. I thought you might have left.'

Stepping Stones

Duval had come to know three Edmées: the Edmée he had met in her journal, fragments of a life unexplained, a woman who had conjured herself out of words; the Edmée he had known through her illness, a brave fighter; and this Edmée, a frail, broken, young woman whose moods were still affected by all that had happened to her.

May was one of Duval's favourite months, and spending time at Muchmore during that time, he came to remember why he loved the place so much. Most days he was to be found out on the estate. For reasons he chose not to examine, he kept away from Edmée. He paid visits, as her physician, in the morning and again at night. Each time he closed the door to her chamber, he felt a longing to stay, to sit and talk, but he didn't, telling himself there was time.

Edmée was still confined to her bed, on his orders. Lady Harriet kept her company, and gradually she became stronger. The sunlight was what Duval noticed now, when he went into her room. Before, he would have said, if asked, the weather was grey, the room was grey. Now, somehow, colour had burst in. Edmée was sitting up in bed, her green-grey eyes smiling up at him.

He had asked her if there was anyone in the émigré community he might write to, who would be able to contact a relative.

She had shaken her head. 'There is no one.'

The concept of there being no one, of her having been all alone with Samuel Hyde, subjected to all his barbaric behaviour, struck him as truly dreadful. But she showed no desire to talk about the past, and he had no desire to confess what he had learned from her diary.

One evening, when he paid his usual visit, she said, 'I think this might be making matters worse.'

'Making what matters worse?' he asked and smiled at her.

'You don't often do that.'

'Do what?'

'Smile.'

'A physician must keep a serious face. Make what worse?' he asked again.

'The scandal of our marriage.'

'My lady, you have lost me.'

She produced a piece of paper from under her pillow. 'I wasn't meant to receive this letter. It was addressed to Lady Harlington, but it is obviously meant for Lady Harriet. All these ladies beginning with H is, I agree, rather confusing.'

She read:

My dear,

I was at Almack's last week and there was a shocking rumour going round, that this woman Duval bought at a wife sale is with child. The rumour is that it is the parson's child she is carrying. I know this to be true because I saw Mr Carson out and he told me that Duval left as soon as he could change into his riding habit after the wedding.

My dear Lady Harriet, if this is true, you must encourage Duval to act as soon as possible to annul this ridiculous marriage. He told me himself he intended to have it ended, but I have heard nothing from him since he was in London, though I have written to ask and have even suggested far cleverer solicitors than Mr Gutteridge.

The lord of such a fine estate as Muchmore cannot be encumbered with a parson's wife and child. The thought is shocking, the scandal too big to be contained. I am afraid that if Duval doesn't rectify the situation he will be cast out from society.

I heard that this woman had had all her hair chopped off and her face – well, without being rude, she is no beauty, according to Mr Audley, who was there at the auction in Thetford. He described her to the journalist for the Comet *as a timid mouse…*

Duval saw tears lacing Edmée's eyelashes and said, 'Stop, stop now.'

Edmée let the letter fall.

'I take it this is from Arabella Gosling.'

Edmée nodded. 'What she says is right… except the bit about me being a timid mouse. She was your mistress?'

Duval sat on the bed beside her, his face serious. 'Yes, she was, before I went to France.'

'Why did you not marry her?'

'The letter might give you a clue. I was never in love with her, and I had no desire to be married for any other reason.' After a pause, Duval went on. 'Yes, I was contemplating the idea of having this marriage annulled, that is true. And also making a settlement that would give you a comfortable life.'

They were silent.

'I understand,' she said. 'I will be gone when I find my feet.'

'No, you don't understand. And what's more, I don't understand either.'

'Please, my lord, you have been more than kind. Hannah told me you never left my side while I was ill, and I owe you my life. I ask nothing of you. I'm only like this because I'm tired and still in pain.'

'I don't want you to go,' he said. 'Now, think no more about leaving and go to sleep.'

'It won't do,' said Edmée. 'Perhaps it would be for the best if you did have our marriage annulled, then the scandal would go away.'

Though her words were bravely spoken, he saw she was terribly pale.

'Damn it, you shouldn't have read that letter. Not ever, but especially not when you are grieving for your child.'

Again, they were silent. After a long time, she said, 'Shall I tell you something shocking? Not one part of me wanted that baby. Yet I told myself it wasn't the child's fault, and if it had lived, I would have had to have found love for it. I would have to think that, perhaps, by raising it differently, it could be a different person.' She sank back into the pillows. 'I am a mess when I cry,' she added with an attempt at a smile.

He took her hand. 'I am sorry,' he said. 'I could give you laudanum to help you sleep.'

'No. Are you tired?' she asked.

'Not at all.'

'Do you play cards?'

He rang for champagne and a light supper to be brought up, and that night they played cards until one in the morning and talked of many things. He wanted to ask her about *ma puce*, but he couldn't bring himself to do that. Curiosity, he told himself, was good for neither cat nor man.

But he did ask her, 'Have you ever been in love?' to which she simply replied, 'No, no I haven't.'

'That is hard to believe.'

She studied his face, then said, 'The past is a place we depart from; the years are stepping stones to where we stand now. This moment is all there is.'

Duval went out on estate business first thing each morning but found himself returning home earlier every evening.

He knew he would have to accept that Edmée, like the heart itself, was destined to remain a mystery to him. Maybe it was easier that way. There would be time enough for all things to be revealed. Perhaps she was right, the past didn't signify – at least he hoped it didn't.

He read to Edmée from *Gulliver's Travels*, which she loved. And when she was stronger, she told him fairy stories that dated from before the Revolution.

The first day out of bed, she fainted. The second day she felt too sick and lay down again. But gradually and determinedly, she began to find her balance.

'*La derrière* is very heavy,' she said. 'It is a bad design.' Duval laughed, as he often did with her these days. '*Mon cher*, you don't have to come each evening.'

'I come because I want to be here.'

'I would have been sad if you'd said anything else,' she said, smiling, and he treasured the fact she called him *mon cher*.

They played draughts and whist, Lady Harriet joining them for the card games.

Often, they would sit, just the two of them. They avoided the topic of the Revolution; they talked about philosophy and Romanticism and the new ideas coming out of Germany.

She said, 'I want a fresh sheet of paper with a pen, to write what has not yet been written.'

He felt he was beginning to know her, but still he felt the word 'love', or at least the way his father used it, to be too weighed down with guilt. He didn't want a love like that. *To love...* he thought, *what does it mean?* To judge her by standards he himself would be horrified by? No, that was not love. Or to accept what was before him and find in that a truth he would never otherwise see?

To his surprise, he knew the real answer.

A month passed; it was the beginning of June. The weather became warmer, and Duval was happy to forget all about London.

He came down for breakfast one morning to be greeted by the unusual sight of his aunt surrounded by the newspapers.

'This is most unlike you,' said Duval, seeing her lost behind *The Times*. 'Is Napoleon defeated?'

'I don't know,' she said tersely. 'What I do know is that this scandal of Edmée's pregnancy is in every newspaper.'

'What do you mean?' said Duval, his voice icy.

'I'm afraid Mr Carson has let it be known that your marriage hasn't been consummated, and the child that Lady Harlington was carrying was that of the parson, Samuel Hyde. Therefore, this estate should, by the terms of your father's will, be his. He is accusing you of purposely swindling him out of his inheritance. He has also thrown aspersions here, there and everywhere, all rather clumsily planted, that Edmée might have, could have, most probably *did*, murder Mr Hyde. Several of the less savoury papers are positively thrilled at the notion. Even *The Times* is saying you will be thrown out of your club and shunned from high society, that this is shocking behaviour from the head of such a noble family.'

Duval sat down, waited until the coffee was poured, then picked up the first paper and began reading.

His aunt, seeing his white face, said, 'We will be isolated all over again. I thought something must have happened yesterday when Mrs Fairlight, who comes regularly to play cards with me, sent a very curt message saying that she would not be here for the foreseeable future and she was sure I would understand.'

Duval was furious at the vile things that had been written about Edmée. This had to stop. He wouldn't have her hurt again by people who had no idea what she had been through, no idea who she was.

'I am going to London.'

'And what, pray, will that achieve?' asked his aunt. 'Duval, personally, I think you should stay.'

'No, Aunt, this needs to be put to bed, once and for all. Why should both you and Edmée be outcast by the likes of Mrs Fairlight?'

'On that I do agree.'

'I don't want Edmée to know about this.'

'She will hear nothing from me,' said his aunt, 'and I wouldn't let anyone talk about her the way they have done in these scandal rags. I agree with you. They don't know her. How long will you be gone?'

'A week, maybe two. I will let you know.' He stood up to leave. 'I will not have you ostracized from polite society any longer.'

Duval went to see Edmée. She smiled when he entered the bedchamber. She was propped up in bed on a pile of pillows with her breakfast tray beside her. He had never wished as much as he did then that he could tell the world to go hang.

'We could have a picnic today,' she said. Then, seeing his face, 'What is it?'

'I must go to London,' he said. 'I have business that needs attending to.'

Edmée's face clouded over. 'Is it to do with the letter?'

'No,' he said.

'You are a bad liar, my lord.'

'I will be back in a week. You are to get better.' He turned to leave, knowing she was watching him.

At the door, he hesitated, then walked back towards her. She looked up at him; he bent down and kissed her gently on the lips, something he had wanted to do for so long. Then, without another word, he was gone.

The Liars' Club

Duval was dismayed to discover that a week had passed and he had found no way to contain the scandal that was whirling afresh, now with the added detail of the miscarriage. He had been banned from his club and from Almack's, and the list was growing. The only invitation Duval had received was to the Wallingtons' ball. Reluctantly, he decided to go, and was surprised to find that his mere entrance caused a stir. The music stopped, and everybody stared until Mr Wallington came to greet him and said how delighted he was to see him.

The amount of trash written about Edmée had shocked him; hearsay and tall tales took up an inordinate amount of space in the daily opinion columns and scandal rags. She was reported as being a woman of little education and no rank, with nothing to recommend her by way of beauty. Meanwhile, the murder of the Riley family in Cheapside had been almost ignored.

'It appears,' said Jameson, 'that Mrs Gosling has been saying that she knows for a fact that the marriage is to be annulled, and that you will soon be married again because—'

'Because?' said Duval.

'She said it hadn't been consummated.' Jameson looked worried.

'I have no intention of ending my marriage. Ever.'

Jameson, who was full of sentimentality, had tears in his eyes when he said, 'That warms the cockles of my heart. And who would have thought it? Though William did bet one whole guinea with Lord Roberts's head groom that that would be the case.'

'What would be the case?' asked Duval.

'William has a very good eye for horses. What I mean to say is he thought that you... my lord.'

'I think you've said quite enough.'

'Has he won his guinea, my lord?'

All Duval wanted was to be back at Muchmore. He knew his longing to be home had everything to do with Edmée. She dominated his thoughts; he felt her absence as a physical pain. No woman had ever fascinated him so much. When he tried to write to her, he once again appeared to be only a three-word writer – but this time, the three words he wanted to say shocked even him.

In prison, he had written many last letters for citizens; words had come easily. But now, each letter felt inadequate. A sentence could be so easily misunderstood. A sentiment might be misconstrued. What fairy magic was this that had dazzled him into silence? Only Edmée could release him from the spell he was under. For that to happen he needed to be with her, to see her, to speak to her, to tell her of the fear he had of walking where there was no gravity. Instead, he screwed up all the letters and threw them into the fire. What stopped his pen from writing was the terrifying idea that she might not feel the same about him. It was that dread of rejection that made him distrust his emotions.

Duval told Jameson that he would be leaving for Muchmore as soon as matters had been resolved. But how that was to be achieved he had no idea, especially after some buffoon in the Houses of Commons had raised the matter of the Harlington affair in Parliament. *Has the world gone mad?* he wondered. England was at war; what on earth did any of this matter?

The next day, Granger came to inform him that Mr Carson and his sister were here. They had been shown into the salon. Duval was impressed at Mr Carson's audacity, given that he must know Duval had had quite long enough to discover the source of the scandalmongering. Here he stood, Mr Carson, looking like a peacock. His sister, drab by comparison, looked frightened. Mr Carson's face was powdered, as was his wig. He was dressed in a style that would have become a younger man with a finer figure, but due to his love of sweet things, Mr Carson's waist was unable to contain itself, and therefore, his waistcoat buttons were pulled to bursting. It struck Duval that the man was a character in want of a play. On the other hand, his sister looked terrified, twisting a handkerchief between her fingers.

'Good afternoon,' said Duval with all the civility he could muster.

Mr Carson and his sister had risen momentarily from their seat; one curtsied, the other bowed, then immediately they sat down again. Mr Carson said, 'I think it's best if I come straight to the point. I have taken legal advice, and I am told that I am in my rights to claim my inheritance that your esteemed father left me. I have spoken to a well-respected lawyer, and

I wanted to inform you that I intend to take the matter to court if you do not relinquish the Muchmore Estate in my favour. Your father made it quite clear that was his intention.'

Duval said nothing. He agreed with Mr Carson in one respect. Why on earth had his father been so foolish?

'My lawyer tells me I have a good case,' said Mr Carson.

'Your lawyer is in Gray's Inn, I believe?'

'Yes,' said Mr Carson.

'That's good,' said Duval. 'I'm glad we had the right address.'

'Right address?' said Mr Carson. 'You mean you see sense and are going to act according to your father's wishes?'

Duval said, 'You have been saying slanderous things about myself and Lady Harlington. Titbits which I believe you have sold to the papers for some not inconsiderable sum of money. I think you will find this all outlined in the letter from my solicitor, Mr Gutteridge, informing you that I will sue you for libel if you carry on with the malicious, slanderous comments about Lady Harlington.'

'Me?' said Mr Carson. Even under his powder, he had gone red.

'Unfortunately,' said Duval, 'there is no one else in the room called Mr Carson, so I must be referring to you. If you think for a minute that the friends you have made at the scandal rags will keep their mouths shut and not tell my handsome purse who it is that has been feeding them endless bits of information, all inaccurate, then you are much mistaken.'

Mr Carson was now standing. 'May I inform you, sir, marriage is not legally binding until it is consummated. My lawyer is quite convinced we have a winnable case and one I am prepared to fight.'

'We don't know each other, sir,' said Duval. 'I had never heard of your side of the family until my father's will. I would hate you to be wasting your money, but I do understand your disappointment. On the day I returned from France, you thought you were two days and seven hours away from having all this. But it really doesn't matter which lawyer you employ, for you have no legal ground to stand on. The codicil of my father's will establishes that the ceremony was all that was required; a year was given for more affection to grow between myself and Edmée, and no amount of your rumours and gossipmongering will change that. I am afraid your expectations were falsely raised. You have, by all accounts, taken quite sufficient funds from the estate already. I would be very careful, Mr Carson, that I don't ask for that money back.'

Carson glared darkly, before retorting, 'You have brought down the name of Harlington. I think many people, many people, sir, would be shocked at your behaviour. And after this unsavoury episode, you will no longer darken the doors of the great and the good of this land.'

Duval had had more than enough of this silly fellow and his sister, so he rang for Jameson to show them out.

Mr Carson, realizing he had lost this battle leaped to his feet, and said, 'I saw your wife with my own eyes, sir. I saw her and her face – an ugly little thing she is, and cheap—'

'Be very careful,' said Duval quietly, 'that I don't challenge you to a duel for these insults.'

Mr Carson suddenly went quiet, and his eyes bulged in unison with his lips. He hissed like a pantomime villain; the effect was quite comical, yet what he was saying was far from it. 'I will not let go of what is rightfully mine. This is far from over. You will be hearing from my lawyer too.'

After they had departed, Duval went for a walk to clear his mind. As he walked, he heard footsteps behind him and someone calling, 'My dear love.' Duval turned around to see Arnold.

'I just went to your house, and Granger told me which way

you were walking. As you have been barred from White's, let me take you to my club.'

'Where is that?' asked Duval.

'It's called the Liars' Club, and it's on the Thames. It serves the best steak and kidney pie, and we can have a window seat, look out over the water, and contemplate the folly of society. This scandal, my dear love,' said Arnold, 'is top-notch. I mean, I don't think anyone even knew the word Edmée before, and now Edmée seems to stand for—'

'I know what's been written,' interrupted Duval, as they reached the water steps of Westminster.

'Of course you do,' said Arnold, as he decided which waterman he was prepared to use.

It was only when they were past London Bridge that Duval felt somewhat calmer. Then he asked, 'Have you written about me too?'

'No,' said Arnold. 'I have not. I don't know the woman who is at the centre of this storm, but I know you, and I don't think you would stand by Lady Edmée if she fitted any of the said descriptions.'

The pub they had gone to was rowdy and loud, not a table to be had. Duval, in his beautifully cut tailcoat and Hessian boots that came up to the knee, appeared as if he were another species of human.

'What are we doing here, Arnold?'

'Don't worry, dear love,' said Arnold.

The bartender, seeing them, opened a thin door behind the bar, and they went up another set of stairs to the room above that had two box windows looking out over the Thames. 'No one here will say a word; this place is tighter than a priest's arse.'

There was only one other man in the dining room; he was eating alone. Arnold nodded at him before they took their seats.

A steaming hot pie had been brought to the table along with a bottle of the Liars' Club's finest claret. Duval asked, 'Why is Arabella on the attack? What does she want?'

'Well,' said Arnold, 'I suppose a title. Lady Harlington would be what she'd like the most.'

Duval looked at Arnold and said, 'But she is happily married.'

'Oh, that must have been last month, dear love,' said Arnold. 'Things have gone slightly awry.'

'What do you mean?'

'It's only a rumour, but it's a fairly solid rumour, not one that I'm going to dangle in front of my public until it's fully baked.'

'What is the rumour?'

'Philip has fallen in love. One really can't blame the man. He has had quite enough of Arabella's metallic heart, and most probably he's sick of putting pennies in it and getting very little in return. He has fallen madly, passionately, to the edge of his reason, in love with an actress.'

Duval looked at him. 'Are you being serious?'

'Deadly. You saw her playing Polly in *The Beggar's Opera* and doing it charmingly. She's also managing to put on quite a lot of weight around the old waist, and rumour has it that there is a baby on the way, and the daddy of the baby is a very proud, happy banker, except he's got one enormous problem – a wife.'

'Does Arabella know this?' asked Duval.

'I would think she has an inkling, but I don't think she realizes the severity of it, or how deep his affection and his wallet goes. He has bought his love a house off Berkeley Square, she rides in his carriage, has servants, the finest modistes in London, but unlike Arabella, she is absolutely, so they tell me, besotted with him.

'The trouble is, my dear love, at the moment, you have the

Carsons, who would really love to make sure that you never surfaced in public again. You have Arabella, who is after you, and was hoping to make Philip a deep shade of green with jealousy. And you have this unknown Edmée.'

Duval looked out of the window. 'Why can't they leave us alone?'

Arnold stared at Duval for a long moment. 'Who would have thought…' He went on, 'You're in love with her, aren't you? Foolish me for not seeing the signs. Well, that should be the headline news.'

'I don't know what to do to make this go away.'

'And he doesn't deny it,' said Arnold with a chuckle. 'My word, Duval Harlington, who swore he would never fall in love.'

'Have you finished?' said Duval.

'Yes, dear love, carry on.'

'I don't want to be involved with Arabella and Philip's affairs.'

'Quite agree, a stop must be put. I have an idea.'

'What is it?'

'Hold a ball.'

'Oh, no, no, no, no,' said Duval.

'Not in London, dear love. Have it at Muchmore, though I must say, it really goes against my grain. I can't stand all that greenery. And so many sheep depress me. What do they do all day? The sheep, I mean. Not to mention the cows. But that's by the by. Invite all the people you already know. Mrs Dent, Lord Sutton, Sir Wilfrid – who I am certain is as lethal as a sword and can drive you to death with boredom – and his rather tantalizing wife, who I do find divine, mainly because she never says anything. Then you'll have to invite Arabella and Philip. And the only way Philip will ever come down is if you invite the Marquis de Soule – you'll remember that Philip is his banker.'

'I can't stand the marquis,' said Duval.

'I know, but he is very important. If Philip doesn't come, well then, it'll give him more reason to think you're having an affair with Arabella. If they are both there, it will be quite clear that you are not in love with her. And let's not forget the vulture Mr Carson and his poor pigeon of a sister. Let them all see you are not available to be played with.'

Arnold could sense Duval's reluctance. 'Leave me to do all the invitations,' he said. 'There are quite a few fine and finely dull families near you. Put on a wonderful ball, one everyone will remember. Soon, all this will be forgotten. Let's say the 9th of July. What say you?'

Duval groaned, but did not say no, and that was all the encouragement Arnold needed.

A Pirate's Island

Edmée saw herself as a strong woman, one who had survived both the French Revolution and Mr Hyde, so she could not understand how she had become so undone by Duval.

When he hadn't returned after a week, she began to wonder what the kiss he had given her meant. After fifteen days with no word, no letter to say when Lord Harlington might return, her spirits began to flounder. And the kiss appeared to have had more farewell than future to it.

She felt furious that he could so easily walk away and seemingly forget her, when she appeared incapable of forgetting him. She tried to think if she had missed anyone in her life as much as she missed Duval and realized she hadn't. The house felt bigger; she felt smaller. And a thought dressed as a villain came tiptoeing into her mind: if he cared for her, he would be back by now, or at least have sent a letter by way of explanation as to what detained him. The old nightmare began to emerge again.

As a child, Edmée had developed a good imagination, one that could turn a story with the wind of thought into something else. With Hyde, she had used it to float out of her body and imagine a different life. With *ma puce*, she had been young, less formed, more malleable, and had believed her feelings bordered on deeper affection, though she had not missed him when he went away. And when she heard talk of love, she could see nothing much to recognize in her own situation.

But this was an unknown country, these feelings she had for Duval. They were confusing, too troublesome for her uncharted heart.

Hannah had told her in detail how well he had cared for her, never leaving her side. He had stayed by her bed all night and all day. Lady Harriet, too, spoke of his devotion to her, and said that, if he hadn't been there, she was in no doubt Edmée would have died. The only thing keeping her from going overboard with romantic thoughts was the letter that Arabella had sent, about a world she was not a part of – a world Arabella wanted to exclude her from – and in her imagination, she played with it until her heart was sore with longing for him. He was there now, probably at the theatre, dining out at a ball, with Arabella encouraging him to leave the timid mouse.

Each passing day when he hadn't returned, she wondered if it was because he was about to put an end to the marriage – how ironic, just when she knew the one thing she wanted was to be with him. She felt irritated with herself, and finally, having no one else to talk to, she was forced, out of a sense of desperation, to ask Lady Harriet for her opinion.

'Is that why you're not sleeping?'

'Yes, I think so,' said Edmée.

'Don't be a goose. Duval is a singular gentleman, in many respects a private man. But I have never seen him so affected as he was by your illness and your time spent together. It is not for me to say, but I have very little doubt of his strong affection for you. An affection, I would like to say, that he never showed for Arabella.'

Edmée laughed. 'Am I that transparent?'

'In the matters of the heart,' said Lady Harriet, 'when feelings are genuine and not motivated by money or status, they are hard to disguise. Personally, I would say he is very much in love with you, and I believe you are with him.'

'Perhaps...' said Edmée. Feeling uncomfortable with where this conversation had strayed, Lady Harriet changed the subject. 'We should see the dressmaker, Mrs Appleby.'

'I don't need any more robes,' said Edmée.

'Well, I do,' said Lady Harriet.

Every time Edmée saw the dressmaker, she became anxious and felt she was walking too close to the edge, never quite sure if Madame Dupont could be trusted. Lady Harriet was looking at Edmée for an answer.

'Then we should see the dressmaker,' she said, attempting to sound light-hearted but knowing her voice was lead-heavy.

'That's the spirit.'

It is and it isn't, thought Edmée. In the past she had let frivolities such as gowns, shoes, bonnets and lace dull her senses. But she knew, however hard she might try to distract herself, at the back of her mind was a terror of a thought – what if all this began to unravel? She wasn't sure she could bear it, for this time she was in love.

The seamstress came to Muchmore from Woodbridge. She told of a rumour she had heard that there was to be a ball at Muchmore House on the 9th of July. Lady Harriet did not trust gossip – she would wait to hear the news from the source.

The following day, a letter arrived from Duval as Lady Harriet and Edmée were having breakfast. It was short and to the point.

'What is it?' asked Edmée, as Lady Harriet put her

spectacles on the end of her long, fine nose. She only wore them when something on the page made no sense.

'Apparently, it's true. We are indeed to give a ball here, on Saturday, the 9th of July. According to Duval, the invitations have been sent out from Lord and Lady Harlington. What, I would like to know, is he thinking?'

Edmée felt a nervous excitement dance in her; at least she would see him again, even if she had to put up with a party from London. No, she told herself, she would not be intimidated. She was more than capable of doing this – after all, it had once been her way of life.

'Who is invited?' Edmée asked.

'He doesn't say, but I would think Mr and Mrs Gosling. No doubt this ball is the doing of the little minx Arabella. I remember him mentioning that he "owed" her a ball.' Lady Harriet fanned herself with the letter.

'Can it be stopped?' Edmée asked.

'Not now the invitations have been sent. But to be quite honest, I doubt if anyone will come. In London, they might have made the effort, but out in the country... it seems a reckless act.'

Edmée went to kiss Lady Harriet on the cheek. 'Then we must make the most of it,' she said. 'It is a beautiful day and the weather is warm. Shall we have a picnic by the pond? I can swim, and you can sit by the water and dabble your feet and read.'

'An excellent idea,' said Lady Harriet.

That afternoon, followed by a procession of footmen carrying blankets, picnic baskets, chairs and umbrellas, they went down to the pond that was hidden away from the house in a small wood. Lady Harriet led the way, holding a large parasol to keep the sun off her, while Edmée was like a cat who couldn't get enough of the warm rays.

'What are you reading?' Edmée asked, when at last they were settled and the servants had left.

'*Pamela*,' said Lady Harriet. 'My heart goes out to her, that's all I can say.'

'You are a romantic.'

'Unashamedly. And you?'

Edmée thought for a while. 'Perhaps. But not like you. I don't believe in happy endings. All endings are tragic because we all die with unfinished business.'

Lady Harriet watched Edmée go out into the water and thought she was one of the most elegant young women she had ever known. Then, having lost her place in the book, she closed her eyes. She suddenly became aware of someone looking down on her. She sat up straight away.

'Duval!' she said. 'At long last.'

'Please don't disturb yourself, Aunt.'

'Where have you been?' she said, standing up. 'You just wander off and all I hear is we are having a ball. No justification given.'

'Aunt—'

'No, Duval, you owe Edmée an explanation.'

'Where is she?'

'Swimming. I will see you at dinner, and hopefully then you can tell me how you came upon this foolish notion. All I can say is this is not the medicine I would have prescribed.' And she walked away, head held high.

Edmée came out of the water in the thinnest of muslin slips. Duval stared at her, mesmerized, and knew he had never wanted a woman more than he wanted her. There was no smile on her face, no look of delight to see him. If anything, she looked furious.

'What did that kiss mean, my lord?' she said. 'Did it not even warrant a letter?' She stood before him, glittering with anger.

He went closer to her. 'I did write to you. I wrote so many letters, and none did I send. What I wanted to say to you needs to be said face to face.'

'That you are annulling the marriage? Then I will pack and be gone.'

'No,' he said. 'I don't want that.' He was silent. She smelled of summer, and he took a step back, shocked at his own desire.

'Do you belong to the fairy world?' he asked. 'For you have much in common with a water nymph.'

'What do you want, my lord?'

'I want to be married to you. I would like to be married to you for as long as I live. I never ever thought I'd say that to anyone. But I do want you, just you.'

'Then… why the ball?' she said, her voice softening.

He sighed. 'To show you off, for people to see that you are the most beautiful woman I have ever known.'

'In body?'

'No, madam, and you are too clever to not know what I mean.'

Finally, she smiled, her face changing from night to day. She said, 'You are forgiven, and I am pleased to see you. Do you swim?'

She went back into the water and disappeared in the shadows under the willow trees. The muslin slip floated on the water all around her. She said, 'Are you coming in?'

Duval kept on only his breeches and his shirt, and swam towards her, pleased that the water was cold. He hoped it might cool his passion.

'There's an island,' she said, when he reached her.

'I know, I swam here as a boy. There is a sandy shore where I fought pirates.'

'I too,' she said. 'There's one who is monstrously bad. I want to bring a picnic here to the island, but Lady Harriet is worried about the willow trees. She says that if you fall asleep under a willow, you can lose your soul.'

He caught hold of her and instinctively she put her arms around his neck, then as if remembering something, she pulled away from him and swam towards the shore.

Yes, he thought, *you can lose your soul to a water nymph*. He watched her walk up to the chair where Lady Harriet had sat, the outline of her body caught in the rays of sunshine that flickered through the emerald leaves. Her skin golden, unfashionably brown. And without any embarrassment, she took off her wet muslin slip and wrapped a towel about her, before putting on her simple chemise. He swam towards the island in hope to calm his fevered mind. She ate an apple, watching him.

Finally, he swam ashore. She looked up at him.

'I apologize,' he said, 'that I never wrote to you, but—'

'They whipped you,' she said, suddenly serious. Duval's shirt, made of the finest cambric, had stuck to his torso and, being wet, was now transparent.

'Was that in prison, in La Force? Show me.'

'No, you don't need to see it.'

She took his hand, pulled him down, and he sat next to her. She looked at him, and he felt as if she saw into his soul, as if she knew the grief that he carried within him. He took off his shirt.

She ran her fingers over the scars on his back. No one else had ever been allowed to touch them, but it was clear she understood what each lash meant. He closed his eyes.

She rested her head on his shoulder, and he felt her tears roll down his back.

'We both have scars,' she whispered.

They sat there a long time in silence, watching dragonflies skim the water. He said quietly, 'Are you some sort of enchantress?'

'No,' she said, her eyes moist.

'I think you are. I counted every day I was away from you, and it hurt more than anything I have experienced, tore at my heart,' he said in a breathless whisper. 'I love you. But how could you ever want me as I want you, after what that monster did to you?'

Without waiting for a reply, he picked up his shirt, coat and boots and walked swiftly towards the house.

Edmée watched him go and returned to the water. She swam on her back, smiled and said aloud to herself, 'He loves me. Oh, thank you, water nymphs and fairies. He hasn't abandoned me.'

The Unwritten Future

For the following two nights, Duval had dined out, once with his steward and the other with an old tutor who still lived in Woodbridge. During the day, he was employed on estate business.

Edmée had no idea what to do for the best or how she could meet him without footmen and formal meals getting in the way. She woke that night, thinking she had heard someone cry out. She wasn't sure if she had dreamed it. Unable to sleep, she lit a candle and decided to write once more in her journal. The last time she had opened it had been before she became ill. Perhaps it would be good to begin again, for writing had always calmed her. Paper doesn't judge the words written there. Edmée took the bound book to the desk by the window and saw her reflection looking back at her. She thought about how far she had come since she first wrote in it.

But the minute Edmée opened the book, her heart missed a beat. Duval's letter, which she used to keep her place, wasn't on the right page. A terrible thought came to her: someone had read her diary. Hannah, she knew, couldn't read. There was only one other person who had been in the room long enough to find it and read it, and that was Duval. Perhaps that would explain why he had been unable to write to her, for fear of giving himself away. So he knew about *ma puce* – what else had she written? She felt her heart beating loudly, her eyes almost unable to make sense of the words. Desperately she went through page after page until her head was spinning.

She re-read it. She had mentioned *ma puce*, but nothing more. Picking up the candle with a sense of dread, she went to the antechamber, and there was the box she had brought with her. She was relieved to find it unopened. She had hidden the key at the back of the portrait of Duval, where there was a small cavity between the canvas and the frame. *Breathe*, she told herself, unlocking the box.

She took out one of the thin notebooks that she hadn't yet transcribed into her journal. Hyde had not taken it from her box, the writing considered too childish, too small for his impatient eye. She picked it up, put it into the embers of the fire, and waited until it caught light. 'Farewell, *ma puce*,' she said. Only when the truth of her was no more than ash did she go back into the antechamber.

She sat on the floor, rested the candle on the box, and took out her precious book. On the title page, at the bottom in small print, was written, *Bernard Simoneau, the bookbinder of rue Jacob*. The pages held the smell that could take her back in time, tinged with a faint odour of burnt paper. She sat there and let the tears roll down her face. This book had hidden within it her prized possession. It wasn't lost, but what would be gained by telling Duval the truth of it? They were all long dead. She thought it better by far they remained that way. She put the key back behind the painting.

*

The next morning, Lady Harriet was in the drawing room going through replies to the invitations, most of which were polite refusals.

'We are being quietly shunned,' she said.

As Edmée entered the room, she said, 'Shunned by whom?' She thought Lady Harriet might mean Duval, for neither of them had seen him the night before, or that morning.

'By all and sundry, primarily the ghastly Mrs Beale,' said Lady Harriet. 'I knew this ball wasn't a good idea. She has spread gossip as thick as cowpats.'

'Do you think, if it is a success, it will silence all this unnecessary talk?'

'Yes, that is the hope.'

'Then I am in favour of it,' said Edmée, 'especially if it can be done without the inconvenience of having to go to London, where I think I would be more on show, and we would have to give dinners.'

What worried Edmée more than the ball was Duval. He had been so distant since telling her he loved her. She wondered if she had dreamed it, whether perhaps he had never said it at all.

One rainy afternoon, Lady Harriet was alone in the drawing room when Watkins came to announce the arrival of Mrs Beale.

She entered the drawing room, overflowing in every sense of the word. Not even her clothes seemed capable of containing her. She oozed insincere condolences. *She really is the most foolish woman*, thought Lady Harriet, as Mrs Beale commiserated on the tragedy that had apparently befallen the great estate of Muchmore.

'I have no idea what you are referring to, Mrs Beale,' said Lady Harriet. 'No one has died.'

'No, Lady Harriet, but Mr Carson came to dine the other night and told us of the dire predicament in which Lord Harlington finds himself. He is quietly confident that this estate will all be his, as entrusted by the late Lord Harlington—'

'Mr Carson?' interrupted Lady Harriet. 'Don't tell me he is back here again.'

'Yes, he is back at Monkton Manor. He said that it is quite tragic to see the great name of Harlington brought so low,' said Mrs Beale. 'I'm sure you agree that this business of a wife sale is too shocking for words. And that's not to mention the consequences.' Lowering her voice to a whisper, she said, 'Perhaps it would have been for the best if Lady Harlington had died. But now this ball puts everyone in a—'

Lady Harriet had been about to ask Mrs Beale to leave when the drawing room door opened and Edmée entered, cutting off whatever Mrs Beale was going to say next. Edmée looked ravishing. Great attention had been paid to her dress: a white muslin, long-sleeved gown, with a green ribbon tied high above her dainty waist. On her head, she wore an elegant lace cap. The whole ensemble spoke of sophistication. Her skin was honey-coloured, and rouge had been lightly applied to her cheeks and lips.

Mrs Beale was quite taken aback by the figure that now appeared before her. For a moment, she was confused. Surely this couldn't be the same woman who was once married to that Mr Hyde? Mrs Beale rose to her feet with a sigh, as if the idea of curtseying was almost too exhausting and unnecessary. She would pretend they had never met, and heaven help this trollop if she wanted to play it any other way.

Lady Harriet made the introductions.

'We meet again, Mrs Beale,' said Edmée. 'I hear your daughter is married to a colonel in the Duke of York's army. May I offer my congratulations?'

'Again, Lady Harlington?' said Mrs Beale, surprised by the assured way with which Edmée spoke. Hardly a trace of an accent. Still, she wouldn't want any home truths coming out here. Mrs Beale carried on, with the smudge of a smile on her face. 'We live mainly at Witchling… I don't think we have met.'

'Oh, but we have,' said Edmée. 'I used to live in the village, as you know. But perhaps you don't recognize me, for back then my face was bruised and swollen.'

Flustered, Mrs Beale said, 'No, I cannot have met you, Lady Harlington. I am sure I wouldn't have forgotten.' She hoped she had said that with more confidence than she felt.

Lady Harriet rang a bell and asked for tea to be served.

'I cannot stay,' said Mrs Beale, now seriously fearing she had misjudged the situation.

'Your memory needs help,' said Edmée. 'It's a shame you have forgotten our last meeting because, if I recall correctly, I had escaped the parsonage and come to you for assistance. I told you what Mr Hyde had done to me, and you said—'

'No, no,' said Mrs Beale, knowing she had been outmanoeuvred. 'Please, Lady Harlington, perhaps it's best forgotten.'

They were interrupted by tea, which was served with full ceremony. The footmen stayed by the door, as requested by Edmée, with strict instructions not to let Mrs Beale leave.

Mrs Beale took her cup with a flushed face and shaking hand. 'The weather has been rather hot,' she said.

'Do have a cake, Mrs Beale. We have an excellent French pastry chef,' said Edmée.

Taking a cake herself, Lady Harriet said, 'Mrs Beale came to tell me the ball was unwise, and to explain why no Christian family could accept the invitation.'

'How very unfortunate,' said Edmée with charm.

Mrs Beale put down her plate and, hearing a distant clock

chime, said, 'Is that the time? I really must go – Jocasta is expecting me.'

'You will sit down,' said Edmée firmly. 'When I came to you for help, you told me that, as an émigré, I shouldn't complain but should be grateful for being given a home at all. You also told me Samuel Hyde had a right to beat me, and that I must have deserved my bruises.'

'Mrs Beale, you didn't!' said Lady Harriet. 'What a vile thing to say. You of all people! In all the years I have known you, you have never once obeyed your husband.'

'I'm not used to such candid talk,' said Mrs Beale. Recognizing defeat, she stood up, nearly knocking over a side table.

'Perhaps we can all pretend you are a decent Christian soul,' said Edmée. 'Though I will need a little practice.'

Mrs Beale looked close to tears. 'Mr Beale and I would be honoured to accept the invitation to your ball,' she said.

'And can we assume,' said Lady Harriet, 'that everyone else in your circle will also overcome their scruples?'

'Yes, yes,' said Mrs Beale, 'and nothing more need be said about... about...'

Edmée stood. 'If you keep your word, madame, it will be my pleasure to forget we ever met before today.'

As she left, Mrs Beale curtsied far lower than she had on entering the room.

'Bravo,' said Lady Harriet, as the carriage was driven away. 'Bravo, my darling girl, for confounding that sanctimonious woman.'

Edmée leaned back in her armchair. 'She is truly dreadful.'

'Your timing was impeccable,' said Lady Harriet. 'How did you manage it?'

Edmée said, 'My maid was in the village and heard Mrs Beale's maid saying her mistress intended to call today. We dressed me accordingly.'

'You were spectacular.'

The drawing room door opened, and Duval strolled in. 'Was that Mrs Beale I saw being forcibly stuffed into her carriage?'

'Edmée stumped that old crab,' said Lady Harriet. 'She was well and truly routed.'

Duval smiled at Edmée. 'Many congratulations, my lady.'

After supper that night, Duval saw Edmée to her bedchamber and wished her goodnight. He took her hand and kissed it, then bowed and turned to walk away. When she caught his hand, he stopped.

'Sweet dreams,' she said.

Duval went back to his study. He liked these hours when the house was quiet – time to think. He smoked a cheroot, drank a brandy. Once again in that witching hour he found himself frustrated by longing for Edmée. Since his return he had been out, mainly walking the estate, hoping to calm his troubled mind. He'd never really seen the possibility of love driving one mad but he had reached a point where he didn't know quite what to do with himself. He needed to talk to her; he needed to hold her. He needed to tell her he loved her again and again. But what if she said she didn't love him? Could he cope with that? The thought of such tragic love took him back to his father. Damn this house. Too many ghosts.

Perhaps he would have to accept that they would never become lovers, that theirs would be a platonic marriage. He found the idea deeply disturbing.

Blast it, he shouldn't have said he loved her. If he had waited, there might have been a more appropriate opportunity. He had been undone by her touching his scars – the way her fingers had gently traced the map left on his skin. She didn't say, 'How terrible,' or gasp in horror. Her touch had felt achingly erotic. He had had tears in his eyes, but he couldn't let her see that. It had taken all his strength to walk away from her that day.

He drained his glass and was about to go to his chamber when a note was posted under the door.

He read:

We have done everything backwards. We married at the wrong end of beginning.

I love you too. There, I have said it. I love you with all my being. I want you not to think of me as a weak and damaged creature. Neither am I a victim of misfortune. To view my life in such a way would be to undo all the blessings that my marriage to you has brought me.

My bed is large, and my bed is empty. I want to be with you, if you want me.

Duval walked down the long corridor, lined with paintings of his father's bad-tempered ancestors, and knocked quietly on Edmée's door. It opened.

He said, 'I thought I should bring you my reply in person,' as he closed the door behind him.

Edmée woke late to find her bed empty. She smiled to herself, relishing the memory of last night, his kisses, his touch, and as cats do when they have cream, she stretched in pleasure. All she wanted was for that loving to repeat again and again.

A maid arrived with the breakfast tray, while Hannah pulled the cover over her mistress to protect her modesty and puffed up her pillows.

'Is there a boat to row on the pond?' Edmée asked.

'There is, my lady,' Hannah answered.

'Good,' she said, and curled back into the soft pillows.

She felt like singing with joy. She couldn't remember when she had last felt this happy. Yes, this was unadulterated happiness. Perhaps, finally, she would be secure.

It was security she had searched for all her life. Here, she hoped she could let the curtain fall on her past; *ma puce* wouldn't haunt her, not now she was Lady Harlington. She was considering the tea on her breakfast tray when the door opened, and Duval came in, still in his dressing gown, carrying a bottle and two glasses.

'Breakfast – good,' he said. 'I'm famished.' He kissed her. 'You know what last night means.'

'What?' she said, concerned.

'It means our marriage is well and truly consummated.' He smiled. 'Don't look so worried, my dove, I'm funning with you.'

She lay back in the bed, modesty forgotten. 'What a relief,' she said, as the champagne bubbled into the fluted glasses.

'Here's to our unwritten future,' he said, lifting his glass.

He knew now he would never ask her about *ma puce*, about all of those things he'd read in her diary. It was irrelevant.

She had been on the verge of speaking, then changed her mind. Duval didn't press her. He said, 'This is where the future starts; the past is gone, the dead are buried.' He took from his pocket a small jewellery box.

She opened it. Inside was a diamond and sapphire ring. 'It's exquisite,' she said.

'I bought it in London, when I couldn't stop thinking about you,' said Duval. 'It can be altered to fit.' He placed it on Edmée's finger. 'No need,' he said quietly to himself, as if the perfect fit proved her worth.

He wrapped her in his arms and kissed her neck, and the breakfast lay forgotten.

*

For the first time since being in prison, regardless of Mr Carson, Duval was feeling optimistic. He found himself sleeping better. The heat of her body, with his arms around her, went a long way to preventing the nightmares that had so often disturbed him. He could honestly say he had never known such contentment.

With the ball two weeks away Muchmore House seemed to have sprung into life, with the happiness of the two lovers, as if the estate had woken from a long and troublesome sleep.

A small army of gardeners was employed to made sure the walks in the park were immaculate, the maze was neatly trimmed, the disused fountains were cleaned and once more gushed water, the lawns were like velvet and the greenhouses full of flowers, ready for the ball. The kitchen took on a new energy. Rooms were aired, carpets beaten, wood polished, until the house gleamed and stood waiting for its guests.

On the dot of six o'clock on his birthday – a day before his guests were due to arrive – Duval was to be found wearing an open shirt, breeches, no stockings, a beautifully cut, embroidered silk banyan coat and a pair of Moroccan slippers. Despite this casual dress, he cut a very dashing figure. Still, there would be no one, except his wife, who had prepared a surprise for him, to see his becoming outfit. Or so he thought.

The day had been hot, there was a slight breeze, and everything about that early evening had a stillness to it, the quiet that comes after the heat of the day subsides. But the quiet was broken by the thunderous sound of carriage wheels on gravel, and not just one, but two carriages arrived.

Watkins and the footmen spilled out of the house and lined up to greet the guests. For an absurd second, Duval felt like running for the woods. The carriages came to a stop and a sheepish Arabella climbed out.

'We thought we would arrive early and surprise you on your birthday,' she said, with a quick curtsey. 'We're here to celebrate with—' The luggage was being taken down. 'Be careful of that bandbox,' she called. Then turning back to Duval, she continued, 'We're here to rescue you from your dull life in the country.'

Duval said sharply, 'I don't need rescuing.'

'I told you,' said Philip Gosling, rebuking his wife and bowing to Duval. 'I couldn't stop her, my lord.'

'Oh, tish tosh, of course you could. You didn't because you thought it a good idea. Don't deny it,' said Arabella.

Arnold climbed out of the second carriage. One look at Duval was enough to tell him they weren't wanted.

'Guests,' muttered Lady Harriet, descending the steps to greet the party with as much enthusiasm as she had for a book with a bad ending.

'I'm afraid I have a prior engagement this evening,' Duval replied.

'You are hardly dressed for one,' said Arabella, pouting. 'Surely you can cancel it?'

'No, I can't; you will have to excuse me,' said Duval. He turned to his aunt. 'You will look after our guests, won't you?'

'Of course,' Lady Harriet said flatly, as she ushered them into the house.

Watkins came out to Duval. 'What can I do, my lord? It's past six.'

'I'm well aware of it. Make sure they are fed and entertained and come nowhere near the woods, or the pond,' said Duval.

From the doorway, Arabella watched him walk away towards the shadow of the trees.

*

Duval closed the gate that led to the path along the stream, where midges flew in clouds. He came to the pond. Waiting near the shore was a small boat. He took off his slippers, lifted his coat and waded out to it, then rowed to the island and climbed ashore. A table and two chairs sat not far from the willow tree, behind them a makeshift tent and, inside, a bed scattered with rose petals. It was a place where Oberon might have wooed Titania – but there was no Edmée. Looking over the still water, he saw her swimming towards him, and he helped her ashore.

'I thought you might not come,' she said, 'so I—'

He took her in his arms. 'Arabella arrived early.'

'Oh, I know,' she said. 'I have just come from the house and saw her in the hall. She asked me to take her bandbox up to her chamber.'

'What did you do?'

'I walked away.'

'May I say, I regret this ball with all my heart,' said Duval. 'I made a mistake.'

'Let's not worry about it tonight. Instead, we will eat and enjoy ourselves.'

'Yes,' he said.

'I have something for you,' she said.

He hadn't noticed the small box on the table that she now pushed towards him. Duval gazed at it suspiciously.

'Have you never had a birthday present before?' she asked.

'No. When I was a child, my birthday was a day of great sadness. Whatever the weather, we wore black, the house had a black sash across the front door, and I was reminded I was responsible for my mother's death. So, this is my first birthday present.'

He opened the box and stared at its contents.

Edmée said, 'Do you hate it? It is, I know, a little sentimental.'

'A locket,' he said. 'It's beautiful.'

'But there is something more to it, look.'

He opened the oblong locket and inside was a painting of her eye. A lover's eye – one of the most glorious fashions of the day – and the artist had captured the look in Edmée's eye exceedingly well.

He stared at it in wonder, and tears came to his eyes. 'How do you do it?' he asked.

'Do what?'

'Live in the moment,' he said. 'Not let the past drown all the love in you.'

'What I'm going to say might sound ridiculous,' she said, 'but I always believed I would meet you, that if it hadn't happened yesterday, it just meant I had to hold on until tomorrow. I thought it was you the minute I saw you. My fear was that you hadn't been waiting for me.'

He wrapped his arms around her. 'Thank you,' he said quietly. 'I believe you are a nymph from the fairy world – there is too much magic in you not to be. This is the best birthday I have ever been given.'

When it was dark, they lit the candles and made love, slowly this time. Never had Duval so entirely lost himself in a woman.

In the early hours of the morning, like thieves, they went back up to the house.

Looking out from behind the shutters upstairs, Arabella saw the lovers strolling hand-in-hand across the lawn and felt the green-eyed devil stirring inside her.

'A lady doesn't walk at dawn half-dressed,' she said to herself. 'No, a lady doesn't. But a whore might.'

The Note

When Edmée woke, her heart was pounding, as it often did when she'd had her recurring dream, though it was more of a nightmare, so vivid that it smothered the day with its disturbing images. It never varied; always the same thing happened:

A woman in a red bonnet of liberty sells petticoats. They hang around her, billowing like ghostly flags. These undergarments have outlived the ladies who once wore them. Cottons, silks and the finest linen – all have found equality here. None too clean, the sad flags flutter in the breeze, the remnants a reminder of all the fallen, headless women of Paris.

Abandoning sleep, she got up and dressed herself. She turned when she heard Duval stirring.

'Thank you for last night,' he said.

He reached out for her hand. She bent down and he kissed her fingers, then pulled her back into the bed.

He smelled of sleep and his skin of oranges and sunshine.

'Are you not going to tell me I'm creasing your dress?' he said.

'Never,' she replied, 'but your aunt is waiting to take me to Woodbridge for a final fitting.'

'That matters…' said Duval, smiling, as she stood up again, 'little.'

For a pleasurable time, the nightmare was forgotten.

'There you are,' said Lady Harriet. She was in the hall, putting on her gloves. 'Let's not dilly-dally.' Her brand-new phaeton had been brought to the front of the house. 'It looks so smart. I'm pleased I chose deep red. I told the carriage builder it must be bright, then no one can say they haven't seen me coming.'

Her last phaeton had ended in a ditch; fortunately, no one had been hurt. Lady Harriet was known to be a reckless driver.

They set off at a trot and Edmée smiled to herself on seeing that the groom – or more likely Duval – had wisely not allowed Lady Harriet to have the fastest horse.

The joy of a phaeton was that you were high up and could see over fences and hedges, as well as having a good idea of what was coming round corners. *If only*, Edmée thought, *you could see into the future so easily*. The sunlight and the warmth of the day went some way to clearing her mind. *It was nothing but a nightmare*, she told herself. It was fantastical to imagine the future could be so simply foretold by dreams. Determined to think no more of it, she asked Lady Harriet if all the guests from London had arrived last night.

'Most are arriving today,' said Lady Harriet. 'Arabella told us that she had persuaded the Marquis de Soule to join her party. I heard he has never left London, hard to believe. But Arnold is of the opinion he has an interest in Duval – though what that could be, I've no idea.'

'The Marquis de Soule?' repeated Edmée. The colour in her cheeks started to rise. 'I am positive he was killed in the September Massacres. Surely, you are mistaken, or thinking of another marquis?' She held on tightly to the side of the carriage as they went round a sharp bend. In her mind's eye, she saw again the petticoats of headless women.

'Did you know the marquis?' asked Lady Harriet, when the phaeton was back on the straight and narrow.

'No,' said Edmée, 'only the name...' Quickly changing the subject, she said, 'You mentioned Arabella was in a foul mood last night?'

'Yes. Arnold said he had his suspicions, but wasn't very forthcoming about them. It's all so tiring. I am very much of the opinion that London society is best when it is in London, and not down here.'

Woodbridge was sleepy in the heat haze. The house where the dressmaker lived and worked was on the market square, but before the Revolution, she had been much sought-after in Paris. She had left France at the height of the Terror, and since she had married a local sailor, Mrs Tom Appleby seemed most content with her new circumstances. Her business was flourishing. As far as Lady Harlington was concerned, she had kept her word. Yet still, Edmée felt the familiar sense of trepidation rise; even more so that morning, after her nightmare, which she had now come to view as a warning.

The gowns were exquisite, and Lady Harriet was delighted. 'Who would have imagined that we should have such a talented dressmaker in our small town?' she said. 'Were you very much in demand in Paris?'

Mrs Appleby said quietly that she was. For the first time it occurred to Edmée that perhaps the dressmaker also had secrets she would rather no one knew about. She wondered what Lady Harriet would say if she knew that her dress had been made by one of the late queen's favourite modistes.

Just as they were leaving, Mrs Appleby said, 'Oh, Lady Harlington, I nearly forgot – Mademoiselle Carson left this note for you.'

'I expect she wants to accept the invitation after all,' said Lady Harriet grimly, though Mr Carson had written to say neither he nor his sister would be attending. *There is no accounting for such people*, thought Lady Harriet, then, turning to Edmée, she said, 'Wait here, I won't be a moment – just need to see if the phaeton is ready.'

Edmée sat down on a chair – the dressmaker had followed Lady Harriet out into the hall. Left alone in the workshop, Edmée wished now there was time to tell Duval the truth. No more secrets.

She opened the note and read it, looked again at the words that made no sense. She went very pale as she realized their meaning and hurriedly tore the note to pieces. Mrs Appleby came back into the room and asked if Lady Harlington was feeling alright. Edmée didn't seem to see her; she murmured to herself, 'How could he ever love me now? It is all too late.'

'Shall we go?' said Lady Harriet, returning.

Edmée stood up unsteadily. Her legs gave way, and she fell to the floor.

Edmée woke with a start to find Lady Harriet crouched beside her.

'Oh goodness, Edmée, my dear girl, you fainted – I will send for Duval.'

'No, Aunt, you mustn't, please,' said Edmée, struggling to

her feet. 'I'm quite alright – I didn't have breakfast, that's all it is.'

'Are you sure?'

'Yes, perfectly,' she said and bent to pick up the scraps of paper.

'Let me, your ladyship,' said the dressmaker.

'Was it the note that upset you?' asked Lady Harriet.

'Oh… no,' said Edmée.

'What did that wretched Carson's sister want?'

'An invitation to the ball,' said Edmée.

'That's all?' said Lady Harriet, when Edmée was seated once more in the phaeton.

Edmée shocked herself and smiled. 'Yes, foolish woman. Do you mind if we go home? My head is splitting.'

As they rode back in silence, Lady Harriet thought, not for the first time, that there was so much still unknown about the new Lady Harlington.

The Past Doesn't Travel Well

As soon as they arrived at Muchmore, Edmée went to her bedchamber and lay down, exhausted. She curled up, wondering what to do for the best. Was the note a hoax? It must be. But what if it wasn't? Outside, she could hear the sounds of carriages arriving.

Edmée felt she would never be able to escape the past. It would hang around her, a chain rattling ever more loudly with every passing year. She tipped her head back and tried not to cry.

Duval found Edmée in the bath, her face puffy.

'Edmée, my dove, you're flushed. Have you been crying?'

'No,' she lied. 'I despise women who cry.' She smiled. 'I think the bath-water is too hot.'

He felt the water. It was tepid. It occurred to Duval for the first time that she wasn't yet fully recovered. He helped her out and wrapped a towel around her. 'Arabella hasn't demanded you fetch her shawl?'

'No,' she said. 'I haven't seen her.'

'You were crying,' he said and held her close.

'It's nothing. I think perhaps losing a baby makes a merry-go-round of one's emotions.'

There was a tap on the door and Watkins' solemn voice announced the arrival of the Marquis de Soule.

'Thank you, Watkins,' Duval called. 'I must go down,' he said to Edmée. 'I'll be back.'

When he returned, Edmée had bathed her face and Hannah had dressed her. She was wearing a simply cut dress, made from a luxurious silk with a train. Over the silk was the finest see-through muslin, embroidered with little black dots. The waistline was high, the sleeves puffed, and the low-cut bodice showed off Edmée's petite bosom, framed in black Belgian lace. The hem of the dress was embroidered with a red design and the ribbons in her hair were also red; the effect was strikingly modern.

'You look stunning,' said Duval. 'Is that the gown you had made in Woodbridge?'

'Yes,' said Edmée.

'What on earth is such a superb dressmaker doing here?'

'She is an émigré,' said Edmée, but stopped. Through the walls they could hear raised voices.

'Is that the Goslings? They sound as if they're in the next room,' said Edmée.

'That happens in this house. Sound travels in the oddest of ways. My dove, are you quite well? You're shivering. There is no need to be nervous. You will outshine everyone.'

She kissed him, then stood back, as if inspecting what he was wearing.

'If you feel too tired this evening, you can retire early,' he said.

'Yes,' she said. 'Yes, of course.' She took his arm and they went down to the salon. As two footmen opened the doors, he turned to look at her and saw her eyes were closed.

*

There was a stunned silence as they entered. Duval realized he had not yet described his wife to anyone, and now most of the gathered guests stared wide-eyed at the new Lady Harlington. Edmée might not have been a conventional beauty, but she was undeniably bewitching.

Duval introduced her, and as bows and curtsies were exchanged, Sir Wilfrid Fairly spoke first.

'Only ten guineas? My word – I would have happily paid a thousand pounds,' he declared. Edmée curtsied.

Lady Anne Fairly, who always stood by her husband, said, 'I'd be most surprised, my dear Lady Harlington, if my husband would have paid so much as a penny for me.'

'Oh, there I go,' said Sir Wilfrid. 'I haven't been here more than ten minutes and already I've upset my wife. Put it down to my nerves being jangled. I've been rattled about like a pig in a pen in my confounded contraption of a carriage.'

Arabella, who was next in line, said, 'Oh, my word, you sly fox, Duval.'

Edmée smiled. 'Did he tell you I was dull-looking?' she asked. 'And resembled a timid mouse?'

Arabella blushed.

'I refuse to take the blame,' Duval said, relieved Edmée had recovered her confidence.

'I was just saying to Mrs Dent that I doubted looks would be much on display at a wife sale,' said Lady Anne, rather tactlessly.

But Edmée replied with good humour. 'Oh, Lady Anne, it was the husbands who looked shocking; the wives fared much better.'

The laughter that followed died away, as the salon doors opened again to reveal the spectral figure of the Marquis

Reynaud de Soule. His face was painted white, as was his wig, and his cheeks and lips had been dusted with rouge.

He stood and surveyed the room. Edmée had moved away from the door. The marquis was about to speak when he saw her. 'Ahh-ahh-ah…' he said, and stumbled, appearing to lose his balance.

'Do you require assistance?' said Mr Gosling, stepping forward.

'No, no,' said the marquis and waved him away. 'There is no need to fuss.' He waited, stood up straight and said, 'Lord Harlington, who is this enchanting lady?'

'May I introduce my wife – Edmée, Lady Harlington.'

The marquis bowed deeply and, composure regained, said, 'Such beauty could only belong to France.'

There was general amusement, and Arabella clapped.

'My dear monsieur,' she said patronizingly, 'you are always so generous when you meet a new lady.'

'No, Mrs Gosling, I am not. Most Englishwomen have too much of the horse about them and not enough of the powder.'

Duval glanced at Edmée and saw the shadow of a smile.

'And may I introduce my aunt, Lady Harriet Haslet,' he said.

Lady Harriet curtsied and said, 'I admit I have something of the horse about me, Monsieur le Marquis.'

'*Mais non*. You, Lady Harriet, are perfect, not a hair of the horse about you. And your gown… no – it cannot be – surely…' He stopped, then looked at Edmée. 'Surely it is the work of Madame Dupont?'

'Indeed it is, monsieur.'

'I remember well the gowns she made for the late queen.'

'Oh,' said Arabella, much impressed. 'You knew Marie Antoinette?'

'Yes, of course. I knew her and I knew the king.' He took

out a handkerchief and, with a waft of cologne, added firmly, 'But I will not talk about them.'

Dinner was a convivial occasion and Duval, who had been worried lest it be too much for Edmée, was relieved. Though it did still seem to him that, for all Edmée's composure, she was not herself.

'I am very much looking forward to seeing the rest of the house in the morning,' said Mrs Dent. 'And the garden. I believe there is a maze, Lord Harlington.'

'My father had it designed and planted, but lost interest after being marooned in it for a whole day,' said Duval.

Arnold laughed at the thought and said, 'Old Lord Harlington was such a butterfly of a man.'

Arabella, wanting to bring herself back into the conversation – or at least to show she knew the Marquis de Soule better than anyone else round the table – asked, 'My dear Monsieur le Marquis…'

He ignored her, much to Arabella's annoyance, and turned to Mrs Dent. 'You rescue women from what?'

'From dreadful households, from brutal marriages. You would be shocked by how many men have no manners in this country. I believe the same goes for France.'

To the relief of all the guests, the marquis laughed.

'Were you ever married?' asked Sir Wilfrid.

The marquis's face clouded over.

'Yes, of course.'

'What was her name?' asked Arabella.

The marquis hesitated, took a deep breath, then said, 'The Marquise de Soule was murdered in the September Massacres.'

The silence that followed was broken by Lady Anne. 'Oh dear,' she said. 'What a sad loss.'

Arabella was about to speak again, when Lady Harriet caught Edmée's eye and gave a slight nod.

Edmée stood up, saying, 'I think it's time we left the gentlemen to their port.'

After supper, the card tables were set out in the drawing room. Having no desire to gamble, Edmée sat with Mrs Dent.

'The marquis is very taken with you, Lady Harlington,' said Mrs Dent, smiling. 'But he did seem to be in an odd mood.'

Edmée shrugged. 'I doubt it signifies anything,' she said. 'Whereabouts in London do you live?'

'In Berkeley Square. Have you visited London, Lady Harlington?'

'No, madam, but I hope to do so.'

'Then you must call on me,' said Mrs Dent.

Arabella, leaving the card table, joined them. She flopped on the sofa, saying, 'I have become so sensible these days. I've set a price on how much I can tolerably bear to lose, and once I reach that figure, I retire. I am in danger of being found dull.'

'Impossible, Mrs Gosling,' said Edmée.

'I see why Duval fell in love with you,' said Arabella. 'Luckily, I am not a jealous soul, otherwise I could easily dislike someone as lovely as you.'

The Day of the Ball

The weather was hot and sultry on the day of the ball, with a feeling of thunder in the air. Duval was up early. He had the boats brought to the lake and the tent put up, to make the hot day more comfortable for the guests.

Arabella and Philip had had another row when Arabella had returned to her chamber to unsuccessfully attempt to rest. What folly was Philip talking of, accusing her of being obsessed with Duval? And now he was speaking about leaving her. How dare he even bring it up. Then Philip had left to see the marquis, one of his most important clients, who had asked him to breakfast in his chamber.

'Oh tosh,' said Arabella to herself when he had gone. From the window she could see Duval out by the lake and decided to make the most of this opportunity to find Edmée alone.

Knowing the house well, she took an educated guess as to which door would be Edmée's chamber and knocked on it. Hannah opened it and said her mistress was not receiving visitors.

'Tra-la-la,' said Arabella, walking straight past Hannah. 'Bring me a hot chocolate, Hannah, and some of those delicious biscuits the cook makes.'

Hannah looked at her mistress, who was standing by the window looking down onto the lake.

Edmée nodded.

'I thought we should get to know one another better, Lady Harlington,' said Arabella.

Edmée turned to look at her. The silence was awkward.

'I always loved this chamber,' said Arabella. 'It used to be mine, when the Viper was alive. Of course, you never met the old earl. I adored him; he was most misunderstood, that's what I used to tell Duval.' She sighed. 'He was also right about Duval not going to Paris. He knew it was a stupid thing to do, but would Duval listen?' She sat down and, changing the subject, said, 'I thought the gown you wore last night was charming, and I want the name of the—'

'Mrs Appleby,' said Edmée, interrupting her. 'You will find her in Woodbridge.'

'Do sit and talk to me,' said Arabella.

Edmée stayed by the window.

'Oh come, there is so much delightful gossip to be had. Let us talk about last night. Do you not think it a little strange, the way the marquis reacted to you? He is a ridiculous man, but honestly, I thought he was going to need smelling salts when he saw you. I'm fascinated to know if you were acquainted with him in Paris.'

'No, Mrs Gosling,' said Edmée. 'I never had that pleasure.'

'Mr Gosling told me the marquis had many mistresses,' said Arabella. 'Then again he spoke last night about his wife who, alas, died in tragic circumstances. I assumed he must have mistaken you for someone else. When I'm back in London, I will get to the bottom of the mystery. The minute I do, I will let you know. Isn't that fun? Still, are you sure he did not know you? Come, you can tell me. You are a dark horse, Lady Harlington.'

'And you are not, Mrs Gosling?' said Edmée.

'I don't know what you mean. My heart is already taken—'

'With my husband?'

'I can assure you; my marriage is a happy one. I am holding out a hand of friendship to you.'

'I strongly doubt that, Mrs Gosling.'

'Oh, really?' said Arabella as she flounced out of the room, nearly bumping into Hannah, who had come back with hot chocolate but no biscuits.

'Shall I dress your hair, my lady?' said Hannah when Arabella had gone. 'Mrs Gosling – Miss Collins as she was then – was never liked when she stayed here,' she told her mistress.

Having received the surprise news of the marquis's impending departure, Duval set out to visit him. The marquis had been given the late earl's Sanctuary. Duval loathed going there, even now. Once the will was settled for good, he planned to have the whole apartment redesigned. Every time he took the long walk to the suite of rooms, he saw himself at varying stages of his life.

Today, he saw the optimistic young man, determined to go to France to study medicine, to do something useful.

'There's a bloodbath coming to that country,' his father had said.

'There's no evidence for that,' replied the young Duval.

'That's because you are too blind to see it,' the Viper had snapped.

He knocked on the door, half expecting to see his father. The Marquis de Soule was sitting there, just where his father used to sit, his bejewelled hands resting in front of him. Duval tried to find a word to describe him; he thought 'broken' would do. The marquis stood and gave an exaggerated bow.

'I have been told, monsieur, you are leaving us before tonight's entertainment,' said Duval.

'I hope you will pardon my little whim,' replied the marquis in French, 'but I should have told you before that I cannot abide green. Here in the countryside, in the summer, there is too much of it.'

This man is as foolish as my father, thought Duval.

'I thank you for your hospitality.'

The marquis's valet helped him on with an embroidered frock coat. It was green.

'Remind me,' said the marquis, 'how much did you pay for your wife?'

Duval hesitated, then he said, 'Three years in La Force.'

There was a silence, then the marquis said, 'A wife sale – a priceless gem wasted on English swine.' And with that he walked slowly out of the room to his carriage.

Taking a walk through the house to calm herself, a memory that she had been trying to suppress overwhelmed Edmée. It was of a wedding in Paris, the one she would never speak of. She was twelve, and in her mind's eye, she could see her father standing there, a serious look on his face, her bridegroom laughing. The priest was drunk and slurred his words when he announced they were man and wife. And what had she been thinking of at that moment? She was thinking that she had never worn such a glorious dress before. It was what a fairy princess might wear.

'Where are you going, Papa?' she had asked, when he left straight after the ceremony.

'Home,' he said sharply.

'I want to come with you,' she had said. 'Please take me home.'

'No, girl, you are not my concern. Not anymore.'

The memory made Edmée feel she was losing her balance. She steadied herself against a stand on which there was a lavish display of flowers in a vase.

She could remember all too well shouting, 'Papa, Papa, don't leave me, don't leave me, not here, not with him…'

Her legs went weak beneath her, and both vase and flowers crashed to the marble floor. Duval came out of the drawing room and found her sitting amid the debris of roses and broken china. He carried her to their bedchamber, calling for Hannah.

'You are to rest,' he said to Edmée.

She held on to his hand. 'Forgive me,' she said.

At the door, he said, 'It was only a vase.'

That afternoon, Duval found his aunt, not in her chamber resting, but in the drawing room alone. 'Do you have any idea what's going on with Arabella?' she asked.

'Why?'

'She came to see me in my chamber just now and left in a furious state, saying that Edmée had been rude to her or some such nonsense.'

'I think it has a lot to do with what is happening in Arabella's life.'

'Yes, Arnold told me. You are talking, I suppose, about this actress in *The Beggar's Opera*.'

'I am,' said Duval.

'An unhappy woman looking for revenge. Alas, my dear, it has always been so. But I think it might be the reason Edmée has been so upset these past days. Apparently, Arabella went into her room and accused her of being only interested in how rich you were, and your title. So Hannah tells me. And that she boasted how that was the room you and she had once lived in.'

'Oh God,' said Duval.

'Let's just hope Arnold's right,' said Lady Harriet, 'and this ball will put an end to all the nonsense.'

'That is what I am hoping too,' said Duval.

'Personally,' said Lady Harriet, 'I don't think it matters two hoots where Edmée has come from. I think what matters, darling, is she is an extraordinary woman, and you will have a long time together to find out about her past.'

'Yes,' said Duval.

The Ball

That night, everything went perfectly. The guests arrived, awed by the splendour of the setting. The hundreds of lighted candles, hanging in trees and lining paths, made Muchmore House seem magical, a fairy palace. The tall windows on the terrace were open and dance music floated from the ballroom into the evening air.

The curious were satisfied that Lady Harlington was indeed enchanting. That she had ever been married to a drunken parson seemed almost unbelievable.

'Why,' said one lady, 'you would hardly know she was French.'

Duval danced the first and last dance with Edmée. The floor was theirs, and onlookers described her as fairy-like in her movements,

Did she leave his side? No, she was there with him the whole night. Or most of the night? Yes, he was sure – most of it – and if she wasn't by his side, he knew where she was. He danced once with Mrs Dent, and Edmée with Lord Sutton, but each time, they returned to one another. Was it one o'clock or two when the musicians finished?

And was it then the guests climbed gratefully into their carriages, saying it was one of most delightful nights they could remember? The wheels turned on the gravel and the coaches disappeared down the drive, the last of the candles flickered and died, and was it three o'clock when the sky fractured with lightning and the rain came down, making the earth smell sweet and drenching the tables that had yet to be moved inside? What time was it when they went to bed? He couldn't remember. He had held Edmée tight and slipped into a deep, contented sleep.

In the morning, when he woke, she wasn't there. He wasn't concerned; Arabella had talked of going into Woodbridge with Mrs Dent and he assumed Edmée was with them. Hannah said she hadn't been called to dress her mistress, but he knew Edmée often dressed herself. When did doubt begin to eat at him? Was it when the stableboy said he hadn't seen her ladyship that morning? Or before that, when one of the servants reported that a door had been left open last night, though Watkins swore he had closed them all? Duval told himself he was being an alarmist for no reason. And yet, he knew, deep down, that something was wrong.

Arabella and Mrs Dent returned just before the main meal of the day was served, full of news about the success of the ball. Duval saw them from the library and the sun was such that he thought he saw Edmée with them… at first.

He felt as if his breath had been taken from him; his bones were almost too heavy to move. Panic flooded through him. Where *was* she? He ran down to the pond, but even before he reached the island, he knew she wasn't there. His reason was on the edge of despair. A frantic search of the grounds took place, and by ten o'clock that evening, no one was in any doubt that Edmée, Lady Harlington, had vanished without trace.

★

Duval hadn't slept that night. He had been plagued by the thought, *How do I survive losing her?* and knew he wouldn't. He was up at first light, organizing a search party. People came from the village and neighbouring estates to help, arriving out of the morning mist, as eerie as ghosts. He went out to join them and saw his guests climbing hurriedly into their carriages, all somewhat embarrassed to be caught leaving so early. Only Arnold was left, promising to make inquiries in London. Arabella had climbed into her carriage without once looking at him. She had left Mr Gosling to say their goodbyes.

Duval tried to soothe his mind and think rationally about where she might have gone.

That night, he paced back and forth in their chamber, going over it all again and again. Who would have taken her – and why? There was no ransom note. All of it bewildered him. How he regretted ever holding this ridiculous ball. What on earth did the scandal matter compared to losing her? He wondered if Arabella had said anything that had upset Edmée so much that she would have left of her own free will.

Still, he was surprised that Arabella hadn't argued that she should stay. Perhaps her own marriage troubles had taken her back to London with all speed. Otherwise he was in no doubt she would have been there, gloating at his misfortune. That at least, he thought, was one relief in a landscape that now seemed completely foreign to him.

The mystery just became harder to explain. No carriage had been seen along the road at that time of night; no stranger had been reported in the area. It was as if she had vanished into the fairy realm.

He wondered if her disappearance could have had something to do with *ma puce*. Was it possible that this phantom of a man was more involved than he had ever thought?

Jameson knocked on his door at midnight and brought him a whisky. Duval drank it, refusing anything else. Jameson and four footmen waited outside the chamber. Jameson was quite prepared to take the consequences of having drugged his lordship on the grounds that he desperately needed to rest. They waited until they heard him stumble and fall.

'Finally,' said Jameson, as they lifted Duval onto the bed, pleased that their sleeping draft had worked.

Duval woke at midday and could not be angry, for his mind was indeed calmer. But as he scanned the room, he noticed Edmée's journal – or rather, he didn't notice it, since it was not there.

Hannah said she hadn't seen it since the guests had arrived. She thought Edmée might have put it away in case it fell into Arabella's hands.

Where was the box she brought with her? Duval wanted to know. Hannah showed Duval its place in the antechamber, still locked. Hannah and Duval meticulously searched the chamber for the key, and Duval eventually found it tucked behind the painting over the fireplace. He felt somewhat relieved; he didn't like the idea of having to take the box to a blacksmith to have it forced open. But when he opened it, the box was surprisingly sparse. It contained a small, badly painted miniature that must have been of her mother, her journal, and one book, *The Picture of Paris*, but nothing more.

'Do you need me to stay, sir?' asked Hannah.

'No thank you,' said Duval. He was grateful for Hannah, who had answered his questions as thoughtfully as she could.

'Can you remember anything strange about that day, or the day – the week – before the ball?'

'No, my lord. The only outing my lady made was to Woodbridge with Lady Harriet.'

Duval reflected on this for a moment, then went on. 'When you were dressing Lady Harlington for the ball, did she say anything?'

'No, I thought she looked sad.'

It was getting dark when Duval returned to Edmée's room. He'd been out most of the day, once again searching, and now his mind was worn out with thinking what could have happened to her. He sat down at her desk and pulled out her journal, going through all the blank pages meticulously. His heart stopped when he came across a new entry, dated the day of the ball. It was addressed to him.

I know, mon cheri, *that you have read this journal and so you will find my message.*

Please forgive me. There was nothing I could do to save you, other than this. You will not find me. Perhaps it is better this way. I love you more than words can say. I will be with you always; not even death will take me from you.

'No, no, Edmée, what have you done?' He hadn't wept when his dearest friends had been guillotined, but those few lines had opened in him a grief that had too long been buried. 'I can't lose you,' he said to the empty room.

Four days after she disappeared, Mr Beale, the local magistrate, came to see how the search was proceeding. He brought with him a constable, and it was decided the lake and the pond should be dredged, but not so low as to endanger the fish.

Duval was stood watching from his study window, a decanter of whisky before him, when there was a light knock and the door opened to admit Mrs Dent. Only she and Lord Sutton had stayed to help.

'We are leaving, Lord Harlington, but before we go, I must have a word with you. May I be frank?'

'You always are,' said Duval. 'Would you like a drink, Mrs Dent?'

'Yes, my lord, I would,' she said.

He poured two glasses of whisky.

'She's not there.' He pointed to the lake. 'When I was arrested and taken to La Force, the warder said, "I hope you won't be with us long." I wonder, now, if I've ever left that prison, for here I am again, in the dark with a curtain drawn on the future.'

Mrs Dent said, 'I know a gentleman, a little on the rough side of life, but he's one of the best at solving mysteries. His name is Joseph Quinn. I think you'd like him. There are too many pieces here, some in the present, but more, I suspect, are hidden in the past. Not all of them connect. Do you want me to talk to him?'

Duval looked at her. 'Quinn,' he said. 'I know that name.'

'He was the main investigator in the Riley murders. I know he's not busy because he was injured when arresting the murderer.'

'I remember reading about that. Yes, if you think he can help, Mrs Dent, I would be most grateful to have him here as soon as can be arranged.'

'Don't let this make you bitter, Lord Harlington,' said Mrs Dent. 'You're a good man, and I'm as sure as I can be that Lady Harlington loves you. She would be heartbroken to see you in so much misery.'

Duval had listened to Mrs Dent. He hardly heard anyone else, their words floating above him, unconnected.

Just before Lord Sutton's carriage departed, the news came that Lady Harlington's body had not been found, in either the lake or the pond.

'I will send Quinn,' said Mrs Dent from the carriage window.

After they had gone, the house seemed oppressive. Duval saw his father in a judge's wig again, heard him condemning Duval to a life of grief.

You will be just like me, but without the Fortnum condiments. I built this tomb of a house for you to be buried in.

He felt as if the past would smother his life, and in his nightmares, Edmée called to him from far away. He dreaded sleep and his despair grew darker. He would lie awake, waiting for the dawn to bring back a moment of hope.

An Investigator

Joseph Quinn was about Duval's age. He had a handsome face: dark brows, brown eyes, the nose of a fighter, and lips that looked thin but weren't. It was his hair that made him instantly recognizable – thick, unruly and cut short. He sat drinking that morning, in the corner of an inn near the Old Bailey. He liked the place, felt at home there, with the cockroaches of crime. It was a fine morning and he had reached a decision: he was going to retire from serving as an officer of Bow Street.

He preferred to see himself as an investigator. He was good at his profession, one of the best. He had a way of thinking that went counter to the facts. But that morning, over the second pint of ale – or was it the third? – he had made a decision. He would retire to the country, live near the sea. He liked the sea. *Somewhere in Sussex*, he thought. He'd grow vegetables, go fishing. He'd tell everyone he used to be a coal merchant or a waiter. He'd already written his letter of resignation, and he would hand it to the chief that afternoon.

The last case had done it for him, nearly cost him his life. A whole family murdered, and the servant girl. It had even shocked London. And it had taken him too long to capture the murderer, a man who bore a grudge against the husband. Quinn had tracked him down to a house by the Fleet. There had been a fight, and Quinn had been stabbed before he could arrest the villain. He didn't need to be told he was lucky to have survived.

He knew who was behind him before he turned round.

'Mrs Dent, I haven't seen you for a while.'

'How do you do that?' she said. 'Know it's me, I mean?'

'Everyone walks in a different way, and I have long known your tread.'

'I hear you nearly died. I doubt drink will make you any better.'

'What can I do for you, Mrs Dent?'

'I have a favour to ask, Mr Quinn.'

'No. I'm retiring.'

'You are not – you'll just become a maudlin drunk. You don't want to turn out like your father.'

'Now that's below the belt, Mrs Dent, below the belt indeed.'

'How's your mother?'

Quinn smiled. 'She's married again – to a good man this time. He works in Covent Garden – fruit and veg – and she does flowers. Don't see her as much as I should. I remind her too much of the past.'

'That's a load of rubbish and you know it. I never knew a mother prouder of her son. Go and see her, for goodness' sake. She would be horrified to know you were in here, drinking.'

'Have you come to tell me to go and see my mother?' He laughed. 'I'm a little old for that. What are you drinking, Mrs Dent?'

'I'll take a port,' she said and sat down. 'I have a friend.'

'You have lots of friends. You are a wicked woman, with a great heart.'

'And you were, and still are, a scallywag. But at least, in

the Runners, you're on the right side of the law.' She lowered her voice. 'I want to talk to you about Duval Harlington and the disappearance of Lady Harlington. I'm sure you've read about it.'

Quinn would like to have said he never read the papers and he was ignorant of the case, but he knew exactly what Mrs Dent was talking about. Scandal seemed to be following Lord Harlington. As if the wife sale wasn't bad enough, now his new bride had vanished into thin air.

The Lord Lieutenant and the Justice of the Peace in Suffolk had both been made aware of the mystery, and a likeness of Lady Harlington, drawn from people's memories, had been circulated. It was displayed in local shops, on trees, in churches and in the town hall. The lack of witnesses made an investigation impossible. None of the local fishermen or sailors had seen a single boat or ship they couldn't account for. The strangeness of the case meant it had been picked up by many regional papers until it appeared in *The Times* and in the *Comet*, rekindling the story of how Lord Harlington had met his wife, setting fire to the curiosity of a nation that had had enough of wars. Here was a news story on a tantalizingly human scale. The leading article that day asked, *Where is the Ten-Guinea Bride?*

'Lord Harlington is somewhat cursed,' said Quinn.

'Edmée Harlington has been missing for over five days,' said Mrs Dent. 'Everything's been done that can be done, and still, no one has any idea what happened to her.' She took a sip of her port and winced. 'Now the scandal rags are suggesting Lord Harlington himself had something to do with her disappearance, which is ludicrous, considering the terms of his father's will.'

'Interesting. It pulls on the old heartstrings. But… I'm retiring,' said Quinn. 'I'm buying myself a place in the country, and—'

'It's a private investigation and you'll be paid well.'

'For a start, there's nothing private about this case,' Quinn said. 'It will be taken up by a London magistrate, and as it involves a French citizen, the Alien Office will also get involved.'

'That's why I'm asking you to help,' said Mrs Dent firmly.

'It strikes me,' said Quinn, 'that nothing is what it seems – that much I'd put a king's guinea on.'

'Just as I thought,' said Mrs Dent.

Quinn knew he was beaten. He sighed. 'What do you know?'

She told him in detail about the days before Edmée's disappearance. 'Now I have your full attention, don't I?' she said.

'You do, Mrs Dent, indeed you do.'

'The Marquis Reynaud de Soule came down the previous day, but without any explanation, he left before the ball.'

Quinn had taken out his red notebook and was writing everything down.

'Here,' she said, and handed him a list of the guests from London.

'Thank you, Mrs Dent,' said Quinn, glancing at it quickly. 'And what about Lady Harlington – what was she like?' He listened intently to Mrs Dent's description.

As she finished talking, Mrs Dent produced another piece of paper. 'And there's this.'

'What is it?' asked Quinn.

'It's a list of things Lady Harlington had in her box when she arrived at Muchmore House. Before she married Lord Harlington, she was the widow of Samuel Hyde, the parson of Witchling.'

'Hyde,' said Quinn. 'I've heard that name.' He looked at the piece of paper. A notebook, a miniature and one bound book. Did Lord Harlington show you these?'

'Don't be daft. I talked to Lady Harlington's maid.'

'Was there anything written in the notebook that might help?'

'The maid said her mistress never took it out, as far as she was aware. But Lady Harlington did ask for a journal to write in. She sent away to a stationer in Woodbridge. She wrote a lot in that journal, apparently. There was another book that was found in the box. She can't read, so I asked Jameson, Lord Harlington's valet, and he told me the title of the book – *The Picture of Paris* by Mercier. The bookbinder was a Bernard Simoneau – rue Jacob, Paris.'

'You're good, Mrs Dent, very good. Did it mention the name of the shop?'

'No, only the address.' Mrs Dent stood up, her port barely touched. 'My carriage is at your service. And speed, I would say, is of the essence.'

'And how will you get home?'

'Lord Sutton is waiting for me.'

'I'd still like to say no,' said Quinn.

'But you won't,' said Mrs Dent.

He escorted Mrs Dent to Lord Sutton's carriage; her own carriage was waiting for him round the corner.

'I'll be leaving for Muchmore House tomorrow, in the morning,' he said to the coachman. 'Pick me up from Theobald's Road at eight.'

Quinn walked back towards Bow Street and remembered how he had first met Mrs Dent.

He had been ten years old when he returned to that hovel they called home one afternoon and found his ma lying on the floor, her arm all wrong.

'Ma?' he'd said.

'It's alright, love.'

He knew it wasn't, though. His pa would be back, and this time he would kill them both.

'We've got to get out,' he said.

'I can't move.' She was weeping.

He'd told her he'd be back.

'Run,' she said. 'Run, Joseph, save yourself.'

He ran that morning with hollow legs; they hadn't eaten for three days. A neighbour told him where he might find help.

'I read about her in the paper, a Mrs Dent.'

When he arrived at the address in Berkeley Square, he knew it was a mistake. The neighbour must have thought it a joke. But then a footman came to the door, and Quinn said, 'I'm looking for Mrs Dent.'

It had seemed hopeless, when he saw her. He couldn't imagine how this small woman, all done up in her finery, could help them. Then she'd spoken with a voice he knew, an accent he'd grown up with.

'Go on, spit it out,' she said, and he had.

It was the first time he'd been in a carriage, but all he could think was that Pa would be home by now and he would have murdered Ma for having nothing for his supper.

The mud was always bad round where they lived, and the wooden boards slippery. Mrs Dent didn't seem to care, though. Quinn had taken her to where Ma lay unconscious, and Mrs Dent set to work. She made a splint for Ma's arm from the leg of a broken chair and sent Quinn to fetch one of the coachmen.

Mrs Dent had set off first, with Quinn, and behind them the coachman was carrying Ma. Then he saw Pa, standing at the end of the wooden boards. He was drunk. *Now we are all dead*, Quinn thought.

'What the devil are you doing?' Pa shouted.

'I'm taking your wife and son to a place they'll be safe,' said Mrs Dent, without one ounce of fear.

'No, you aren't. She's my wife and I can do what I bloody well—'

Before he'd finished, Quinn had charged at him, head down like a bull, sending Pa slip-sliding down into the mud. He tried to grab Quinn's leg and received such a blow from Mrs Dent that he fell backwards into the mud again. 'You're a witch,' Quinn's pa yelled.

'And you,' said Mrs Dent, 'are worth less than the mud you're lying in.'

He was still tapping the resignation letter in his pocket when he was called into the chief's office. This was the most interesting case to have come his way for a long while. It was a mystery worth solving.

The Alien Office had been attached to Bow Street for three years – the two couldn't be separated. The city was crawling with French spies, and the chief didn't like spies. French, English, they were much of a muchness to him. He thought of them as shadowy creatures, needing the padding of other people's secrets to make them believable.

'Do you know anything about this case, sir?' Quinn asked.

'There's not much to go on,' said the chief.

'Does the name Hyde, a parson, ring any bells?'

He thought for a moment. 'Now you mention it...' He called into an outer office.

Quinn waited while the chief was handed a piece of paper

'Yes, here it is. Some months ago there was a gentleman by the name of...' He paused, screwed his face up and said, 'Wish I could read my writing... Mr Carson, yes, that's it, a Mr Carson. He wanted inquiries made into the death of a parson named Hyde. It seemed a waste of time, nothing suspicious had been reported, as I told him. But he was a pompous prick, so to get rid of him, I gave him Walter Veldt's name.'

'Veldt, who now runs a pub in Sailor Town?' said Quinn.

'The same. He does a bit of private work. Wasn't a bad investigator, but not the brightest either. He's retired now. But what's this to do with Lady Harlington's disappearance?'

'It might be nothing,' said Quinn, 'but Lady Harlington was Samuel Hyde's widow.'

It was twilight by the time Quinn reached the water steps at Lincoln's Inn, where he took a ferry downriver to Canary Wharf. Even at this time, the river was so busy with shipping that Quinn could hardly see the water.

Quinn tracked Veldt down to his pub, The Cocked Hat, located next to a ship-chandler in one of the many dark alleyways that made up Sailor Town. Veldt's weakness, in Quinn's view, had been his liking for the criminal class and a slight addiction to the card tables. But, as Veldt said himself, he could talk the ears off a rabbit if required.

'Talk,' Veldt had once told Quinn, 'even if half-garbled, comforts fools.'

The pub was full, and Veldt sat where he aways did, up on a small dais, with a pewter tankard before him, watching his customers.

'So, you're still alive,' Veldt said.

'I am,' said Quinn.

'What can I do for you?'

Quinn noted that Veldt was better dressed than the last time he'd seen him. He was wearing the costume of a sea captain.

'You have a ship?' asked Quinn.

'No,' said Veldt. 'But a uniform inspires more respect than your ordinaries.'

'Can I join you?' said Quinn.

Veldt nodded to a seat and a beer was put before Quinn.

'So, what brings you here?' asked Veldt.

'I heard you investigated the death of a parson, a Mr Samuel Hyde.'

'Oh, that was some time ago,' said Veldt. 'The parson died of a sudden heart attack. My client, Mr Carson, wanted cause of death pinned on the parson's widow, who'd remarried and become Lady Harlington. He had some interest in the matter, due to the terms of a will.'

'Which were...?'

'As I said, it was a long time ago. I don't remember.'

'Was there anything suspicious?'

'The parson didn't have many friends. There was one slow-headed woman – a Miss Weekly... no, *Weeks*. Her house is opposite the parsonage, and she saw the parson at his desk the morning he died. Asleep, she said, but that wasn't unusual. She didn't see anything more, and when she looked again, the shutters on the parson's window were closed.'

'Can I see your report?'

'You can, but I wouldn't waste your time if I were you.'

'You've heard Lady Harlington's missing?'

'Vanished,' said Veldt, 'in a puff of smoke. You thinking of taking up the case? Tell you who I suspect? That husband of hers, Lord Harlington.'

Quinn didn't answer, but drank his beer.

Quinn wondered if it was too late to call on Fleur. She lived with her mother in three rooms in a noisy house off Bloomsbury

Square. It was full of émigrés whose money hadn't stretched as far as they'd hoped. Fleur and her mother had escaped the September Massacres of 1792. Like so many émigrés, they were both dressmakers, but unlike many, they were doing well for themselves.

Quinn went up the stone stairs to the top floor and knocked lightly on the door. Fleur opened it and smiled up at him.

'*Maman*,' she called, 'it's Monsieur Quinn.'

Madame Clément, a small, neat woman, came to greet him.

'I'm sorry to call this late,' he said.

'Come in,' said Fleur. 'You are always welcome.'

He marvelled at the way they kept the rooms, the tidiness of everything. Fleur put a bottle of wine on the table, with bread and cheese.

'There's no need to go to any trouble,' he said.

'It's no trouble,' said Fleur. Her fingertip touched his hand and sent a shock of desire through him.

'We have news,' said Madame Clément. 'We have found a new shop to rent, so we can take on more customers.' She raised her glass. 'So, we must drink to that.'

They talked for some time, before Quinn said, 'Was it the rue Jacob, where you lived in Paris?'

'No. But it wasn't far from there,' said Madame Clément. 'All the streets have been renamed, though. It's hard to remember what it is called now. Definitely no saint or king.'

'Do you recall a bookbinder?'

'You mean Bernard Simoneau? Yes, he had his workshop there. He was famous for his work before the Revolution.' Madame Clément stood. 'It is hard to find out if people are alive or dead. *La Terreur* is over; I hear many papers have been burned to hide the true horror of what the Revolutionary Tribunal did. So, I'm afraid I don't know what happened to him or his child. Anyway, if you will excuse me, Monsieur Quinn, I am going to bed. It is good to see you are so well.'

When the door was closed, Quinn found Fleur's fingers wrapped around his. Silently, she kissed him.

'I have to go away, just for a few days,' said Quinn. 'When I return, may I take you out?'

She kissed him again. 'I would like that.'

'You could bring your mother.'

Fleur said, 'Do you want me to?'

'No,' he said.

'I remember the bookbinder's daughter,' Fleur said. 'She was such a scruffy little thing, with short hair like a boy. *Maman* didn't like me to talk to her.'

'Come here,' Quinn said, and kissing her, he nearly forgot everything in that moment. 'You do this to me every time,' he said.

'Do what?'

'Make me long for you.' He pulled her back into his arms. 'I'll write to you while I am away.'

Ralph's Handkerchief

Duval didn't want to leave Muchmore; he had a prayer at the heart of him that she might just come back. He knew he was sinking into a dark place, and he recognized it for what it was. When he was released from prison, he had told himself he would not look at this part of himself again, but the loss of her was a turnkey, and now he could almost smell the walls of his prison in the darkness. That place the devil could comfortably have called his hotel, bursting with souls waiting to be sacrificed on the red altar.

Here he found himself every night, in his mind, incapable of escaping. Whisky helped, up to a point, before it tipped him too far into the nightmare, until he could no longer count how many turnkeys, how many gates opened and closed. The only way to free himself from the nightmare was to say his mantra over and over again: 'Dear Lord, don't let her be harmed. Please may she be alive. Return her to me safe. Return her to me unbroken, please, dear Lord, bring her home. Please may Quinn be on his way.'

*

The only people Duval hadn't spoken to were the Carsons. Although they hadn't attended the ball, they had an undeniable interest in Lady Harlington's disappearance.

When Mr Ralph Carson had taken on Monkton Manor, Duval had had a terse exchange with him, telling him firmly that he would not pay for the rental. It was a large house which required many servants. He had strongly advised his cousin against renting it unless he could afford it.

That morning, Duval took his horse on the short journey to Monkton, arriving just after eleven o'clock. The front door was opened by a grumpy-looking servant, who slunk away. Duval was left in the hall – a gloomy affair, with a domineering Tudor staircase. The place was cold and the combined effect was to sink his spirits to his boots. He was contemplating leaving when he heard, from upstairs, a conversation between Ralph Carson and his sister. Sarah Carson was being severely reprimanded for taking Ralph's handkerchiefs.

It was Sarah Carson who came downstairs first, clutching a handkerchief and looking as if she half expected Ralph to be on her heels. Duval had an opportunity to study her. Without the excessive powder and paint, she wasn't as plain as he had first thought. Her hair, though mousey, had a natural curl. She had a snub nose and smallish grey eyes, and gave the impression that not long ago she might even have been considered a beauty.

Sarah was startled and a little alarmed to see Duval, saying, 'Oh, I am so sorry… I wasn't told you were here.'

'Where are all of your servants?'

She let out a nervous laugh. 'They refuse to work until Ralph pays them. Sorry…'

'No, need to apologize,' said Duval. 'I would like to speak to you.'

'Sarah,' shouted her brother, 'bring that handkerchief back now!'

'Lord Harlington is here,' she said, standing straight and shaking.

'You think I would fall for that?' Ralph, not yet dressed, ran down the stairs, then stopped. At the sight of Duval, he puffed himself up, hoping to make a more aristocratic impression, and, regaining a calmer posture, he bowed, his expression changing to one of forced serenity.

Until now, Duval had not altogether taken these two seriously, but this small, strange interaction changed his mind. There was something cruel in Ralph's face, and it was plain his sister was truly frightened of him. He remembered the conversation about Sarah Carson with Minnie in Soho.

'To what do we owe the pleasure, Lord Harlington?' asked Ralph Carson now.

'I want to ask Miss Carson why she wrote to Lady Harlington the day before the ball.'

Sarah let out a squeak. 'I didn't… It wasn't… Why would I?' Then looking at her brother, she said, 'I just…'

'Just what, Miss Carson?' said Duval.

She had turned white.

'Oh, the note,' said Ralph Carson. 'We talked about this, didn't we, Sarah?'

'Yes, Ralph,' she said.

'My sister wanted to attend your ball, and she unwisely wrote to Lady Harlington, saying she would accept. I strongly rebuked her. We didn't attend the ball because I felt it was not the correct thing to do.'

'May I ask what you were doing on the night of the ball?' said Duval.

'We were here, at home,' said Ralph Carson. 'Though, of course, we have heard about the dreadful business of Lady Harlington's disappearance. I suppose there is still no news?'

His tone irritated Duval. It was unbearably cheerful.

'May I ask if anyone dined with you that night?'

Sarah said, 'Oh, yes, it was—' She was silenced by a gesture from her brother.

'An acquaintance, new to the parish,' he said. 'But I can't see it's any business of yours, Lord Harlington. We were not guests at your ball, so our movements are irrelevant, and really, I have nothing more to say on the matter. Sarah, go up to your chamber now.'

'Mr Carson,' Duval said firmly, 'my wife is missing, and I am trying to gather all the information I can. You have a vested interest in her vanishing, as I am sure you are highly aware, due to the terms of my father's will, which stipulate that, if she was to die, you would inherit.'

'Are you suggesting,' said Ralph Carson, squaring his shoulders, 'that my sister or I have anything to do with this sorry, sordid affair of yours? When you pick up a strange woman at a wife sale, you cannot be surprised by the consequences. It is obvious to me that Lady Harlington ran away, that she wanted nothing more to do with you. There is no mystery at all. I wish you a good day, Lord Harlington.'

Duval had an urge to throttle the smug boiled capon, but instead, he left that house, mounted his horse and rode as if a tempest were bearing down on him.

Who was it who had dined with them? Sarah Carson had been on the verge of telling him before her brother interrupted her.

He wondered why Ralph Carson's fury had been so quick to ignite. There was something about the way he had spoken that struck Duval as unnecessarily defensive. But logic argued there was no way a foolish gentleman, obsessed with handkerchiefs, could possibly be embroiled in the abduction of his wife.

A Jockey Hat

Early the next morning, Quinn sat in the barber's chair, being shaved.

From the barber's, he had the carriage take him to a respectable tailor he knew who owed him a favour. He came away with riding boots; a brown wool double-breasted coat, with a high turned-down collar and wide lapels; a double-breasted white waistcoat; long, close-fitting buckskin breeches; white stockings; two white linen shirts with a matching cravat; and a greatcoat with a gold-edged collar. At the last minute, he asked to borrow an outfit for the evening. The boots didn't fit too well, but at least he looked presentable – a man to be reckoned with.

'A hat, sir,' called the tailor, coming out of his shop, as the bandboxes containing the garments were loaded onto the carriage.

Quinn looked at the tall hat. 'What is it?'

'A jockey hat,' said the tailor. 'It's all the rage in France. Wear it at an angle.'

Quinn settled back in the comfort of Mrs Dent's carriage.

As it made its way out of the rain-swept city, he read Veldt's report.

It was exactly what he would have expected from an old Runner, desperate to impress his client but knowing there was not enough evidence to take the case further. Yet, Veldt's conclusion baffled him. Surely Veldt would have at least hinted at Lady Edmée's guilt to appease the Carsons? But he hadn't. Instead, he had written – and it was underlined – that there was no evidence of foul play. Case closed.

Quinn was not sure why Veldt had come to this conclusion. If he had to guess, it was because Veldt had realized there was something altogether bigger to be gained here. But what?

A village is like a beehive, Quinn would say. Find the queen bee and the rest is relatively easy. The queen bee in Witchling, he quickly discovered on his arrival there, was Mrs Beale.

The carriage he had been kindly loaned from Mrs Dent was impressive and not easily dismissed, even if the occupant spoke with a cockney accent. And the way Quinn was dressed made him look as if he were a countryman.

On learning that Quinn was investigating the disappearance of Lady Harlington, Mrs Beale, who introduced herself as the magistrate's wife, offered him refreshments.

'The parsonage is not far from here,' said Mrs Beale. 'That's where the late dear Mr Hyde lived with his then-wife – who, a matter of days after his death, became Lady Harlington.'

'Miss Weeks lives next to the parsonage,' said Quinn. 'Is that correct?'

'Yes, she's a spinster, and is responsible for spreading some very unpleasant remarks about the late Mr Hyde. Her dog died, and she swore that Mr Hyde had poisoned it. Of course he did nothing of the sort, though her dog could have driven anyone to distraction… As I said, a terribly nosy and boorish woman. But it being a small community, it's hard to exclude her from social events without appearing rude.'

This information was offered without a blush. Then, seeming to meet a crossroads in her thoughts, Mrs Beale changed direction.

'The Carsons have been *so* shabbily treated by Lord Harlington. They didn't go to the ball – they felt they had been slighted. As you know, it was after the ball that Lord Harlington's wife went missing. Shocking, utterly shocking, but I always thought she was untrustworthy. It mattered little if she was married to a parson or an earl.'

Quinn, sitting on a delicate chair, felt decidedly uncomfortable.

'Would you care for another slice of cake, Mr Quinn?'

Quinn disentangled himself from cutlery and crockery and said, 'You must have known Lady Harlington well, to come to that conclusion.'

'Not really. I didn't like her. And Mr Hyde died in mysterious circumstances that—'

Quinn interrupted her. 'And the Carsons, madam – are they staying in Witchling?'

'No,' said Mrs Beale, suddenly unsure if she should have trusted this cockney. 'I think, Mr Quinn—'

Quinn bowed and left before he was forced to hear any more.

The parsonage was a double-fronted house, with a graveyard on one side and the village on the other, so it gave the impression of being sly: one eye spying on its parishioners, the other eye noting their graves. Quinn couldn't tell if this was the fault of the builder, or if it had more to do with the influence of its previous resident.

It was raining when Quinn, wearing the jockey hat, knocked on Miss Weeks's door. Her maid, a pretty young woman, regarded him dubiously and told him to wait. As soon as Miss Weeks came to the door, he introduced himself and offered his condolences about her dog. Miss Weeks invited him in.

'He was a little terrier called Alfred,' she said, once they were seated in front of the meagre fire in her cramped drawing room and she had asked her maid to bring sherry.

'I had a little terrier myself, when I was a boy,' said Quinn, remembering the mongrel cur his father had drowned. 'I was wondering, Miss Weeks, if you would tell me how Alfred died.'

The oddness of the request took Miss Weeks by surprise, just as he thought it would. Loneliness was something he understood well; it had been his constant companion throughout childhood. Here, with all her fuss and manners, was an isolated lady not as old as he thought she would be, who had no social standing in the village and was desperate for company.

'Alfred was my father's name,' she said.

If Quinn had been the type of investigator who looked into the workings of the mind, he was certain he could have made something of a little terrier being named after the owner's father.

'He died suddenly, and he wasn't old,' she added.

'Your father?' asked Quinn.

'My dog. There had been nothing wrong with him.' She lowered her voice. 'He was poisoned.'

'And when was that?' he asked.

'A week before the parson died.'

Quinn sipped his sherry. Overwhelmed by her mistress's call for the sherry decanter and two glasses, the maid had failed to draw the curtains, and he saw the drawing-room window looked directly into the parsonage.

'Is that where Mr Hyde wrote his sermons, Miss Weeks?' asked Quinn.

'It was Mr Hyde's study. And it was there I saw him slumped over his desk. He died that same day.'

Quinn, standing up, went to look out of the window. Miss Weeks would have had to press her face against the glass to see into the room.

'Was it raining that day?' he asked.

'I don't rightly remember,' she said. 'I do remember I had cooked some of my little muffins; I took them over for Mr Hyde. He was rather partial to a muffin. I enjoyed making them and I always had too many left over,' she said. 'Nellie was pleased to have them. She didn't like cooking. Mr Hyde was a greedy man.'

'Was there a candle alight in that room opposite?'

'Oh yes, there always was. It's the way the parsonage was built – at such an angle it hardly got any direct light, even in the sunshine.'

'Do you know who was in the parsonage the day Mr Hyde died?'

'Nellie Moore, the housekeeper. And that poor wife of his. I once saw from here what he did to her – I had to close my shutters.' She paused and said in a low voice, as if they might be overheard, 'Samuel Hyde was not a nice man. He killed Alfred, I am sure of it.'

'Did you see Mrs Hyde in the study with Mr Hyde the morning he died?'

Miss Weeks looked worried. She brought out a handkerchief and twisted it through her fingers. 'No, no, I only saw her that one time, when I...'

Quinn, seeing how distressed the question made her, changed the subject. 'It looks as if no one lives in the parsonage now,' he said.

'No, it's been empty these past months. The new parson,

a younger gentleman with a private income, has taken Yew Tree House – near the Beales.'

'Did you ever talk to Mr Hyde's housekeeper?'

'Only occasionally, when the parson was away. Nellie was a coarse woman. But my maid sometimes passed the time of day with her.'

'Where is the housekeeper now?' Quinn asked.

'She was taken ill, and I believe she is in the care of her sister in Woodbridge, but I cannot say for sure.' She paused, and then said, 'There was another gentleman asking about Mrs Hyde, you know.'

'Who was that, Miss Weeks?' asked Quinn.

'A Mr Veldt.'

Quinn sat with this information for a moment, then, with a bow and many condolences, said thank you and goodbye.

He returned to Mrs Dent's carriage, waiting just round the corner. It was less than ten minutes before, predictably, Miss Weeks came out of her door, adjusting her bonnet and shawl, and set off to inform her neighbour what had happened that afternoon.

When she was out of sight, Quinn walked back to the parsonage, found the key to the building under a stone, and went inside. Ever since childhood, Quinn had been able to read the inside of a house. This ability came from studying the poky rooms he had grown up in. The walls held on to the misery of all they had witnessed, all they had heard.

Inside the parsonage, the hall was narrow and damp. He went first into the study and nearly cracked his head on a low beam. It was an odd-shaped room, with a desk that looked as if it had been thoroughly rifled. No doubt Veldt had found a window to climb through – there were muddy footprints to prove it. Quinn went into the kitchen, hearing the mice scurry away.

'You must have been desperate, Mademoiselle Edmée,' he said aloud, 'to have married Mr Samuel Hyde, and have come to this hovel of a home.'

Upstairs, there were three bedchambers. The smallest, he sensed, was Edmée Hyde's. The shutters in that room were closed, and when he tried to open them, he found they had been nailed in place.

Quinn found a candle and a tinderbox in the kitchen and, having persuaded the candle to light, went back upstairs to the room. He could now see there were cords tied to either side of the iron bedstead and scratch marks on the wall. Under the bed, there were traces in the dust where the bed had been moved. One floorboard came up easily. He took off his coat and jacket, rolled up the sleeve of his white linen shirt, slid his arm in and found a small knife. Curious. He left it, replaced the floorboard, and went downstairs.

As he returned the key to its place under the stone, he thought he'd never been so glad to close the door of a house behind him. But perhaps that wasn't true. He remembered how it had felt the last time he had seen his pa.

'A new beginning,' Mrs Dent had said.

That's why I'm good at my job, he thought. *I know all about torture like this.*

Everything Is Upended

Quinn stopped at the Tollgate Hotel in Thetford. Not having eaten for a while, he ordered the dish of the day and sat down to write to Fleur. He had forgotten to ask her the most important question, one he now needed an answer to rather urgently. He carefully wrapped it round with sentiments of love, none of which were artificial. But his main question was simple. Could she remember the name of the bookbinder's daughter? He paid a high price for the fastest messenger in Thetford to deliver it and asked for a reply to be sent to him at Muchmore.

The sky had cleared, and it was no longer raining as Quinn continued his journey to the Muchmore Estate. He asked the coachman to stop when they came to the drive and he climbed out, so he could look down onto the house. It was one of the finest he had seen. In front was a lake that reflected the façade, the gardens were beautifully laid out and woodland framed the property. It looked magnificent in a sudden burst of golden sunshine.

Not for the first time that day, Quinn could see the merit in arriving in Mrs Dent's carriage. As they rolled up the gravel drive, two footmen and a butler immediately appeared.

'I am Joseph Quinn,' he said to the butler. 'I've been sent by Mrs Dent to investigate the disappearance of Lady Harlington.' The butler looked visibly relieved. 'Is Lord Harlington at home?'

'No, sir, he is not. Lady Harriet is, however.'

'May I see her?' asked Quinn.

He waited in the hall, and finally, he was shown into a long drawing room, blessed with a roaring fire – even at this time of year, such a large room held on to a wintry chill. Sitting in a wing-backed chair was a woman of about fifty. Quinn could see she had once been a beauty.

'Mr Joseph Quinn, your ladyship,' said the butler. 'He has been sent here by Mrs Dent.'

Lady Harriet stood up, a tall lady of noble bearing.

Quinn gave his most courteous bow.

'Everything is upended,' said Lady Harriet. Seeing that Quinn was still standing, she said, 'Oh, sit down, Mr Quinn, please. You look like an ornament that I haven't decided what to do with.'

Quinn lowered himself into an elegant chair.

'Do you know where Lord Harlington is?' he asked.

'He went out early this morning and hasn't yet returned. Oh dear, what a time for you to arrive. The papers are reporting that Lord Harlington might have had something to do with… It's a terrible accusation… as if he hasn't suffered enough. To be honest with you, I fear he might have, on an impulse, left for France to look for Edmée.'

'Has he taken a horse?' asked Quinn.

'No, I don't believe he has. That would have caused the alarm to be raised. But if he has gone to Paris, I feel sure he will be arrested and executed.'

'I would like to talk to his valet,' said Quinn.

'Of course.' She rang a bell.

A servant came in with two decanters.

'Oh,' said Lady Harriet. 'Is it that time of day already?' She sighed and asked the servant to send Jameson down.

She poured two glasses of sherry and Quinn saw her hands shake as she gave him a glass.

'I am all nerves,' she said. 'This affair has been most upsetting.'

'Can you tell me about Lady Harlington?'

'I was appalled when Duval told me he had bought his wife in a sale, but what choice did he have, given my brother's foolish will? He left for London straight after the wedding. But Edmée was a charming young lady, and once the bruises had faded from her face and her hair had been attended to, she looked quite lovely.'

'Bruises?' said Quinn.

'Yes, the parson—' Lady Harriet stopped.

Quinn waited.

'How much do you know?' she asked.

'Nothing, your ladyship,' said Quinn.

'What I am going to say is not to be repeated, though heaven knows, enough has been made of the scandal already. Edmée discovered she was with child, not by Lord Harlington but by the late Mr Hyde. It took time before she told me of the shocking circumstance of her marriage to him and how he... how he drugged her and... do I have to say more?'

'No, your ladyship,' said Quinn. 'When was this?'

'She had been here about two months when I found out. I sensed it before, though I never asked her directly. Then she collapsed and lost the infant. Lord Harlington – he's a qualified physician – nursed her back to health, then fell in love with her. So much so I regretted I had not—' She stopped. 'But this is not about me.'

'Before Lord Harlington returned, did her ladyship meet anyone? Go anywhere alone?'

'No. No, never.'

The sherry was good. When Quinn put down his empty glass, it was immediately refilled.

'Not even to a dressmaker? A shoemaker?' he asked.

'We went together to see Mrs Appleby, the dressmaker in Woodbridge. We did that often. We last went... it was the day before the ball, I think – yes, that's right, Lady Harlington hadn't breakfasted.'

'What's important about her not having had breakfast?' asked Quinn.

'It was only that she fainted.'

'Where was this?

'As we were leaving the dressmaker's. Come to think of it, I really should have mentioned this sooner.'

Quinn knew the softest steps were needed and silence must be the guide. He said nothing.

'I went out to see about the phaeton; it was new, and I was anxious not to leave it too long in the street. I went back inside the dressmaker's house to find that Edmée had swooned in the passage. She said it was because she hadn't eaten breakfast, but it happened just after she had received a note from the awful Carsons.'

'What happened to the note?'

'She tore it up and threw it away, I imagine.'

'Did Lady Harlington say what the note was about?'

'Just that it was Miss Carson asking if it was too late to accept the invitation to the ball... Mr Quinn, your questions are too many. They take me at a gallop over umpteen steeples.'

'Forgive me, Lady Harriet. It's just—'

'That you are doing your job.'

'Yes.'

They sat in silence until Lady Harriet said, 'The Marquis de Soule left the morning of the ball. It was so impolite of him. He reminded me of my late brother. If you're going to ask me why he left, I honestly have no idea. The more I live, the stranger I think people are.'

Quinn noted all this in his red book. 'Who invited him?'

'Sir Arnold Prescott, I believe, was responsible for the invitations,' said Lady Harriet.

Quinn took another sip of sherry.

'Among the guests were Mr Gosling, the marquis's banker, and his wife, Mrs Arabella Gosling. She had been in a very bad mood,' said Lady Harriet, 'and she had an argument with her husband. What it was about, I have no idea. I think she was jealous of Edmée.'

'Why was that?' asked Quinn.

'Mrs Gosling had long ago been the mistress of my nephew. She likes to think that will be able to save Lord Harlington from a scandal.'

'I see. And may I ask what Lady Harlington is like?'

'She has a gentle nature, is intelligent, well-read, very perceptive; I think still waters run deep in her. It was due to Edmée that I changed my style of dress. She is very *à la mode*, you know. She was, I suspect, the daughter of a count, though she never said that.'

Lady Harriet was interrupted by a discreet knock on the door.

'Good,' she said, as a serving man entered. 'This is Jameson, Lord Harlington's valet. Jameson, this is Mr Quinn. He is here to find out what happened to Lady Harlington.'

Quinn rose to his feet. 'Do you think, Mr Jameson, that your master would have left for France without your knowledge?' he asked.

'No, sir,' replied Jameson. 'I know all that he does. He has been heartsick since her ladyship went missing, which is only to be expected.'

'Would you call your master a defeatist?'

'No, most definitely not. He is a pragmatist.'

'Thank you, Mr Jameson,' said Quinn. 'There is nothing else for the time being.'

When Jameson had gone, Quinn said, 'I believe there's no need to worry, Lady Harriet. Lord Harlington will be back.' Quinn didn't think for a minute Lord Harlington had gone to France – there was no logical reason to do so. He could, however, understand his lordship wanting time alone. That, to Quinn's way of thinking, made much more sense.

The day was rapidly turning to twilight and the minutes ticked past as they waited. 'Would it be possible to talk to Lady Harlington's maid?' asked Quinn.

'Yes, of course,' said Lady Harriet. 'I should have thought of that,' and she rang the bell again and called for Hannah.

A pretty, alert young woman entered the chamber and bobbed a curtsey.

'This,' said Lady Harriet to Hannah, 'is Mr Quinn. He is here to investigate Lady Harlington's disappearance.'

'Can you tell me anything about the night of the ball?' asked Quinn.

Hannah's cheeks coloured a flaming red. 'There are two things I didn't tell Lord Harlington. I thought they would distress him further. My mistress made me promise not to say a word to him, but I have been brooding on it, and now I think they might be important.'

'Both happened on the day of the ball?' asked Quinn.

'Yes. Firstly, Mrs Arabella Gosling came to see her ladyship while she was dressing—'

'The guest I told you about earlier,' interrupted Lady Harriet. 'Married to Philip Gosling, the banker.'

'Thank you,' said Quinn. 'Go on, Hannah.'

'Mrs Gosling sent me off to fetch hot chocolate, so I didn't hear all that was said, but as I returned, Mrs Gosling left in a temper, and my mistress seemed distressed. When I was getting her ready for the ball, she was still upset. She said, "None of it matters, for he will never forgive me."'

'Do you know what she was referring to?' asked Quinn.

'No, sir, I don't.'

'And the second thing?' said Quinn.

'Happened earlier that morning, before Mrs Gosling paid her visit. My mistress went out to the garden. I followed in case she needed my help. I stopped when I saw her at open French windows in the wing of the house called the Sanctuary. I couldn't see who she was talking to, and I didn't understand what she was saying because it was in French, but heated words were being exchanged. I thought it might be with one of the marquis's men...'

'Did Lady Harlington leave in her ball gown?'

'No – she was wearing a simple cotton gown.'

'I would like to see the ball gown, if that is possible.'

'I can show you, sir, do you want me to get it? It is a fine gown.'

'Don't worry about that just yet. Can you tell me about the dressmaker, and how she met Lady Harlington?'

'I told my lady the story of the dressmaker, a French émigré by the name of Mrs Appleby. She was rescued by a local sailor from a small boat while trying to cross the Channel. She married the sailor,' said Hannah. 'I had ordered an evening gown from her for Lady Harlington. After I told Lady Harlington the story, she insisted on some paper and wrote to Mrs Appleby.'

'Lady Harlington wrote to her? Do you know what she wrote?'

'No.'

Quinn wondered whether this was not an odd way to get in touch. Why didn't she just ask her to come to Muchmore?

'You said Mrs Appleby was French. Do you know what her name was originally?'

Lady Harriet interjected, 'We didn't until the Marquis de Soule surprised us all by knowing her. She was called Madame Dupont, apparently, and made gowns for the late queen of France. I, too, am rather shocked to hear that Edmée wrote to the dressmaker. They gave no indication of knowing one another when we visited.'

'Hannah, did you get the sense that Madame Dupont knew your mistress?'

'I didn't think about it. She was a nice woman. I was pleased to see my mistress speak with someone in her native language.' Hannah started to weep. 'My mistress is deeply loved. She will be found, won't she?'

The clock in the hall struck half past seven as Hannah was leaving.

'Oh dear,' said Lady Harriet. 'This is most distressing. You don't think the dressmaker had anything to do with this?'

'At the moment, your ladyship, I'm only asking questions. I'm looking for answers to a riddle.'

Lady Harriet, registering the clock strike in the hall, said, 'I hadn't realized the time. We usually dine at four. But still, he's not back.'

'He will be,' said Quinn. As he spoke, he heard the footsteps of the butler outside, followed by an assured step he didn't recognize. The door opened and Duval Harlington came in.

Quinn's first impression was that he had the intelligent face of a Frenchman; Lord Harlington was far better looking than many gentlemen of his class. It was his eyes that were his most striking feature: they shone. But at the same time, Quinn could see in them a haunted look, one he had seen in other men who had been imprisoned during the Terror. Lord Harlington's boots and long frock coat were covered in mud, his dark hair windswept.

'There you are,' said Lady Harriet. 'Where have you been?'

'Walking.'

Duval turned to Quinn, who had stood and bowed, and said, 'You are Joseph Quinn.'

Quinn smiled and bowed again. 'At your service, my lord. I'll return in the morning, my lord, after I've paid a visit to Mrs Nellie Moore, if that would suit.'

'Nellie Moore…' said Duval. 'Samuel Hyde's housekeeper?'

'Yes, my lord,' said Quinn. 'I hear the housekeeper is not in good health, and she might have much to tell me about her late master that would help my investigation.'

'Would you mind if I accompanied you, Mr Quinn?'

'Not at all, my lord.'

'Where are you staying?' Duval asked.

'I'll find an inn in Woodbridge. I have the use of Mrs Dent's carriage.'

'No. That's out of the question,' said Lady Harriet. 'And unnecessary. You will stay here.'

Quinn was shown a room with a four-poster bed, and he thought how much he would like Fleur to see this house, this bed. Hot water was waiting for him in a basin, along with towels and soap. He was grateful he'd had his hair cut and that he had the loaned clothes in the carriage.

Half an hour later, he had changed into his evening dress (which fitted, he thought, remarkably well). He had struggled somewhat with the tying of the cravat, and this had delayed him.

Downstairs, Lord Harlington and his aunt were waiting in the drawing room.

'Shall we go through?' said Lady Harriet.

Dinner, Quinn had been told, was one of the most tedious meals in grand houses, lasting four or five hours. The first two hours were entirely occupied with eating. There was no choice but for Quinn to resign himself to indigestion, for after each dish, Lady Harriet asked if he liked the food and whether he would eat some more. Quinn gave in and ate solidly from the minute he arrived at the table until, at last, Lady Harriet left the gentlemen to their brandy.

'How is it you're acquainted with Mrs Dent?' Duval asked Quinn.

'She takes in mistreated servants, slaves and battered women. My mother and I were used by my drunken father as punchbags. It's an old story, a lonely one to live through.'

Duval looked across at him. 'I thought you'd be unsympathetic but you're not.'

'I'll take that as a compliment, my lord,' said Quinn. 'Can you tell me more about Lady Harlington? You met her where?'

'I first saw her through the window of a coffee house in Thetford. I saw her steal a purse from a maidservant's basket. It woke my curiosity.'

'You bought her at the wife sale and married her. Then what, my lord?' said Quinn.

'I am sure you know that I left here, straight after the wedding.'

'Am I right in thinking you spent a lot of time in London with Mrs Gosling?'

'Yes, I did.'

'Did Mrs Gosling seek you out, or was it the other way round?' asked Quinn.

'She wanted to help me be accepted back into society. After the scandal of the wife sale, she introduced me to her friends.'

'Including the Marquis de Soule?'

'Yes.'

'Is she in love with you, my lord? Are you with her?' asked Quinn.

'That is a very impertinent question, sir,' said Duval. 'No. She is married.'

'That's not what I am asking,' said Quinn. 'I am asking, is she in love with you?'

'No, she isn't,' said Duval. 'And I long ceased having any feelings for her.'

'In London, did you accompany her to parties, or the theatre, without her husband?'

'I truly regret ever getting embroiled with Arabella and her friends. My own folly. But it's no good looking back. I seem to be doing it far too much, thinking of all the time I wasted when I could have been with Edmée. But are you suggesting, Quinn, that Lady Harlington left me… that she had cause enough to go, without a word of explanation?'

'No,' said Quinn. 'Let's say, I don't think it helped matters, and it does account for the scandalous speculation flooding the papers. Which leads me to the Carsons. I wonder – would it be possible to see Mr and Miss Carson as soon as possible? Do you think that might be arranged?'

'Yes,' said Duval. 'Though I should tell you that I paid a visit to Mr Carson recently, and it did not end well.' He sighed and, having written the note, he handed it to a footman.

'Who's that for?' asked Lady Harriet, entering the dining room.

'The Carsons. An invitation to dine tomorrow.'

'Oh lord, not those odious people. Have you lost your mind? Melancholy is one thing, madness quite another.'

Duval smiled. 'I doubt they will come at such short notice.'

'Oh, they will,' said his aunt, in a resigned tone. 'Those two won't be able to resist having another look at all the contents of the house and gloating over what they hope to inherit.'

'Where are you off to before that, Mr Quinn?' asked Lady Harlington.

'To see Nellie Moore,' said Quinn.

'I have no idea who she is,' said Lady Harriet, 'and as my mind is already full of useless information, please don't add to it.'

It was just before Quinn retired for the night that he said to Duval, 'I hear that Lady Harlington kept a journal, and wondered whether I may see it.'

'Yes.' Duval looked sheepish for a moment before going on. 'I read the journal when she was very ill in hope of finding someone who might have known her.'

'Did you?'

'No. The only person she talked about was *ma puce*. It could have been a woman, but I suspect it was a man. You may, of course, read it for yourself, but it is in French.'

Quinn smiled and replied, '*Ce n'est pas un problème*.'

Let Me See the Devil

Two fine Arabian horses stood saddled and waiting on the gravel drive for Duval and Quinn. Quinn was grateful Lord Harlington didn't patronize him by asking if he had ridden before. As a boy, he had worked in Lord Sutton's stables, even being his tiger for a while, and there, he had learned to ride. Even so, Quinn had never been on such a fine horse as this one.

They set off at a trot. Quinn's horse was easy to handle. It had a long stride and relished being given its head. They rode through the park, into the woods. Quinn was glad of the ride – it gave him time to think on all that he had read in Edmée's journal. It had been in the early hours when he came to her final entry. Now, to the rhythm of his horse's hooves, he tried to piece everything together. Two pheasants' feathers flapping rose up from the hedgerow into a sleepy morning sky, bringing him firmly back into the present.

Woodbridge was nestled on the banks of the River Deben, lost in the mist that had rolled in from the water and wrapped itself around the market town. They left the horses at the Angel Inn and went down to a port crowded with boatyards.

'You are a good horseman,' said Duval.

'I am an adequate horseman, on a good horse,' said Quinn.

Duval smiled and Quinn saw how everything about his face changed with that smile. You could see a handsome and unworried man, without the shadow now hanging over him.

They walked along the riverbank to where Quinn had been told that Nellie Moore's sister lived in a small cottage. It had a stable door and, outside, seated on an upturned barrel and smoking a pipe, was a soldier, his red jacket faded and worn. He looked surprised and concerned when he saw Duval. He stood up and bowed.

'Good morning to you, Mr Hyde,' said Duval. 'I don't know if you remember me?'

'I do,' said Gilbert Hyde. 'Is this about Edmée? I can't take her back, if that's why you're here.'

'No,' said Duval. 'We're here to talk to Nellie Moore.'

'My mother? Why? And who's this gentleman accompanying you?' asked Gilbert suspiciously.

'I'm Joseph Quinn. I'm an investigator and I'm here to help Lord Harlington find his wife.'

'What's the law doing looking for your wife? Do you mean Edmée's bolted?'

'She's missing,' said Duval.

'Missing?' repeated Gilbert. 'That doesn't sound—' Then he stopped. 'Blood and thunder! I've just worked it out – Lord Harlington, and she's Lady Harlington. Do you know, I never thought to put it together. No,' he said, looking into his pipe, which had gone out for the lack of tobacco, 'never thought it could be her in the papers. Where did you lose her?'

'That's what we're trying to find out,' said Quinn. 'It's your mother we want to talk to.'

'She's very ill. My aunt's gone to get more medicine.'

Gilbert opened the door and let them in. The place was dark, and it took time for their eyes to adjust to the gloom.

It was a small, poky cottage, lit by a pitiful fire in want of more coal.

'Gilbert,' came a call from behind a curtain that partitioned the room. 'Who is it?'

'It's Lord Harlington, Mother,' said Gilbert, pulling back the shabby curtain that had seen better days. The whole cottage had once seen better days, though when that might have been was hard to imagine.

Nellie was propped up on a trundle bed and looked as if half of her had sunk in the middle, like the bed itself. As far as Quinn could tell, this part of the room didn't benefit from any warmth from the fire.

'Your mother is shivering,' he said.

'I know,' said Gilbert. 'We need coal, candles, food, blankets and linen. Instead, we pay a quack, who gives us medicine that might turn a hen's ears green, but won't help my mother. As for anything else, it goes by the name of Everything.' He shrugged. 'In short, there's no money.'

Duval took from his greatcoat, a notebook and an elegant thin silver pencil holder. Quinn watched as Duval wrote out a list.

'Take this to the draper's and tell them to hurry. Give my name, say they will be rewarded for their speed.'

'Thank you, my lord—'

'I will stay with her,' said Duval. 'I qualified as a physician, if that reassures you.'

Gilbert was gone.

Duval lit the stub of a candle. He took off his frock coat and laid it over the woman in the bed, while Quinn went to see if there was any way of making the fire come to life.

'Who are you?' said Nellie.

'I am Duval Harlington.'

'Lord Harlington from Muchmore! What an honour to have you come see an ill woman.'

And, finally warm, she fell asleep.

The draper himself arrived, as did all his assistants, carrying a bed frame, mattress, linen, blankets, pillows and a nightshirt. Gilbert lifted his mother up while the old trundle bed and the sunken mattress were taken out, along with the old curtain dividing the room, then a new one was put in place. The whole thing was done with speed. The draper oversaw all the proceedings as the other things requested were left on the table, in a basket.

When she was finally placed back in the bed in a clean nightshirt, she cried. 'This is like heaven on earth,' she said as Gilbert put a lace cap on her bare head.

'Money,' said Gilbert, amazed. 'If you have money, anything is possible.'

'Here,' said Duval, taking some coins from his wallet. 'Go take this list to the grocer and the coal merchant. Get some tobacco for yourself. And have a drink.'

'Gadzooks,' exclaimed Gilbert. 'That's kind, mighty kind, Lord Harlington.'

Duval pulled up a stool and took Nellie's hand. 'Do you think you could tell me about Samuel Hyde?'

'Yes, what do you want to know about that turd?'

'I want to know why he went to Paris, where he ended up meeting Edmée.'

'Mrs Beale had his name put forward, didn't she, for a mission to retrieve religious things, you know?' Nellie started to cough, her breath shallow. Finally, her cough subsided.

'Religious texts?' said Duval.

'Yes, she came to see him, all full of wind about the good English Christians all stuck in Paris. There was a mission to go out there and give them support and religious guidance. Hyde was supposed to bring back any texts – what did she say... she said it all la-di-dah – "*to bring back any text threatened by the anti-clerical sentiment*".' Nellie wheezed with laughter.

'Mrs Beale said there was no one more suited to retrieving such valuable artefacts. So, they gave Samuel Hyde his papers, free passage for him and one other, hoping he would bring back a good English Christian. Instead, he brought a Catholic French wife. You should've seen Edmée's face when she saw the parsonage, that was a picture. Mr Hyde, he blamed her for his life, as he said, going downhill from then. Because Mrs Beale, that good Christian lady, stopped asking him to dinner, didn't like her.'

'*Her* being Edmée?'

'Yes. She was beautiful. And those high up in the Church were angry too because he hadn't brought back any religious artefacts. Do you know what he brought back from Paris? Naughty etchings of priests doing everything they shouldn't. That made me laugh. Oh, how I laughed.' She stopped as a thought came to her. 'When you are gone, will this bed vanish too?'

'It won't, I promise. It's all paid for,' said Duval.

'You should hate me for what we did to her. I hope the Lord forgives me, I truly do. I don't deserve your kindness. I don't deserve any of it.'

'In prison,' said Duval, 'under the threat of torture or death, people do and say things they would otherwise never do or say, trying to save themselves.'

'I was frightened of him, of his moods. But I was also jealous when he brought her back from Paris. So cross with him. I wasted so much of my life with Samuel. I was his whore, his housekeeper; I was nothing to him. Then she came. Edmée spoke no English; she was so lost. It wasn't her fault. I could see she was hurting inside. She was like a… She was like a fairy, all delicate, a butterfly for him to pull the wings off. And have you guessed who I was?'

'I would imagine Mr Hyde's common-law wife.'

'I was. I had his son, Gilbert, though my upturned-nose

sister and my mealy-mouthed mother took my baby from me.' She paused. 'Mrs Beale was furious with Samuel – she made it quite plain what she thought. She stormed out of the parsonage, he running after her, begging her to understand the situation. He was shouting, "*She means nothing to me.*" Imagine, a parson married and shouting that his new wife meant nothing to him? What a great example for the village.

'To begin with, when he returned, he slept in my bed as he always did. She didn't mind. That went on for a while. Her English got better. She asked for her books back from the small trunk that she had brought with her. That's when it started; he wanted to know what was in the books. She said, "Words."

'He became obsessed with those books. He sensed that there was something valuable hidden in them. She wouldn't tell him. Then he started drinking. By then, he was so stirred up by her that he believed she had the devil inside her… or rather he wanted her that much and didn't know what to do with himself. I was to help him take the devil from her. But she fought against the wine that would save her soul and make her become an obedient wife.'

There was another long silence, then she said, 'Samuel cut off her hair. I left him to his troublesome work until I heard him cry out. I went to him. He had blood on his face and his breeches about his ankles. I knew then it was he who was the devil.'

'Did you poison Samuel?'

'I wish. I did kill Miss Weeks's dog, though – I couldn't stand its barking. When it was dead, I regretted it, because then all I could hear was him… fucking her.'

Duval stood up.

'Shouldn't have said that, my lord, should wash my tongue. I'm sorry, I'm sorry for what we did. You're going to take the bed and everything away with you…'

'No, Nellie, I'm not.'

'Truly, I am sorry. Edmée just had that thing about her; she stirred him up. She made women jealous. I think she could send a man mad with longing, and even when you thought you had her, she could still escape you.'

Duval was now by the curtain. He went back to where she was lying.

'What do you mean, Nellie?'

'In her head, she escaped Samuel. She knew exactly what to do to frustrate him as well. She would move about. He couldn't do it if she did that. Don't think he was the first. I think she was someone important and Samuel Hyde had no idea.'

Gilbert came in with a coal merchant, carrying two sacks of coal. 'That goes out the back,' he said, and put down the rest of the goods he'd bought. 'I spent the lot,' he said. Then he stopped, wondering what Duval had been doing, only now realizing his mother, for once, was quiet. 'Is she dead?'

'No,' said Duval.

Nellie looked up at her son. 'Are you the Angel Gabriel?'

Duval and Quinn walked out of the cottage.

'Wait,' Gilbert cried, marching up to them briskly. 'Thank you, my lord, for your help. I don't know what she told you, but I know her life was ruined by that bastard.'

'Mr Hyde,' said Duval, 'is there anything you didn't tell me about Edmée?'

Gilbert took his time before he said, 'I've no idea why she's taken off, or where she might be, but I can tell you one thing: there was hardly anything of her, but she had a will of steel. I don't say that lightly. Some soldiers profess bravery and talk about courage, but that's a woman who says nothing and has survived a Revolution and a violent bastard of a husband. Lord Harlington, she would be a hard candle to blow out.'

*

They returned to the Angel Inn. Quinn suggested they stop to have a drink before they set off once again. Seeing Duval hesitate, he said the horses, if not the riders, had earned a good pint. Duval wavered, fearful of being recognized, then shrugged and agreed. They sat in the corner, near the fire.

As Quinn had expected, the coaching inn was busy with people coming and going, serving maids with trays of food, and servants carrying bandboxes and trunks. Tired passengers trying to get used to solid ground after being so long jogged and jiggered about. The chatter was loud, and in all the hullabaloo, two gentlemen, peacefully enjoying their ale, would hardly be noticed.

Duval looked weary.

'That was difficult,' said Quinn. 'It was impressive the way you encouraged her to tell her story. You have a knack for it.'

'I survived prison by listening to people without judgement. I was there from the beginning of ninety-three to October ninety-five. I heard too many desperate last confessions. Did you read Edmée's journal?'

'Yes I did.' said Quinn. 'She obviously knew that you had read it too.'

'I hoped that wasn't the case,' said Duval. 'But I was mistaken. You saw the last entry. Did you finish it?'

'Yes, and like you I was very interested to read about *ma puce*. You have no inkling about who he was?'

'No, we both agreed we would start the clocks again on our lives, we would leave the past behind. But you can't. Someone once said, *What is true by lamplight is not always true in sunshine*.'

Just then, a serving girl dropped a pile of plates and the noise resounded around the inn. There was much confusion and changing of places, while the broken crockery was swept up.

'Can I ask you, my lord,' Quinn said, 'do you think a count's daughter would be good at thieving?'

Duval shrugged. 'I don't know, and I don't care. What does it matter?'

'I ask because, when I was a lad and my mother and I were starving, I learned to pick pockets to survive. I was taught by the street urchins and thieves who lived down by the river near the hovel we called home. And I read about Edmée's nifty skills in her journal too. May I ask, my lord, have you about your person your silver pencil holder… and the locket?'

'I hope so,' said Duval as he patted his waistcoat and his frock coat.

Quinn put the missing items on the table.

'That's very impressive, Mr Quinn. But what does it prove, other than that you are a good thief who I hope works on the right side of the law?'

'There is an art to thieving, my lord,' said Quinn, 'even from such an open target as a maidservant's basket. There are many émigrés in London who were born into aristocratic families, and they can hardly feed themselves, mainly because, always having had servants, they have no idea how it's done. I asked the question because I want to know: who was the lady who stole from that maidservant?'

Duval nodded. 'In answer to your question, I don't think a count's daughter would do that, even in a Revolution – not without being caught.'

'And after Edmée stole from the maid, did you see the maid come back, looking for her purse?'

'No,' Duval said, opening the locket Edmée had given him and looking at the painting of her eye.

'Which shows she had no idea she'd been robbed. And that is the art.'

Duval drank his brandy then said, his voice breaking, 'Do you have any idea where she is?'

'I will know more this evening,' said Quinn.

'You think the Carsons are involved?' asked Duval.

'What I know is there isn't much time. If she is alive, whoever has her hasn't as yet shown their hand, maybe because they already know they are cornered, or they are waiting to see what we do next.'

Quinn had other inquiries to make that afternoon and said that he would see Duval back at Muchmore. They parted. Quinn stayed in the inn. He wondered how he would feel if he discovered that Fleur had been so badly abused, and then been told that Samuel Hyde probably wasn't her first.

A picture of Edmée was beginning to form in Quinn's mind. The one thing he was certain of: she was a thief, and she had probably stolen something of far greater value than coins from a maid's basket.

Madame Dupont

Quinn had decided to learn French when the Bastille fell. He could see how the tide was turning, as émigrés started coming to London. Without French, he would never be able to comprehend the nuances of reports about the community. More importantly, he wouldn't truly understand what was in Fleur's heart.

A maid opened the door at Mrs Appleby's, saying that her mistress wasn't in.

'Will you tell her that I am an investigator from Bow Street, London, inquiring into the disappearance of Lady Harlington?'

The maid disappeared, only to reappear a moment later, and Quinn was shown into a busy workshop. Three seamstresses were working on a gown. With a clap from Mrs Appleby, they stood up, and with a curtsey to Quinn, left the room.

The dressmaker was a neat and tidy woman in her late thirties who took great pride in her work. Quinn told her again who he was and why he was there.

'I want to ask you some questions. Firstly, your name was

Madame Dupont. Can I ask why you didn't choose to keep it? I would have imagined it would serve you well in your profession.'

'My husband thought it unwise because of my work in Paris, and I agreed with him.'

Quinn looked at the gown on the workshop table. It was an exact copy of Lady Harlington's ball dress, the one that Hannah had shown him. 'Who is this for?' he asked.

'Mrs Arabella Gosling,' said Madame Dupont.

'When did she come here to order it?' asked Quinn.

'The day after the ball.'

'Do you know what time?'

'When I opened in the morning; she came with another lady.'

'Did the other lady stay with her?' asked Quinn.

'No, she went to look at the hat shop.'

'So, Arabella Gosling was here alone?'

'Yes.'

'And what did she ask you?'

'Sorry, I don't understand. My English…' said Madame Dupont.

'I would imagine she came here to ask you questions about Lady Harlington. Am I right?'

'…Yes.'

'Did she ask you lots of questions?'

'Yes.'

'What did she ask you?'

Madame Dupont shrugged. 'She asked if I knew of the Marquis de Soule. And if I had known Lady Harlington in Paris.'

'What did you say?'

'No.'

'And she believed you?'

'Yes, of course. Because it is true.'

When Quinn spoke again, it was in French. 'The problem is, Madame Dupont, I don't believe you. I also happen to be rather good at what I do, just as you are rather excellent with your needle. And I can tell when someone is lying. I really do not wish to waste a whole afternoon listening to fairy tales. Do you understand me?'

Madame Dupont looked at him, amazed. 'Your French is excellent!'

'Did Arabella question anything you told her?'

'No, she did not.'

'Did you tell her Edmée's full name?'

Madame Dupont said nothing.

'Lady Harlington wrote to you,' said Quinn. 'I know this because Hannah, her maid, saw the letter. Not its contents, but she knew it was addressed to you. What did it say?'

Reluctantly, Madame Dupont went to a drawer in her workbench and handed a letter to Quinn.

'You are doing much better,' he said. 'Let's try and keep this up, shall we?'

Dear Madame Dupont,

We have both been washed up on these shores, for better or worse. I would be immensely grateful if you did not mention anything to do with the past. We both went through a terrible time, and, like you, I want to try and start again. I need some gowns, and there is no one better than yourself. I hope I can rely on your discretion.

Madame Dupont was silent for quite some time, studying Quinn.

'Madame, I am here to help find her.'

'I was relieved when I saw her again, but I was careful to say nothing, as she requested.'

'What was her name?'

Madame Dupont, seeing there was no way out, responded, 'Albertine Edmée Simoneau.'

'Do you know who her father was?'

'A bookbinder in the rue Jacob.'

'Tell me about when you first met her.'

'She was twelve. She used to come to see me with a Madame Rouchette.'

'What was she like?'

'Madame Rouchette?'

'No. Albertine.'

'She was cheeky, funny, very skinny.'

'And Madame Rouchette?' said Quinn.

'She was a chaperone attached to the Royal Court, at the Palace of Versailles.'

'Did she work for the Marquis de Soule?'

'I don't know. That is the truth. Madame told me that if I wished to be paid and have a flourishing business, best that I kept my tongue still, my ears closed and my eyes shut.'

'Did you make lots of dresses for Albertine?'

'Not many at that point. But Madame Rouchette did call me back again when Albertine was fourteen. Then she was not so cheeky, more anxious.'

'Do you know why she was anxious?'

Madame Dupont hesitated. 'I swore I would not talk about this.'

'I know. I'm aware that's what you said. But I am not going to find her unless I have some idea of her past.'

'Albertine was tall for her age. She had been born with a natural elegance that I haven't seen in many young girls. She was wise. Wise enough, I think, to know what was coming.'

'What was coming?' asked Quinn.

'Madame Rouchette said it must be a seductive gown to woo a man with. I was to use near see-through muslins and silks of the finest quality. It was very radical for its day.'

'Radical for a whorehouse?'

Madame Dupont was quiet for a moment. 'I don't know. I heard a rumour that Albertine had been bought. There were many fantastical stories and much gossip about the Royal Court before the Revolution. I never saw Madame Rouchette again after that. I heard she was guillotined in the Terror. And I did not see Albertine – Edmée – again until Muchmore.'

'Did Edmée say anything to you about what had happened to her?'

'No. I think she was worried that I might know more than I did. She would only talk to me about the gowns and fabric. Though one time she was here, she did say something…' Madame Dupont looked close to tears. 'When Lady Harriet went out to her carriage, after Albertine had read the note, she said, "How could he ever love me now? It is all too late."'

'Who brought the note to you?'

'It was brought to me by Miss Carson.'

Madame Dupont went to her work desk and took out a small drawstring bag. 'In here,' she said, 'are all the pieces that I found on the floor. I thought they might be important.' She handed the bag to Quinn. 'I hope I have done the right thing in talking to you. There are powerful men who have come over from France, and this might be more complicated than it first appears.'

'Complicated in what way, madame?'

'It doesn't matter what I think.'

'You're wrong; it matters. When you're looking for grains of corn in a sea of mud, it matters.'

'I think she was connected to someone important. Who it was, I swear on my life I don't know. Much happened in the Revolution that those of us who survived would rather forget, I just pray she is alive.'

'So do I,' said Quinn.

The Bell for Dinner

It was late afternoon when Quinn returned to Muchmore. He went up to his chamber and, standing there, marvelled at the comfort of it all. He carefully took off his frock coat and put all the pieces of paper that Madame Dupont had given him on a side table, anxious to make sure every scrap was there. He told himself he would try and piece it together before this evening was over.

Then, taking out his notebook, Quinn went through all he had discovered so far. What he knew for certain was there was not enough evidence to wrap around the bare bones of this mysterious case. He knew that Miss Carson had delivered the note to Madame Dupont, that her brother Mr Carson was desperate to claim his inheritance. They were on his list of suspects. The Goslings he wasn't so sure of, but he definitely wanted to talk to the Marquis de Soule, who had left on day of the ball. He wanted to know about the heated conversation that Hannah had overheard between Edmée and one the marquis's manservants. Without doubt the marquis had the means to stage a kidnap, but what would be his motivation? There was also Madame Dupont herself. She was frightened, but of whom? Then again, he supposed, that wasn't unusual. He had meet many émigrés who were certain they were in danger; he thought it came from having lived too long with the guillotine. Quinn stood up, stretched, and looked out of the window. It had begun to rain.

The thing that niggled him the most was Veldt's report of Hyde's death. There was no doubt in Quinn's mind that Mr Hyde had not died of natural causes. Nellie Moore had confessed to killing the dog. He wouldn't have put it past her to have done the same to the man who, as she had said, ruined her life. Why, then, had Veldt decided it was not a murder case?

An hour later, he was almost dressed for dinner – apart from his cravat. Last night, it had proved tricky to tie, but this evening it struck him as impossible. He rang the bell and asked for Jameson, who arrived remarkably quickly, took one look at Quinn and said, 'They can be devils to tie. Would sir like help?'

'Yes,' said Quinn. 'Does it go under my shirt collar or over it?'

'His lordship,' said Jameson, 'always wears his over, so that the side of the collar frames his face.'

Quinn laughed. 'That explains his good looks.'

While his cravat was being expertly folded and tied, Quinn said, 'When the marquis was here, did you talk to any of his servants?'

'No, Mr Quinn, the marquis's servants were all French. They came over with him from Paris. But I have some information that I think I'm safe to pass on, which might be helpful. Word is that Mr Carson hasn't paid his servants since he first arrived here, and they are on the point of mutiny. His sister, so I was told, is frequently subjected to his rages, and often locked in the attic. Rather like those he employs, she lives in fear of his erratic moods.'

'Thank you,' said Quinn. And, seeing Jameson hover by the door, asked, 'Is there anything else you want to say?'

'I noted, while I was tying your cravat, the pieces of torn-up paper on the table. It looks like you are trying to put them back together,' said Jameson. 'Could I help you with that, sir?'

'It's something of a puzzle,' said Quinn. 'Yes, if you are patient enough to do it. But the information that it might reveal is, I hope you understand, sensitive, and not to be repeated to anyone.'

'Sir, I never would. I gather this is about Lady Harlington, and I assure you I am discreet – as well as being rather good at puzzles,' said Jameson.

'Well then, have a try, by all means.'

Jameson was just about to leave, torn paper in hand, when Quinn said, 'I am told a good valet can sniff out a commoner. Can I ask, do you think Lady Harlington came from an aristocratic family?'

'It is harder to tell with citizens from another country, so I am not sure. I would say any whiff of trade is hardly discernible.'

'Why is that?' asked Quinn with interest.

'She seemed well acquainted with the structure and the manners of a great house like Muchmore and her role as the wife of a lord, sir.'

'Thank you, Mr Jameson.'

Quinn set off for the drawing room. He caught sight of himself in a long mirror and wished that Fleur could see him now. Taking a deep breath, he braced himself for what lay ahead and was pleased to find he was hungry again.

*

The drawing room had about it, that evening, the solemnity of a wake. Lady Harriet sat upright in her armchair, looking formidable. Seated on the sofa at some distance from her, like a tableau in a wax museum, was Mr Carson. He was dressed in baby-blue silk, which did much to emphasize all the wrong parts of him. His head appeared to be served up on a plate, the effect brought about by there being so much linen tied around his neck. He looked not unlike an overgrown schoolboy who had decided to put on fancy dress.

'At last,' said Lady Harriet. 'Mr Joseph Quinn, may I introduce Mr Ralph Carson.'

Mr Carson rose to his feet, looked Quinn over, and then dismissed him as unimportant, giving only the slightest of bows before sitting down again.

Duval entered the room. The contrast between Mr Carson and Duval could not have been greater. Duval wore his clothes with an effortless elegance, his neck cloth tied over his shirt so that the tips of his collar framed his face. He wore a frock coat in a steel grey, a waistcoat of golden yellow embroidered with flowers, and breeches made of black velvet that went down to black silk stockings and shoes.

Ralph Carson, breathing in, performed an unnecessarily elaborate bow, which made his wig, styled in two horns, wobble in a comical fashion.

'So kind of you to invite me, Lord Harlington,' he said. 'It shows, if I may say so, such cordiality. As I said to Sarah, when we received the invitation this morning, here is a gentleman of understanding and wisdom beyond his years.'

Duval said, 'Your sister is not with you tonight?'

'No, she is not feeling well. I must apologize on her behalf – and if I may, in addition, ask your forgiveness for the way I reacted when you paid us the most courteous of calls.'

'Enough, Mr Carson,' said Lady Harriet sharply. 'No more play-acting. I can go to the theatre for that.'

The bell rang and the butler announced that dinner was served. The footman opened the doors.

Lady Harriet took Duval's arm and patted it, as they went through to the dining room. Quinn walked with Mr Carson.

The table was decorated with two large candelabra, both ablaze. Lady Harriet sat at the head of the table, much to many disapproving sniffs from Mr Carson.

The courses kept arriving, as did the wine. Only Mr Carson constantly demanded his glass be refilled. Quinn watched, as the now babbling blue baby grew in confidence.

'The problem is...' Mr Carson paused. 'The problem is, Lord Harlington, that even if your dear lady wife were now to be found, your father's will states that if she was ever to leave of her own free will, then...'

Duval, who had hardly spoken all evening, said, 'What is your point, sir?'

Carson let out a high-pitched squeal. 'My point is, then I would inherit the estate. I have spoken to my solicitor, and we feel that, in light of these circumstances, we won't be pursuing our probate claim, Instead, I will simply let events take their course—'

'Mr Carson,' interrupted Lady Harriet, 'do you like the food?'

'Yes, yes, I do indeed, Lady Harriet, a fine table. We were dining last week at—'

'Then you must have more.'

This, Quinn thought, was the perfect moment to ask a question. 'Mr Carson, I believe you employed a colleague of mine to investigate the death of Samuel Hyde.'

The wine glass was again at Ralph Carson's lips. He hastily put it down and patted his mouth with an over-scented handkerchief. The colour rose in his cheeks.

'I did,' he said curtly. 'What business is that of yours, Mr Quinn?'

Quinn continued in a most good-humoured manner. 'Mr Veldt was an investigator in Bow Street. As am I.'

This sobered Mr Carson.

'You are a Runner?' he said.

'I have that honour, sir,' said Quinn.

Mr Carson, now feeling superior in every way, said reproachfully, 'Mr Quinn, there is a lady present.'

'There often is,' said Quinn.

'What buffoonery makes you think that Mr Quinn saying he is a Runner is not suitable for me to hear?' said Lady Harriet. 'Duval employed him to find lady Harlington.'

'I only meant—'

'I was wondering,' interrupted Quinn, 'if you could explain your reasons for employing Mr Veldt. Were you acquainted with Mr Hyde?'

'No, I was not.'

'Then it's strange that you should feel the need to pay for an investigation. Was it, perhaps, out of the goodness of your heart and a desire to see justice done? Or do you have a special connection with the village?'

'I am an upstanding citizen of this country who abides by the laws of the land. And it's ill-mannered to ask such questions at the dinner table.'

'So, there was no connection between yourself and the parson? Do you do this for every death you read about in the paper, or is it limited to a certain locality?' asked Quinn.

'What right have you to question me?' said Mr Carson. 'I didn't come here to be interrogated. I came to enjoy good company and delicious food.' He reapplied himself with great gusto to the dish before him. 'Lady Harriet, may I compliment you on your cook. This is the best beef I have had this year.'

Duval said, 'Mr Carson, I, too, am baffled by your philanthropic approach to the death of a stranger. Tell me, does it only apply to those deaths where you might gain financially? Because, when you think about it, paying to have Mr Hyde's death investigated was arguably for your own benefit and no one else's.'

Mr Carson seemed somewhat concerned. 'I don't follow, my lord,' he said.

Duval said calmly, 'Supposing Mr Veldt had found evidence to prove Lady Harlington guilty of murder; the question surely is, how would that have benefited you?'

Mr Carson let out another false laugh. 'I hope I have not been brought here to be cross-examined.'

Quinn watched this with interest. Now he had an idea what Veldt had been up to. 'I would like to know if you were satisfied with the service Mr Veldt provided,' said Quinn.

'Yes, thank you, I was,' said Mr Carson. 'It was Sarah's idea. She worries about such things. She has an anxious disposition, and the idea that there might be a murderer in the vicinity played on her nerves.' He scowled. 'This is most distasteful talk. I'm sure it's rather upsetting to Lady Harriet.'

'Not in the slightest,' said Lady Harriet. 'What is upsetting is to listen to you not telling us the truth and blaming your sister, who isn't here to defend herself. Your argument, Mr Carson, is utterly preposterous. This was obviously your idea; it seems to be a cowardly tactic to lay it on her.'

Mr Carson put down his fork and knife. 'Is this meal to be ruined by unsavoury conversation that does so little to compliment the cook's skills?'

Ignoring these ridiculous sentiments, Quinn said bluntly, 'Tomorrow, I would like to speak to your sister about her concerns, and what she knows about Veldt.'

'I don't think that will be possible.'

'Mr Carson,' said Duval, 'you were aware it was the late

Mr Hyde's widow who had become my wife. You went to Thetford to find that out, did you not?'

Carson, salmon pink under his white powder, now turned to Lady Harriet. 'Have *you* no objections to the name of Harlington being brought so low? And now that Lady Harlington has run away, it's only right and proper that I—'

To Mr Carson's utter surprise, Lady Harriet rose to her feet. 'I have had enough, Mr Carson,' she said, glaring at him. 'Ever since you were informed of my brother's foolish will, you have confidently assumed that this estate will be yours. Now I've been led to wonder if you haven't purposely tried to sabotage Lord Harlington's attempts to keep his inheritance. And heaven help you if you are involved in Lady Harlington's disappearance.'

Mr Carson stood up. 'These are serious accusations,' he said, and threw down his napkin, knocking a glass to the floor. 'You will be hearing from my solicitor. And when I inherit Muchmore… there will be changes.' He moved swiftly to the door, only to find the footman had his hand on the doorknob.

'Mr Carson,' said Duval, 'do you know where Lady Harlington is?'

'No, I don't. Now, please let me pass.'

Duval nodded to the footman, who stood aside to let the flustered Mr Carson leave.

In the hall, Mr Carson gathered up his righteous indignation, called for his carriage and complained loudly about the appalling behaviour of embittered, entitled people like the Harlingtons. 'There will be changes round here!' he shouted again.

Watkins suggested he wait outside for his carriage. The night was dark, drizzly and cold.

In the warmth of the dining room, Lady Harriet told a

footman to go to the stables and make sure Mr Carson was kept waiting as long as was politely possible.

Puddings were served: plums in brandy, gelée de muscat and sugared almonds.

Seeing how little Duval had eaten, Lady Harriet said, 'These are your favourites. Do try and have some.' Duval took a little of the jelly. Quinn took everything.

Watkins came back to say that one of Carson's horses was lame and William wondered if it would be alright to loan him one of Muchmore's horses.

Duval agreed.

'Wait,' said Quinn. 'Sorry to interrupt you, my lord, but would it be possible for you to make him write a note, with the name of the horse, in capitals, and say that it belonged to Lord Harlington, also in capitals? It must be in capitals, otherwise no horse.'

'Make sure he does it,' said Duval.

'I will, my lord,' said Watkins.

'That is most specific,' said Lady Harriet. 'Can I ask why?'

'Yes, my lady,' said Quinn. 'The note that Edmée was given – I retrieved it from Madame Dupont. She kept all the pieces. While I could not work out what it said, I did notice that it was written in capitals. I want to know if the two writings have anything in common.'

Cheese was served along with port and brandy.

They were interrupted when a footman brought Carson's note from the stables. He said quietly to Duval that Mr Jameson had something for Mr Quinn.

'Show him in,' said Duval.

Jameson looked sheepish as he entered the dining room and put on the table before Quinn the note Edmée had received at Madame Dupont's. He had successfully pasted the fragments onto another piece of paper.

'Thank you, Mr Jameson,' said Quinn, impressed. He

handed the piece of paper to Duval. 'This is the note Lady Harlington tore up at the dressmaker's in Woodbridge.'

Duval read it aloud.

YOU WILL COME TO THE MAZE AT FOUR O'CLOCK TOMORROW MORNING. IF YOU RAISE THE ALARM NOW, OR IF YOU FAIL TO FOLLOW THESE SIMPLE INSTRUCTIONS, LORD HARLINGTON WILL BE SHOT DEAD.

'Oh my word,' said Lady Harriet. 'Who would have sent such a vile thing, and why didn't she tell us?'

'Because she believed whoever wrote this would carry out the threat,' said Quinn. He lay the note that Carson had carefully written out about the loan of the horse side-by-side with the note that Jameson had pieced together. There was no mistaking his writing.

'But I don't believe for a moment that she thought the note had come from Carson.'

'Who then?' said Lady Harriet.

'I don't know,' said Quinn.

Duval stood up. 'He has her. He must have her. I am going to kill him.'

'Mr Carson has signed his own death warrant,' said Quinn. 'I wouldn't put yourself to too much trouble. The state will willingly hang the bastard for you. But first, we need that toe-rag to tell us what he has done with Edmée.'

Duval was by the door.

'Wait,' said Quinn. 'I have a plan. Mr Carson has not paid his servants since he hired them. You, my lord, might have to do that for him. We also need to speak to his sorry sister. It could be the only way we'll find out where Lady Harlington is.'

'Edmée must be at...' Duval stopped, took a deep breath.

'Of course I'll pay the servants,' he said. 'If Edmée was at Monkton Manor,' he said, 'Carson would have been less bold.'

'I agree,' said Quinn. 'But I can still arrest Carson and question his sister, for I am—'

'Let's go,' said Duval.

Mrs Dent's coachman was in the kitchen, enjoying a generous slice of apple pie, when he was told that Lord Harlington and Mr Quinn were in need of the carriage and were determined to set off to London by way of Monkton Manor.

The coachman, who had been thinking of a second helping, stood up, looked lovingly at the pie, and bid the cook farewell.

Duval had changed his attire. For the journey, he now wore a well-cut greatcoat over his frock coat, with a simple waistcoat and buff-coloured breeches and his hessian boots.

The bags were packed and the carriage loaded. Jameson was seated at the back with two of Duval's footmen, both armed with pistols and known to be excellent shots.

When they were seated in the carriage, Quinn said, 'You do have both Lady Harlington's journal and her book in your portmanteau?'

'Yes,' said Duval.

'Good,' said Quinn, falling back with a jolt as the carriage set of with more speed than Quinn remembered.

'Are we going faster or is it my imagination?' he asked.

'I thought it would be wiser to take my horses. There are posting stations all the way down to London that keep my horses ready for me,' said Duval.

'Magic,' said Quinn.
'What is?' asked Duval.
'Money,' said Quinn flatly.

The sky had cleared, and the rain had stopped. A moon shone silver on the road as they made their way towards Monkton Manor. The carriage drew up, just out of sight of the house. Quinn told the coachman and Jameson to wait with the carriage, and if they saw Carson, not to hesitate to restrain him. Having walked down the short drive, it didn't take Quinn and Duval long to find where the kitchens were, for the only light in the whole house came from that window. Duval knocked gently on the tradesman's entrance, while Quinn stood by the front door, certain Mr Carson would try to escape that way.

A butler opened the door, with a mouthful of words that stopped immediately at recognition of Lord Harlington.

'I am here to pay what's owed to you by Mr Carson,' Duval said.

The butler was so taken aback by seeing his lordship that he swallowed whatever he was going to say next and let him in. The kitchen looked clean but empty. Cook was seated at a scrubbed table; she had heard what was said and looked equally startled.

'I understand none of you have been paid.'

'Not a penny,' my lord, said Cook, standing and giving a curtsey.

'Is Mr Carson here?' asked Duval.

'No, my lord, he didn't return from Muchmore. We are expecting him any minute now.' Duval sent the butler to let Quinn in, then asked Cook, 'How much are you owed?'

When she said her figure, Duval promptly produced a bag of money and placed it on the table.

Cook looked dumbstruck.

'The rest of the staff will be paid tomorrow by my steward, who will be here in the morning,' said Duval. 'I need to urgently speak to Miss Sarah Carson.'

Quinn came into the kitchen. 'He has bolted, I would wager.' It was then that they heard a carriage drive up to the house.

Quinn said to the butler, 'You are not to say a word as to our presence.'

The butler put on his jacket and went out into the hall. A moment later, the coachman came into the kitchen. Seeing both Quinn and Lord Harlington, he looked shocked.

'Where is Mr Carson?' asked Duval.

'He is not with me, your lordship.'

'We been paid,' said Cook bluntly. 'And if you want your money, then the truth might be your best friend.'

'My word... paid! Well, then... we took him to Woodbridge... We woke up a sailor and his crew who had accepted him, but they do not sail until the morning. He made a right scene and promised double if they left there and then, and the last I saw of him was his buckled shoes stuck in river mud.'

'What if he has her and we let him escape?' said Duval. 'Damn it. I should have gone after him.'

'He hasn't got her, of that I'm quite certain,' said Quinn, coming back into the kitchen. 'As you said, he would never have been that calm, and he wouldn't have dared risk coming for dinner. He'll be caught in London. Hopefully, by then, we might have found Edmée.' He turned back to Cook. 'Where is Sarah Carson?'

'She is in the servants' quarters,' said Cook. 'He locked

her in there this evening, and we're not allowed to open the door.'

'You have the key, though, don't you?' said Quinn.

Cook took a key from her apron pocket and said, 'Mr Carson beats his sister regularly, and tells her it's all her fault. She's that scared of him.' She added, 'We all are.'

'Did you see anyone here on the day before the ball at Muchmore House, or the day after?' asked Quinn.

'A gentleman dined here that evening.'

'Did he stay the night?'

'Not to my knowledge, though one of the serving girls was certain the house was haunted because she heard noises in the night. In the morning, there was nothing there; we went to look.'

The butler said, 'I had strict instruction that I wasn't to open the door to anyone.'

'You didn't see Lady Harlington?'

Cook let out a gasp. 'You don't think that was she up there – not a ghost?'

The clock had ticked past midnight when Cook went upstairs and came back with Sarah Carson and a hurriedly packed bag. Sarah was shaking and sobbing as she was brought down. 'Lord Harlington, what are you doing here?' she said, surprised.

Lord Harlington bowed. 'Miss Carson.'

'That will be all,' he said to Cook and the butler. 'Tomorrow, as I said, my steward will be here to pay the rest of those employed by Mr Carson.'

Sarah stood there, twisting a handkerchief between her fingers. Quinn saw it was embroidered with the initials R.C.

'Are you going to arrest me?'

'No, but you are going to tell us all that you know,' said Quinn. 'If you don't, then yes, you will be arrested, for aiding and abetting in a kidnap.'

She let out a sob. 'I never wanted any part of it,' she said as she was led weeping out of the house.

The coachman lit the lanterns on the carriage before they set off at a gallop into the darkest part of the night, Jameson praying there would be no highwayman that needed shooting.

It was only when they were underway that Quinn asked Sarah how long she had suffered her brother's bullying rages.

'I hate him,' she said. 'I absolutely hate him. But I have never had any money of my own, so there has been no means of escape.'

'I can help you,' said Duval. 'But in return, I need to know what has happened to Lady Harlington. Time is not on our side; do you understand?'

'Yes! But I don't know where she is – if I did, I would have said. I think my brother does, though… Oh… Ralph will find me and bring me back and it will start again and be worse.'

'Your brother is in a lot of trouble,' said Quinn.

'He told me I was, too. He said I was involved.'

'You're not,' said Quinn. 'But you are a witness. So you must help us. Did you know Veldt?'

'Yes. I didn't like him one jot. He was a deceitful man.'

'Why do you say deceitful?'

'He appeared to be one thing, then another. You never knew which way the tide went with him. He came to Monkton Manor with his report—'

'His report,' said Quinn, 'on Mr Hyde's death?'

'That is correct. And Ralph was furious when Mr Veldt said he didn't think Lady Harlington had murdered Mr Hyde. He flew into one of his first-rate rages. Mr Veldt was not alarmed by him at all; he found him amusing.

'Then Veldt said something more sinister. He said he was certain Lady Harlington could be made to disappear, and then my brother would inherit the estate... but not if he gave into his tantrums. Ralph calmed down after that. The ball, he said, would be the best opportunity, because there would be so many people around. I didn't think he was serious – it seemed such a far-fetched notion, until I realized my brother believed every word.

'And... I know it might sound suspicious that I know so much, but the two of them paid me no mind when they were scheming. My brother told Mr Veldt that I was a blunderhead with a feeble mind, and it didn't signify what they said around me.'

'Don't worry, Miss Carson. We are most grateful for your help. When did Veldt come again?'

'The day before the ball. Veldt had Ralph write out the note that I was to deliver to Madame Dupont. Told my brother that Lady Harlington would come like a lamb to the slaughter anyway.'

'Why did he think that?' Quinn asked.

'He said he knew something that was more deadly than a bullet.'

What on earth, thought Quinn, *did he mean by that?*

Miss Carson let out a sudden sob. 'Oh, what will become of me?'

Duval said, 'You need not worry. There is a lady in Soho. A friend of mine; I believe you might know her – Minnie?' Even in the dark of the carriage, he was sure that Sarah had coloured bright red.

'Or if you would rather, there is Mrs Dent,' said Quinn hurriedly, 'who looks after women who have suffered all sorts of ill-treatment. You will be safe with both women,' Quinn assured her.

Though, Duval thought, *perhaps not safe from temptation with Minnie*.

Seeing Miss Carson still looked worried, Quinn added, 'Fear not, Miss Carson. Your brother will not find you at either establishment, of that I assure you.'

This Pleasant Land

The day broke in a red dawn and, true to words of shepherds, by the late afternoon such was the rain and thunder. Duval was reluctant to stop but had to acknowledge it was too dangerous to continue. An inn should be found and the last stage of the journey undertaken in the morning.

Duval had been silent for a long period of time, lost in his own thoughts. Quinn had been more obliged to speak to Sarah, if only to reassure her that she was safe until she fell asleep. What he had to do next was get an arrest warrant for those two bastards, Veldt and Mr Carson.

Duval's thoughts had run along a different path. He was thinking about Edmée, of all the things they hadn't told one another. That you can never be free of the past; it follows you wherever you go, and in the end, it is your story and your story alone. It cannot be taken from you by the promise of a different future. If he had confessed to having read Edmée's journal, that would have given her an opportunity to talk about *ma puce*. He wondered why he hadn't. Deep down, he knew the answer: he had not wanted anything to break the enchantment he had found with her. Did he think it could have lasted without reality? The answer was a bleak no. But with Edmée, he had found the freedom to be himself, to be loved for who he was. No, he didn't care what she might have stolen. He had given her his heart, his soul, his body. She had robbed him of nothing.

All three travellers were relieved to find a coaching inn, with a good cook and a wine cellar, though Sarah asked if she might be able to have her meal in her room. Quinn looked uncertain, but Duval shrugged and said, 'Jameson will keep an eye on her. I don't think for a moment that she will run away. This must be the safest she has felt for a long while.'

The inn, being a Tudor building, was beamed. This always put him in mind of being inside a spider; he had no great liking for the period or the architecture. It was a private dining room they were shown into. The table was laid with a clean white cloth; there was a good fire in the grate and a hearty rabbit pie with thick puff pastry, fluffy mashed potato and a dish of leeks, while outside, the wind howled and the rain fell heavy on the leaden windows.

The two men ate in silence. Duval wasn't in the mood for talking, still too wrapped up in his own thoughts. It was only after the pie dish, which was scraped empty and had been cleared away, and the latch on the wooden door had been closed, that Duval said, 'This is the book that was in Edmée's box. You asked to see it. I've looked through page by page and can make no sense of its significance. It is a book that was famous in its day, *The Picture of Paris* by Mercier. The author survived the Revolution. It was said that the book was composed in the street, written on a doorstep.'

Quinn examined the spine of the book. 'I have seen this kind of contraption before. These books are ingeniously made – it's hard to fiddle with them, if you don't know what you're doing. They need to be treated with great care. The

Alien Office uses a man in Burlington Gardens to open them. This one might be nothing; it is impossible to tell.'

Duval sat listening, staring into the heart of the fire, and saw in it a crooked road.

'You think she was a spy? A thief?'

'I don't know,' said Quinn. 'What I do know is her father was a bookbinder. I believe her full name is Albertine Edmée Simoneau.'

'Her father…' said Duval taken aback. 'No, that…'

Quinn looked at Duval intently. 'It doesn't matter to me who my Fleur's father was, but I can see the identity of Lady Harlington's father matters to you.'

'It doesn't,' said Duval quickly, stumbling in his eagerness to get the words out.

'May I have the boldness to suggest that's a—'

'Lie?' said Duval. 'You would be correct.'

'And I might go so far as to suggest that Edmée would have known this, and be worried about telling you the truth.'

'No,' said Duval, shaking his head as if having an argument with himself, 'that can't be the reason for all this.'

'That's the problem with the aristocracy. It has such a shallow pool in which to fish. Consequently, there are too few ladies with beauty and too few gentlemen with any brain.'

Duval looked at Quinn and burst out laughing. 'Touché,' he said.

They set off early the next morning. Sarah slept in the corner of the carriage, while the two men came up with a plan.

'Jameson will make sure we stay in touch,' said Duval. 'I will let him know my movements and you will send any message to me at St James's Square.'

'I am going first to the Alien Office to get an arrest

warrant for Veldt and Mr Carson. I will have my men on the lookout for a clipper from Woodbridge. The weather was bad – I should think that delayed them. Then I will arrest Carson.'

'The sooner the better,' said Duval. 'I will take Sarah to Minnie's.'

Quinn, letting down the window, inhaled the air as they descended Highgate Hill, the city laid out before them. 'Good old girl, I missed you,' he said. Sitting back in the carriage, he added, 'If this job has taught me one thing, it's that I could never live in the countryside.'

'I am pleased it has been of some benefit,' said Duval.

'I will find her, my lord,' said Quinn.

'I fear it is too late,' said Duval.

All My Days

They parted near The Strand, Duval agreeing to meet early in the evening. He hailed a hackney carriage, Sarah worrying all the time what would happen if Minnie turned her away. Though he would not have said so, Duval was having the same fear, regretting that he hadn't decided to take her to Mrs Dent's after all. What would Minnie say to them both?

Having started out a bright morning, the day was becoming overcast, and by the time they reached Minnie's, a fog had begun to set in.

'They say it's going to be rogue's veil today, over the Thames,' said the cabbie cheerfully when they stopped outside Minnie's house.

Duval helped Sarah down, paid the cabbie, then knocked on the door. He guessed the hour was far too early for a lady of the night. Scrap opened the door to them, Duval half expecting her to snap, *What o'clock do you call this?* Instead, much to his surprise, she said, when she saw Sarah, 'Come in, luv. It's good to see you, Sarah! There I was telling

Minnie something would turn up, and it has.' Sarah looked uncertainly at Duval.

'It's Lord Harlington,' Scrap called, 'with a friend.'

'Male or female.'

'Female.'

Show them up,' came her mistress's reply.

Scrap took them upstairs and opened the drawing-room door. There was Minnie, fully dressed, walking back and forth across the room. Sitting on a chair was a lady with a harp, who looked fairly miffed. Beside her, standing up, was a woman dressed in a dressing gown.

'It's no bloody good,' said Minnie, 'you can't just stand there like a wet Thursday and tell me you won't take your clothes off. If that is the case, all I can say is you are in the wrong bleeding business. Go on, get out.'

'Willingly,' snapped the lady. 'Anyway, I like men better.'

'They might like you a darn sight more if you washed,' snapped Minnie. Then, seeing Sarah, she said, 'Well, what has the wind blown in today?'

'I'm h-h-here,' stuttered Sarah.

Duval explained quite why they were there. 'Perhaps it's not suitable,' he summarized at the end.

'No,' said Sarah, finding her voice at last. 'I would like to earn my living, and you said, Minnie, if I needed help, you had a job for me.'

'I did, love, and I do, love. I need a naughty lady for tonight. It's a little show I put on for my ladies.'

Sarah was silent then said, 'I know, I came and saw it.'

'Then if you feel you are up for it, it involves being in a state of undress, and a little bit more than just kiss and tickle. Quite honestly, love, I can't take on another prude. Do you really think you could do it?'

'Yes.'

'Scrap,' called Minnie. 'Take her and get her ready.'

Sarah looked on the verge of tears. Duval said calmly, 'As we said, there is always Mrs Dent.'

'No,' said Sarah, 'you don't understand. I've dreamed of doing this.'

Duval looked at Minnie as Scrap came into the chamber with some brandy and two glasses, and put them down inelegantly. 'Come on,' said Scrap, 'let's get you presentable.'

'Thank you. I don't ever want to go back to living with my brother. I want a life to live; I would love to work and be with ladies who think... and are... like me.'

'First step,' said Scrap, 'get you out of those dowdy clothes.' And with that, the door closed.

'I must thank you, Lord Harlington, for bringing her. You know she came here in such a state about that brother, but there was something about her, and I thought, *She'll do*. She doesn't look very prepossessing now, but get those shy repressed ones going, and they're the best. A bit of flattery, rouge on the cheeks, on the lips and...' She stopped and turned to the harpist. 'Have a break, Maud. We will start again in quarter of an hour.' Maud left the chamber.

Duval had turned to study the erotic etchings hanging on the walls. 'I remember this one – you used to have it downstairs,' he said. 'I thought it would be impossible.' It was of a man making love to a woman, seated on a donkey.

'I think you're right, but I find it humorous,' said Minnie. 'I gather you haven't found Lady Harlington.'

'Everyone seems to know my business,' said Duval.

'Have a drink before you go,' said Minnie. 'Brandy?'

He turned once more to look at the pictures. 'I can't stay,' he said. 'There are things I need to do.'

'Here you are. A brandy isn't going to hurt you. I'm not going to keep you long.'

Reluctantly, he took the glass.

'The trouble with you is...' said Minnie. 'The trouble is...'

He didn't want to hear what the trouble was. He knew it, or he thought he did.

'You have no story for what has happened to you,' said Minnie. 'Neither do any of the survivors of the Terror. You are rudderless souls looking for an anchor; that anchor can be love, as in your case, religion, as in others, or sex, but in all honesty, there are no words powerful enough to keep you afloat. Most of the émigrés, and other survivors, have fiddled with the truth, to make sense of the unacceptable.'

'I know that,' said Duval. 'I don't know what Edmée's truth is, but I wish she had told me it.'

'The newspaper said she was married to a parson who was very cruel, and she was reported as being black and blue at the wife sale. I would imagine that's the reason she lost the baby, am I correct?'

'You always are, Minnie,' he said.

'You, my lord, are a particular man where it comes to women. You have a lot of experience – not into amateurs, don't think you ever were. You say you wish she had told you the truth. Didn't she tell you her truth in another way?'

'What do you mean?'

'Do you think she would have known how to satisfy you in bed, if she had just had the weaselly sod Mr Hyde to go by?'

Duval said nothing.

'And what about you? You never lied?'

'No, yes. No, I didn't lie. Oh God, where is she? I want her back. I don't care what her truth is. I didn't lie...'

'You came to London after you were married and slept with me. You went everywhere with Arabella Gosling, and people thought you were having an affair with her, gave Mr Gosling the perfect excuse to go and live with his mistress. Arabella told lies, you told lies, and he told lies. It is only right that a marriage collapses under the weight of all those lies.

'May I ask – what do you think happened when you were

young and paying for the use of my girls? Do you honestly believe none of them got pregnant? How many children do you have?'

'None,' said Duval.

'None you know about. Between you and your friends, there were at least three babies born during the stag years. Two of my girls never came back to work; one of them died. As for the babies, I couldn't say what happened to them. It's the reason I do ladies only now.

'You look shocked, Duval. Are you going to tell me it was different because the girls were whores?'

'No, I never—'

'Don't tell me I didn't just see the thought flicker in those deep eyes of yours.'

'No.'

'That borders on a lie, my lord.' She refilled his glass. 'Drink up. All I am trying to say is, we all carry more in our bandboxes than we should.'

The Spine of a Book

Duval felt as if he had done a round or two at Mendoza's Academy for Boxing. He had been saved from Minnie by one of his footmen turning up with a message. It was a hastily written note from Quinn, giving the address of a Mr Weinrich's jewellers' shop in Burlington Gardens.

He will be able to open the book, and will know the value of what's inside.

Duval walked from Soho towards Burlington Gardens. The building he was looking for was painted black and, on the outside and inside, was a model of good taste. It was busy with the bon ton, buying pieces of jewellery, and they reminded Duval of a mischief of magpies all pecking at glitter. The young man behind the counter had been expecting him.

'I wonder if I could see Mr Weinrich?' asked Duval. 'I am here on behalf of Joseph Quinn.'

He was taken up some steps into the smallest of chambers whose only merit was its window that looked out onto the garden – or at least that's what Duval supposed it was, when the fog hadn't swallowed it whole.

Mr Weinrich stood up and bowed. 'How can I help?'

'I am not sure that you can.' He took out the book. 'I was told by Joseph Quinn that you might recognize this book, and if you did, you would be about the only person able to open it.' Duval was already beginning to feel that this was a wild goose chase. He wondered if he should just tell the jeweller not to worry about it and leave.

Mr Weinrich's put his pince-nez over one ear, then the other, and picked the book up. First, he took it to the window to examine it in the fading light, then he came back to his desk, put the book down, and looked up at Lord Harlington.

'Bernard Simoneau was renowned for these books; each one really is a masterpiece of engineering. I became involved in opening them for another client. This book is incredibly rare; the marbling inside the cover tells me it was a part of Simoneau's private collection.

Duval was about to pick it up only to find Mr Weinrich's hand firmly on the cover. 'I take it you are the Lord Harlington whose wife has mysteriously vanished?' Mr Weinrich said.

'I am.'

'Bernard Simoneau books are highly prized. I have never actually seen an original book that belonged to him – his bookshop burned down. It was said he had the gift of a magician. See, you can't tell if there is anything in this book. Many people make a mistake when they try and open his books. Look, you can see the spine is thicker than many bound books.' Mr Weinrich took it over to the candle, then with a tiny instrument, found what he was looking for and pressed it into the spine. Duval heard a click as the spine flapped back to reveal its treasure: a small, fine muslin bag. In it, a gem shone bright and green.

Mr Weinrich carefully took it out it. Rays of green light

flashed about the small chamber. They both stared at it in silence.

Duval felt the hair on the back of his neck stand up. It was the biggest emerald he had ever seen. 'That can't be real,' he said. Why would Edmée have it? Another, more worrying thought came to him. *Who had she stolen it from?*

'Ah,' Mr Weinrich said, examining it carefully. He put it under a magnifying glass. 'Beautiful. Such fine craftsmanship – you don't see that often.'

Duval felt sick. 'Is it real?' he asked.

'No, it is a fake – an excellent fake.'

'Of what?' said Duval, fearing he knew the answer.

'Of an emerald called the Eye of Envy.'

'That emerald belongs to the Marquis de Soule.'

'It does,' said Mr Weinrich. 'There is a story that goes with this emerald – whoever owns it is sent mad with envy, certain that their lover will be unfaithful. This one is very valuable, for the simple reason the marquis has offered to pay two thousand pounds to whoever returns it to him. It's a goodly sum, but nothing compared to the value of the original.'

'How much is the original worth?'

'I would say, just under one million pounds.'

Duval was staggered at the sum. 'A million?' he repeated.

'Maybe more. And there really is little difference between the two. Only an expert eye can tell that one is a gem, the other a stone made into a gem.' Mr Weinrich put the fake emerald back into the bag and closed the spine. 'You just press. It locks only once – cannot be relocked. It was a way of showing whether the book had been tampered with.'

'Do you know why there would be such a reward on this fake gemstone?'

'No. But the marquis is an… unusual man.'

*

Duval walked back to St James's Square. Mr Weinrich's words echoed in his head. *One is a gem, the other a stone made into a gem.*

He was determined to go and see the marquis, but knew that first he must go home and send Quinn a message with his best footman, telling him what he had found out from Mr Weinrich. He had just arrived when Granger came to tell him that Mrs Gosling was there. 'She wouldn't listen when I told her you were not at home. I sent her up to the drawing room.'

'It's not like you to let in an unwanted visitor,' said Duval.

'I know, sir.'

Reluctantly, Duval went upstairs.

The chief was waiting for Quinn that morning when he arrived at Bow Street. He was wearing a serious expression.

'Good day, sir,' said Quinn.

'Is it?' said the chief. 'I haven't noticed.'

Quinn said, 'I need warrants for a Mr Ralph Carson and Mr Veldt. There is strong evidence to prove they are involved in the kidnap of Lady Harlington.'

'No,' said the chief. 'Will not happen. The Alien Office is closing the case.'

'Has Lady Harlington been found?' asked Quinn, trying to keep the sudden panic from his voice.

'No,' said the chief.

'Then why close the investigation?'

'Because a lady of her description was seen boarding a ship for France last night. Don't be too harsh on yourself, Quinn. The case was closed this morning, and as far as the Alien Office is concerned, she left of her own free will. It was all planned.'

'Wait, sir,' said Quinn. 'Where is the evidence? This lady could have been anyone.'

'The case, as I said, is closed.'

Quinn tried to stay calm. 'You must read my report, sir,' he said.

'I haven't time, Quinn. There was a near riot yesterday in Whitechapel – the usual problems – but those in power, being jumpier than a bag full of frogs, wanted all such disturbance quashed. And you expect me to sit down all cosy, feet warming by the fire, and read a bleeding report into rich sods who have more money than sense?'

'So, you're doing nothing? Please, I insist you read my report,' Quinn said firmly.

'I'm sorry, Quinn,' replied the chief, 'but, for the third time, the case is closed.'

'Does Lord Harlington know?'

'No, not yet. The Alien Office will be in touch with him.'

Quinn picked up his hat and put it on. Without another word, he walked away.

'Where are you going?'

'To find Lady Harlington.'

Fog on the Thames

Quinn was now on his own, with only Duval's footman to run messages. He didn't even have the luxury of having the Runners to help him. He had been down to the dock before going to Bow Street, but no clipper from Woodbridge had arrived. When he went back again the boat had docked, but the captain swore he had never seen or heard of a Mr Carson. Quinn's next stop was Sailor Town, to see if he could pin down Veldt. He was stopped from taking a ferry by one of Duval's footmen, who handed him a note. He read it, then wrote back.

Don't go to the marquis until I return.

Only when he was in the boat did he remember he should have written that the Alien Office had closed the case. 'Tell Duval,' Quinn, shouted, 'that whatever he hears about Lady Harlington he is not to believe. The Alien Office have closed the case, but they are going on false information.' And with that he left.

The ferryman who rowed Quinn was full of talk.

'Read about the vanishing lady?'

Quinn nodded, not listening, annoyed that the Thames had become so choppy. He doubted now that he would be back in time to meet Lord Harlington.

He wished he felt calmer. The trick would be to catch Veldt out – but how? He read Duval's detailed note about the book: it had contained an emerald – a fake. The real gem was known as the Eye of Envy.

Quinn was too tired to make sense of what Duval had told him. Why and how had Edmée come to be in possession of the fake gemstone? Did she know that was what the book contained? He thought of what Madame Dupont had said. And there was still a piece of the puzzle missing. A fake emerald... but was it a big enough maggot with which to catch a pike...?

'Fog,' said the ferryman. 'Slows things down.'

At last, they arrived.

'Do you want me to wait?'

'No,' said Quinn as he paid. He couldn't take any more of the ferryman's chatter.

By the entrance to Sailor Town, a drunken woman was slumped on the ground. A man was trying to pull her to her feet. Quinn was surrounded by barefoot children, dogs, and any other creature short of a bob or two, all longing for shelter and seeing each stranger as an opportunity. This was not a place to which a Bow Street man would willingly come. And for the second time in three days, Quinn wondered what the hell Veldt was doing working here while claiming to be on the right side of the law.

Down the dark alleyway he went, until he came to The Cocked Hat. He had already convinced himself that Veldt had cleared out and this journey had been a wasted venture.

He certainly hadn't expected to see his old colleague seated exactly where he had been last, on his dais, overlooking his customers. The only difference was that now he wasn't dressed as a sea captain.

'Sold your ship, then?' said Quinn.

Veldt turned a distrustful eye on him, and Quinn wondered if he had perhaps misjudged the man. Could he be losing his abilities? But then Veldt started to talk.

'Back again, I see,' said Veldt cheerfully. 'Still no luck finding Lady Harlington?'

'No, I haven't found her yet,' said Quinn.

'I have heard she took a ship to France,' said Veldt.

'How do you know that?' said Quinn.

'I have my sources.'

'Sauce for sausages,' said Quinn. 'I don't think anyone knows that for certain.'

Veldt backtracked, eager to change the subject. 'Or perhaps she is under your bleeding nose, if you knew where your nose was.'

'I don't follow you,' said Quinn.

'Because, half-wit, you've been dining with the devil, who *does* know where she is. Lord Harlington – he's the one you should be investigating, rather than wasting your time down here in Sailor Town.'

Quinn listened to Veldt, and the idea that had begun to form on his journey now emerged with startling clarity. 'No, I don't think he has her, but what I heard was that she had stolen an emerald from the Marquis de Soule – the Eye of Envy. It is believed to have been brought over to England by Mrs Hyde – now known as Lady Harlington – but no one knows where it is. If Mr Hyde had found it, he would have sold it, but I've been through all my connections in Bond Street and it hasn't turned up.' With no reaction from

Veldt, he changed direction. 'Mr Weinrich, who deals with the marquis's gemstones, says the Eye of Envy has gone missing.'

'Lady Harlington could have sold it,' said Veldt, suddenly more interested.

'I don't think so. It's worth around a million pounds,' said Quinn, trying his best to look foolish. 'It is more than likely hidden somewhere.'

He watched Veldt's greedy eyes nearly pop out of their sockets.

'Do you know, Veldt,' said Quinn, 'I think that last case did me in. I don't feel I'm up to this, and quite honestly, I'm not sure I really give a damn about rich folk anyway. Bow Street and the Alien Office have closed the case; they want nothing more to do with it.'

'Have a chair,' said Veldt, changing his tune. 'Let me get you a beer; you do look a bit peaky. Did you get into the parsonage at Witchling?'

'No,' said Quinn, 'maybe I should have done. I know what you're thinking – I'm not as bright as I used to be – and you might well be right. But still, I can't see someone just giving away a million-pound emerald, can you?'

'No, no, I can't,' said Veldt. 'You sure it's worth that much?'

'It could be worth more,' said Quinn. 'Anyway, that's all I know. You haven't heard anyone talk about it in Sailor Town, have you?'

'No,' said Veldt.

A beer was placed before Quinn by a young lad. One of the more inebriated customers came up to Veldt.

'I heard,' he said, slurring his words, 'that you'll be leaving us. This place won't be the same without you.'

'Not now,' said Veldt.

The man wobbled away.

'Where are you going?' asked Quinn.

'Taking a tour,' said Veldt.

Quinn took his time drinking his beer, watching Veldt get more and more impatient. Finally, he stood up. 'That's the end of this case, as far as I am concerned,' he said. 'I am going to Covent Garden to ask Fleur to marry me. I thank you for the beer. I wish you safe travels.'

Vanishing Lady

Veldt had a lad follow Quinn to make sure he was not hanging around. He waited until the lad came back.

'He's gone.'

'Are you sure?'

'Yes, I watched the waterman ferry him away.'

'Good. You go and get the carriage. Tell the coachman to be quick about it,' said Veldt. He went out of the tavern and up the stairs of the chandler's shop to the storeroom, where Edmée was tied up and gagged.

He took the gag out of her mouth. 'Scream and you are dead. Come on, wake up. You need to tell me about this emerald.'

He now regretted giving her so much laudanum.

Edmée said quietly, 'Emerald?' Her eyes closed once more.

'Where is it?'

'Where's what?'

'The emerald – wake up, woman. Where's the emerald, the Eye of Envy?'

Edmée was battling to think. 'Wake up' – the words a drum in her head, as she tried to fathom what he was talking about. How would Veldt know about the Eye of Envy? He wouldn't, so who told him?

'Where is it?' he asked again.

His breath was so foul that it acted like smelling salts on her.

Desperately she tried to think, before her mind disappeared back towards sleep again. She mumbled, 'The parsonage.'

He smirked. 'And you think I believe that? If you had such an emerald, why didn't you take it with you? You could have sold it. Come on – speak.' He shook her.

If only her eyelids would stay open, if the room would just stop spinning. She couldn't make her brain work. Then out of the haze, she grabbed at the only thing that made sense to her.

'St-stolen... would have been stolen from me.' She felt as if she was on a rolling sea, with all the words and thoughts swimming away from her. 'C-can't sell...'

Veldt let go of her and she closed her eyes, as sleep overtook her.

Veldt walked back and forth, the wooden floorboards creaking under his weight. He knew there wasn't much time. He couldn't leave her here. If she was telling the truth, the gem would be fair payment, especially if Carson failed him. He opened her mouth to pour in more laudanum and she swallowed it. He gagged her again and went down the stairs and back into the tavern.

'The carriage is ready, the horses a little on the old side,' said the lad.

'Then you better tell the coachman that, if he wants to keep the fingers with which to hold the reins, he better find me good horses and fast.'

'Yes,' said the lad. 'And there's a man asking to see you.'

'Who? Not Quinn back again?'

'No, he left, like I said. Him.' The lad pointed to the unmistakable figure of Ralph Carson.

Veldt quickly looked around to see if anyone had noticed the arrival of this overdressed stuffed turkey. He was relieved to find that none of his sharper-eyed customers were yet in for their evening ale.

'What are you doing?' asked Veldt, holding tightly to Carson's arm. 'I told you – you were to stay at Monkton Manor.'

Carson was out of breath and looked frightened.

'I came to tell you we are in trouble.'

'No,' said Veldt. '*I'm* not in trouble, but *you* might be. What's happened?'

'My sister.' Carson spoke too loudly.

'Shut up,' said Veldt and, still holding his arm, manoeuvred him into the room at the back of the tavern, closed the door and locked it, before putting the key in his waistcoat pocket. The room was full of sacks and barrels; it had a window and a door that led outside to a small raft.

'Keep your voice down,' he said.

'Quinn took Sarah,' said Carson. 'The runner told the captain of the ship I was on that she had told him everything… We will be discovered.'

Veldt felt a quiet rage come over him and went quite still. If Mr Carson had known him better, he would have realized this was a worrying sign.

'All you had to do,' Veldt said under his breath, 'was keep your sister under control. But you couldn't even manage that. And now you're here, when you should be waiting for me in Witchling. We have a ship to catch at Felixstowe.'

Carson, who had been certain he had done the right thing by coming to warn Veldt, was now less sure.

'Quinn will come and arrest us,' said Carson. 'We have to get rid of the French bitch.'

'Then what?' said Veldt. 'We pretend none of this ever happened? And where's my money?'

'What?' said Carson.

'You heard me. We had an arrangement. I put myself to trouble and expense – for which, I was told, I'd be well rewarded. But there was no evidence to prove she had killed Mr Hyde because Miss Weeks, her servant, and that bloody housekeeper all swore they had seen her being beaten by Hyde, and the conniving Windfucker of a housekeeper would've given evidence that the French bitch was tied all the time to the bed. We went through this, remember? That's why we didn't accuse Edmée in my report. We didn't want to draw attention to her innocence. So, I helped you come up with a better plan. All we had to do was show that she had left of her own free will, and it worked, simple as licking cream off a spoon. Then you could inherit the lot and pay me my 25 per cent of your inheritance, but oh no, you had to ruin it all by coming here and saying... what? That there's no money?'

'I'm sorry,' said Carson, 'but the plan hasn't worked.'

'I suggest, then, you pay me – and fast – to avoid any more misunderstandings.'

'I can't,' said Carson. 'I have nothing.' He pulled off his wig as if a bald head would emphasize the point. 'Believe me, there's nothing I can do. I'm sorry.'

'Sorry, sorry, sorry,' repeated Veldt. 'You sound like your sister. And I'm supposed to be satisfied with sorry? How much is a sorry worth? What am I to buy with this putrid sorry of yours? You tell me, you miserable little shit. Lady Harlington is perhaps the most wanted woman in this land. So, what do you think we should do with her?'

'Push her into the river,' suggested Carson.

'You want me to do that?' asked Veldt. 'Or will you?'

'I'm not very good at pushing,' said Carson.

'Imbecile,' said Veldt.

He wrenched open the back door. A lighter was moored to the raft. The tide was high, and a fog was rolling in.

Veldt pulled him outside. 'How did you get here?' he asked, shutting the door with a quiet click.

'I thought it would be wiser to travel by clipper from Woodbridge. The weather was bad, and I was rather sick.'

'And who knows you're here?'

'Only the sailors and the captain of the clipper who you said were friends of yours, and the waterman who brought me to Sailor Town,' said Carson, beginning to shiver.

'Take off your rings,' said Veldt.

'They won't come off,' said Carson. He was suddenly frightened, and moved back towards the door, trying to pull it open, finding it locked.

'Let me help then. Give me your hand.'

'No, no, I can do it,' said Carson. 'Listen, Veldt, if you give me a little longer, I will have the money. The only trouble is, if Sarah talks, then we will be arrested…' Carson paused. 'And I made a mistake.'

'You made a fucking mistake?' said Veldt.

'Should we go back inside?' suggested Carson, desperately trying to open the door. 'I'm getting wet out here.'

'Oh dear, you poor little man. What mistake did you make?'

'I don't think it matters. I'm sure it won't be discovered.'

'What mistake?' said Veldt, his patience all but exhausted.

'The note Sarah delivered to the dressmaker, saying that, if the French bitch didn't do as we asked, we would kill Lord Harlington. It was written, as we agreed, in capitals. But we…'

Veldt gave Carson a stony stare. 'It's always "we", isn't it; you don't do a bloody thing. You sit in your clouts and hope someone wipes your arse for you. You're pathetic. Well, you're on your own this time. It's your handwriting, and your note. You've just signed your own death warrant.'

'No, no – surely, she would have destroyed the note. It won't have been found. It doesn't signify.'

'Why did I ever bloody believe you?' said Veldt. 'Why did I ever think this was a good idea?'

'All we have to do is get rid of Harlington's wife and it all might come right.'

'Do you know what you are? A spoiled little idiot. You lost your mind over that inheritance. You thought you were just two days and seven hours away from owning everything.'

'It's mine by rights, and if I go down, so will you. Don't think I won't tell everything,' said Carson. 'Old Lord Harlington's will—'

'I'm not going to be sent to the gallows by a little shit like you.'

Carson felt a punch in his ribs. He put his hand to his side, stared at his palm in disbelief. It was damp and bloody. 'What have you done?' he asked and stumbled backwards towards the river. He missed his footing, hit his head on the edge of the lighter, and, with eyes wide open, fell with a loud splash into the foggy grey waters of the Thames. No ship, no ferryman sober enough saw him. Only one bargeman out on the river was there to witness the end of Mr Ralph Carson's unremarkable life, and he promptly reported it to a constable.

Veldt put away his knife and went back into the tavern.

The lad was waiting for him. 'Who was that dandy?' he asked.

'What dandy?' said Veldt.

'That short, chubby man.'

'Nobody you ever saw,' said Veldt.

'Never saw no one, Mr Veldt,' said the lad. 'The carriage is ready for you, and the coachman has better horses.'

'Tell him to wait,' said Veldt. Then he went out of the tavern and back to the upstairs room, where Edmée was held.

'Get up,' he said. He was still unsure as to whether to believe the emerald story. She was struggling to keep her eyes open. Damn it, he'd given her too much laudanum again.

'If you're lying—'

She murmured inaudibly.

He looked at her. It might be simpler if he ended it here and now, sent her the same way as Carson. After all, he had his escape route. But not the money he wanted. He pulled her to her feet, then made his decision. He knew what he was going to do. It was a gamble, but hadn't he been right so far? He still had possession of his good instincts. Yes, he decided. He would take her to Witchling. Then, if she was lying, he would do away with her somewhere near Rendlesham Forest, and catch the ship to the New World.

Quinn was walking back towards Sailor Town, the fog thick down by the river, when out of it came two horses, eyes wild, being urged on at unruly speed. Quinn threw himself out of the way, certain he'd caught a glimpse of Veldt and a woman, but of that he couldn't be sure. He picked himself up and dusted himself down. He was about to set off in the direction the carriage was going, when through the fog, he caught sight of the boy from the pub. Quinn sprinted after him. Down by the river, the fog was impenetrable, and the boy appeared to have all but vanished. Quinn stopped, then smiled – an old trick, one he himself had employed as a lad. He found the boy crouched at the bottom of the river steps. He tried to dart past Quinn and failed.

'Where were they going?' Quinn asked.

'He'll kill me if I tell.'

'I will arrest you if you don't.'

'Witch something or other,' said the boy, shaking with fright, 'and then to catch a ship.'

'Did he have a woman with him?'

'I couldn't say,' said the boy, now fighting to free himself and finding he couldn't. Finally defeated, he said, 'Yes'. Quinn still had hold of the lad as he took from his pocket two shillings. 'Here,' he said. 'Go on, off with yourself.'

All Quinn had to do was hire a horse and follow them. But then he heard a whistle being blown, then another. Out of the fog came one of his colleagues, a Bow Street Runner.

'Quinn,' he shouted, 'there's been a murder up near Sailor Town.'

Quinn's heart nearly stopped. 'No,' he said. 'Man or woman?'

'Think it's a woman, not sure.'

'Oh Lord, *no*,' said Quinn. If they had killed Lady Harlington, he'd never forgive himself, for he was certain he knew where she was. He shouldn't have left Veldt's pub.

The fog sat heavy now on top of the water as they went once more upriver, stopping short of Sailor Town. Never in all his long time serving as a Runner had he ever been more pleased to see the murdered body was the unmistakable corpse of a man, and a Mr Carson at that.

But now he knew where Veldt was heading and, he was positive, he had Lady Harlington in tow. He asked the sergeant who had just arrived to tell the chief that he had had to go after Veldt.

'No,' said the sergeant. 'Not happening, not again. I have my orders. You are to go nowhere, unless you want to lose your job. You may think you're above us all, Quinn, but this is now a murder inquiry. I mean it,' said the sergeant. 'One step…'

*

Upstairs in the drawing room of the house at St James's Square, Arabella was walking back and forth. The minute she saw Duval she threw herself at him.

'Oh, thank God you're here,' she said. 'I don't know what to do. I'm broken. You've heard, of course, about Philip and the baby. It's a boy; he has always wanted a boy. Everyone wants a boy. If Fanny had been a boy, then he'd have stayed with me. You must help me. I saved you from scandal, and now you can save me. See, it works in harmony.'

Duval looked at her and thought to himself, *The last thing I need today is Arabella Gosling.* It occurred to him, the last thing he had needed all along had been Arabella Gosling.

She said, 'You must tell Philip that you want him to divorce me because you are going to marry me, and that will make everything right.'

Duval decided it was best to remain silent, hoping she would eventually run out of steam. There was no one who didn't come under her attack: Mrs Dent for being sanctimonious, Arnold for being so will-o'-the-wisp. Not one person in her circle of friends was excused from blame for her husband leaving her.

Finally, when she ground to a halt, Duval said, 'You have not once asked if Edmée has been found.'

'Oh, that's yesterday's news. You have been usurped by Philip having a baby.'

'You talk about nothing and have absolutely no idea what happens outside your own foolish circle.'

Arabella looked at him, shocked. 'But nothing *does* happen outside our circle. This is our world; this is all that matters.'

'No,' said Duval. 'This is where we disagree. We always did. I just managed to momentarily forget that. Go home, Arabella.'

'No, no,' she said. 'You care for me. I know you do. I can't go home in this state. I look awful. I need another brandy.' She had already had half the brandy in the decanter.

Duval wondered how he might rid himself of her. There was still not a word from Quinn.

Outside, the horses clopped past. A street vendor could be heard shouting, and among the other street criers, one voice made his blood run cold: 'Read all about it! Lady Harlington seen leaving London docks for France! Vanishing lady reappears to disappear once again!'

Arabella, hearing the news, dried her eyes, sniffed loudly, and said, 'Well, I'm glad she's gone. Now you have no excuse not to stand by me.'

Duval rang for Granger. 'Escort Mrs Gosling out, please,' he said, his voice icy cold.

'You see, after all that,' said Arabella, standing far away from the door in the hope that she would not be dragged out, 'she didn't even love you. All this drama for nothing.'

'Arabella,' said Duval, I'd like you to leave now, please. Go home and look after your daughter.'

'I, at least, could give you a son, which is more than Lady Harlington could. I hear she can have no more babies after Samuel Hyde.' She dried her eyes, pulled down her veil, a wicked smile passing her lips. 'Shall I tell you a secret about your beloved wife? I looked through Philip's papers – the silly man left them behind in his haste – and I found a line of payments to a Madame Rouchette, paid by the Marquis de Soule.' She started to laugh.' Do you know what her role was?'

Duval said nothing.

'She was Edmée's keeper. Your wife – your beloved wife – was the Marquis de Soule's whore. You may have survived the ridiculous scandal so far, but this one will be the end of you. You will be ruined. Your servants will leave. You will be disgraced. And all for a *cheap whore*,' she spat.

'Goodbye.' said Duval 'We will not meet again. Granger, please show Mrs Gosling out now.'

'My Lord, there is a crowd at the front of the house.'

'Then be kind enough to take her through the servants' quarters.'

'No,' said Arabella. 'I will leave by the front door.' Her voice was drowned out by the news-sellers. *Read all about it! Lady Harlington returns to France!*

Mrs Gosling stood on the front step of Duval's house in St James's Square. She described Lady Harlington to the many reporters gathered there as nothing more than a common trollope, and hinted at her being a lady of the night.

'What did Lord Harlington expect from a wife sale?' she said. 'That he would have bought himself a marquess?'

There was nothing Granger could do to stop her. And there was yet more bad news to deliver.

With a heavy heart it was Jameson who returned to the drawing room. Duval was standing with his back towards him.

'I am sorry to inform you, my lord, that a gentleman from Bow Street came to say that Quinn had been taken off the case. He is now dealing with a murder up in Sailor Town.'

His lordship's left hand, with the signet ring on his smallest finger, held tight to the chair in front of him.

'Man or woman?' he asked.

'It's a man, my lord.'

The hand relaxed.

'May I speak, my lord?'

'Yes, of course you may.'

'Lady Harlington was one of the kindest women I have met. I don't believe she would have willingly gone to back to

France. Mrs Gosling had no right to speak of her like that. None of your servants will be leaving you, I assure you.'

Slowly Duval turned to face his valet, who was in tears.

'Thank you,' said Duval. 'I am going out. When Quinn arrives, tell him to wait for me.'

'Can I tell him where you are going?'

'To see the Marquis de Soule.'

The Portrait

Duval reached Marylebone at about half past six. The Marquis de Soule's house was one of the most opulent in that part of London. The wrought-iron gates were open. Duval rang the bell, and a footman answered the grand door.

'I am here to see Monsieur le Marquis. I am Lord Harlington,' Duval said. 'I want to see Monsieur le Marquis,' he repeated, refusing to let himself think about what he was going to do, what he was going to say.

The footman showed Duval into one of the most magnificent drawing rooms he had ever seen. The tall windows, their shutters open, looked out onto a garden that was half lost in fog. He could well believe he was back in Paris. He turned to take in the rest of the chamber; the doors dividing this room from the next had been folded back. The fire was lit in the adjoining chamber, making it an enticing scene. On the mantelpiece was a vase of white roses, and hanging above it, lit by candles on either side, was a painting. Drawn to the fire, Duval stopped, glanced up, and immediately felt as if he had been hit hard in the heart. He closed his eyes, then looked again. He was staring at Edmée. A younger Edmée, her spirit shining through, in her eyes a look of defiance. He thought that the room had begun to spin. The walls were closing in on him and he steadied himself against the mantelpiece.

Duval had no idea how long he had been staring at the painting. He thought on what Mr Weinrich had said. *Only an expert eye can tell that one is a gem, the other a stone made into a gem.*

The voice behind him was gentle. 'This masterpiece is a portrait of my wife.'

'Wife?' Duval whispered. He didn't trust himself to turn round.

'I realized the moment I entered the salon at Muchmore... It is hard enough for...' The marquis stopped and cleared his throat. 'I was expecting you.'

'Is she here?' said Duval.

'No,' said the marquis. 'I take it she hasn't been found.'

'No,' said Duval.

'You bought her for ten guineas,' said the marquis. 'I didn't know such a thing could happen in this country.'

'How old was she?' Duval said at last.

'How old was she when...?' said the marquis.

'When you married her.'

'She was twelve. She climbed into my garden, looking for the lion I was supposed to keep there. I thought she was a boy. No one had ever spoken to me so fearlessly.

'Monsieur Simoneau, the bookbinder, was her father. I offered him an emerald for her. He rightly said it wasn't enough. Simoneau was worried the arrangement wouldn't last long and that she would be returned to him. Albertine, that is her real name, Albertine, was *un garçon manqué*, a hoyden – his words, not mine. She had grown up without a mother, behaving as a boy. He said that he would only let her go if I married her; he knew that alone would give her status. I liked farce and, never having been married, I thought, why not? It was the first time she had dressed as a girl. She was more interested in what she was wearing than in the vows. She told me they were silly, with which I agreed. Immediately afterwards, I put her in the paid care of Madame Rouchette, to bring her on and teach her how a lady should behave in high society.

'Albertine took to her new life in the salons of Paris. She learned quickly. When she was fourteen, I thought I should see my wife again for myself. I was about to have the marriage annulled, but I invited her to dine. Far from obliterating the spark that had so entertained me, Madame Rouchette had polished and perfected the gem. Albertine truly became my wife that night.

'I indulged her in every way. I dressed her in the finest clothes. I bedecked her in jewels. There was still a wildness to her, a wickedness I relished. To my surprise, I could hardly bear to be apart from her. What I found intolerable were the attentions paid to her by other, younger men. She grew more enticing, more desirable. I believed myself to be a master at understanding human emotions, but I was blinded by her. Every man who smiled at her, who caught her eye, would cause the green-eyed monster to dance in me. *She would be unfaithful*, I told myself, *her devotion to me would fade* – ironic that I should have bought her with an emerald known as the Eye of Envy. Perhaps it *was* cursed; perhaps *I* was cursed. Then in all the chaos of the September Massacres we became separated. News reached me that Albertine and her father had been murdered. It broke my heart.'

'You were *ma puce*,' said Duval.

'Yes,' he said. 'I was. Albertine came to me early in the morning at Muchmore House, before I left, to ask for a divorce. But I am now a devout Roman Catholic, so I am afraid I had to say no.

'She will come back to me. It is her duty as a wife to do so. I understand it was a shock for her to see me again, believing, as she did, that I was dead – just as it was a shock for me to see her too. Perhaps that is why she ran away. But once she has had time to think about it, Albertine will return to me. I know she will.'

Duval stared again at the painting. 'You tricked her father, and instead of giving him the Eye of Envy, you bought her with a stone, an imitation, a worthless piece of glass. Your dishonesty cursed you, not the Eye of Envy. Edmée was a child, and you stole her childhood from her. For what? For your vanity, for your entertainment. You are no better than a thief. She will never be yours again. Never. And no god of any religion will ever forgive you.'

Duval turned and walked out of the house.

All Her Days

'Love,' said Veldt. 'That's what does a man in, makes him weak in the head.' The carriage he had hired had one merit as far as Edmée could see – it wasn't fast.

She had long given up trying to concentrate after many hours of Veldt's unsolicited rants, all of which illustrated how such a man had ended up alone and embittered. His main gripe was against a Bow Street Runner called Quinn.

'Lapped it up like milk, he did,' said Veldt. 'One look at me sitting there, and Quinn thought to himself, *Veldt isn't going anywhere*. The trouble is he don't really appreciate how bloody clever I've been. I suspected you would be in love with Lord Duval. You see, your fate was sealed when I heard about the ball. I thought, a man of his position don't go giving balls and inviting all the toffs unless he wants to show off his new wife. After Hyde, I reckoned you must have thought you'd found heaven with him. I gambled that only love would make you put your life on the line. Love – far more precious than a bullet. It'll be one of my unsung achievements. Do you know what's sad about Quinn? He was so bloody close. I would like to tell him that, yes, but I won't, because by then, I will be living the life I've always wanted. That's if you're not lying…'

And on Veldt went. The more he talked, the more Edmée was sure of one thing: he was not going to let her go. Her only hope of escape lay in raising the alarm on the journey. But Veldt had that covered. He wasn't going to let her out of his sight.

'If you need a piss,' he said, 'I'll have to come with you, and if I need a piss, you'll have to come with me.'

There were no lights; they were surrounded by a thick, soupy, starless night, as if they were travelling on the rim of the world. She wondered where Duval was and what he was doing. Had he found out the truth about her? She shivered. And what would he make of it when he knew?

Edmée lay back and thought that she was destined to be alone. She remembered the day she had been abandoned in Paris. She tried to remember all her days there. But one night and one day, only, came back to her.

She and the marquis had been dressed in all their finery; he was determined they should be defiant against the Revolution. The news on the street, that night of the 1st of September, was frightening. Still, the marquis, undaunted, had refused to allow the ravings of a mob to upset his plans. They had been out to dinner that evening. Several officers were present. One, a particularly striking young man, had paid her many compliments over the course of the meal. He had been charming and attentive. She hadn't been paying as much attention to the marquis as perhaps she should have. Halfway through the meal, he had stood up and said abruptly that they were leaving. They had returned home in silence.

'What is wrong?' she had asked him at last.

'You flirted with that officer. You are supposed to be *my* wife.' His rage had ignited. Edmée had no fear of him, but was fascinated by this outburst of anger that echoed what she saw happening on the streets.

'You are worth nothing,' he finally said. 'You are nothing to me. Do you really think I would have bought you with the most precious of all my gems? No. Your father couldn't tell the difference, stupid man. I bought you with a stone made to look like an emerald – a bride stone worth a few pathetic denier.'

'A bride stone,' she repeated, stunned.

'I could give you everything, but I do not believe you love me. Do you…?' he had asked, his words filled with desperation.

She said nothing.

He made love to her that night, and held her in his arms. 'I have loved many women,' he said, 'but not as I love you.' She had been on the cusp of sleep when she realized he was crying. She had never seen him cry before.

She relit a candle.

He kissed her. 'Forgive me,' he said. 'Forgive me. Tomorrow, I will put it right.'

She had slept deeply with what the marquis called the luxury of youth, and had woken to none of the usual sounds that the great house made in the morning. Neither could she hear the marquis getting ready for his day – he took cleanliness for a religion.

She had lain there, still sleepy, wondering why she couldn't hear the chatter of the hairdressers waiting to attend to him, and found herself suddenly wide awake. '*Ma puce*,' she had called. '*Ma puce*!'

No maid came at the sound of her call. The house was eerily quiet. She got up and went into his antechamber, calling all the while, '*Ma puce*!' He wasn't there; neither were any of his servants. She began to run from room to room, panic overtaking all rationale, until a window was broken by a stone and it dawned on her he had left her there all alone.

With great presence of mind, she had gone to the servants' quarters – they too were deserted. She went into the library to where he kept his gemstones – all gone. Knowing now, for sure, that she had been left alone, calmness overcame her. She found a maid's costume, washed and dressed herself, all the while the mob calling for the whore marquise. She thought it must mean he hadn't managed to escape. As she was about to go out the servants' door, she saw her shoes had a red heel – the symbol of aristocracy. Shaking them off, she searched for something plain to wear and found a simple pair of boots. She left her wedding ring behind and, to the sound of breaking glass and the baying of a bloodlust crowd, she escaped onto the street and into a living nightmare, a hell she could not have imagined.

The sights she saw terrified her. A tumbril went past, with butchered human remains dripping blood and entrails, then came a woman, holding a man's head on a pike. The air stank of iron and terror, and a river of blood ran down the rue Jacob towards the Seine. She heard the mob baying for the Marquis de Soule and his whore of a wife. Maybe he had escaped after all. She stayed close to the buildings, following the crowd, all calling for murder.

The only place she knew to go was to her father's workshop, which she had lived above as a child.

The door was swinging on it hinges. Once inside, she pushed it shut as best she could and bolted it. The place looked like a mausoleum, or the scene of a crime. The glass-fronted bookcases were broken, papers were scattered on the floor, and it seemed as if the workshop had been left in a frantic hurry. She stood quietly and listened.

'Papa,' she said into the darkness. Nothing. Not a sound.

Her father's tools lay in the racks, the fine leather he used, stiff as if with rigor mortis, hung on lines across the room. She could hear the mob outside, pikes and knives sparking against the brick of the building, the noise like a thousand drums of thunder, mingling with the wail of human madness.

Quickly, knowing there was not much time, she searched for the book, the one in which her father kept what he had believed to be an emerald worth a million louis – the Eye of Envy. A fake, she now knew, but it was all she had. If it had been enough to convince her father, perhaps that would be enough to save her.

There was a sound. She stopped. *A rat*, she thought, and then she saw him in the corner of the workshop – petrified, shaking, and holding the book she was looking for.

'Who are you?' she asked.

'I'm an Englishman,' he said, his voice trembling with fear. 'I'm not French.'

She took the book from him.

'And you… you are?' he asked, stammering. Then, not waiting for her reply, 'I will not get out of here alive,' he said, weeping.

'Break it down!' shouted a man outside.

'No one's there, citizen,' said another. 'The bookbinder was one of the first to be slaughtered.'

'I'm…' She hesitated, then dropped her first name, left her married name behind and took her mother's maiden name. 'I'm Edmée Sartine. We must leave, before they come back.'

The shop door rattled again. 'I have papers,' he whispered. 'They guarantee me safe passage to England.'

'Can I come with you?' she asked.

He paused, before he said, 'It would only be possible if you were my wife.'

She knew he wanted her. His tongue came out of his mouth as he spoke, as if trying to prevent the words from leaving a stain on his lips.

And she, a fish in hardly any water and desperate to breathe, said, 'Yes.'

He had insisted on taking some of her father's books. Books of a certain kind, she discovered later, were his only true love in life.

Samuel Hyde bribed an official and they were married amid all that death, and she became plain Edmée Hyde. She told herself the marriage was irrelevant. She had seen Mr Hyde as a way out of Paris and thought no further than her escape.

Her mind drifted back to the carriage where Veldt had fallen asleep, though any movement from Edmée brought him suddenly wide awake, his small ferret-like eyes missing nothing. The carriage drove all night.

At dawn, the light broke, and a sea of yellow sky appeared larger than the land through which they were moving. *Dear Lord*, she thought, *if I survive this, I promise to tell Duval the truth. That's if he will ever want to see me again. There will be no more secrets.*

Miss Weeks

It was nearing eleven o'clock when the old-fashioned carriage arrived at the parsonage in Witchling. Veldt, bone-stiff, climbed out and ordered the driver and postilions to wait. It wouldn't take long.

'What day is it?' asked Edmée, still battling to stay awake.

'Tuesday,' said Veldt. 'What does it matter?'

It was, she thought, a day when little happened in the village. Her only hope was that the carriage might attract some attention.

Veldt looked around and pulled Edmée out. She could hardly stand.

The horses were steaming and pawing the ground. She hoped the sound of their harnesses was louder than the church bells.

Veldt held on to her as he walked her to the back of the house, where, without letting her go, he put his shoulder to the back door. It opened easily. Inside was the narrow hallway, and Edmée felt sick as they mounted the stairs. Her only hope now was the small knife she had hidden under the floorboards.

Seeing she had paled, Veldt said sharply, 'Don't you dare faint on me. The sooner this is done, the better.' He took out his pistol. 'In case any uncalled for ideas come into your head.' He unlocked the handcuffs. 'Where is it then?'

Edmée led him to her old room, feeling bile rise in her throat. Unwanted images flashed in her mind as she pushed the bed aside. Kneeling, she lifted the loose floorboard.

'What are you waiting for?' asked Veldt.

She put her arm in deep, her hand searching among the cobwebs, the mice droppings. She felt the knife. Veldt was standing over her.

'It's not here,' she said. 'Someone has taken it.'

'Don't mess with me, bitch,' he said. 'I know what you are – a lying little thief. Look again.' He cocked his pistol and aimed it at her head.

Downstairs someone called, 'Cooey – is anyone there?'

Veldt hissed, 'Quiet.'

'Hello,' came the voice again. 'Who's up there?'

'You stay here and don't move,' said Veldt. He went to the top of the stairs, with the pistol behind his back and, looking down, saw Miss Weeks in the hall, leaning on a walking stick.

'Oh,' she said, surprised. 'Mr Veldt, what are you doing here?'

'There is no need to concern yourself. It's just a part of my investigation. Go home, Miss Weeks.' There was menace in his voice.

Edmée took off her shoes and tiptoed out of the bedchamber, holding her breath. She was almost behind Veldt, her view of Miss Weeks partly obscured. Edmée waited, with a thumping heart, for Miss Weeks to say her name, but she didn't.

Instead, she said, 'I don't think you should be here, Mr Veldt. No, I don't.'

Edmée saw Veldt was about to aim the pistol at Miss Weeks and, summoning all her courage, she stabbed the small knife into his arm. He span around, wobbled on the top step and nearly regained his balance. She pushed him with all the force she had left in her and, losing his footing, Veldt tumbled down the narrow stairs, followed by the pistol that had fallen from his grasp. He landed, dazed, on his back. Coming to himself, he looked back up the staircase and shouted, 'You fucking little witch!'

What he didn't see was Miss Weeks, who had slipped a sword out of her father's old walking stick and pinned him through his jacket to the floorboards.

'I advise you not to move,' said Miss Weeks. 'Are you hurt, Lady Harlington?'

'No,' said Edmée, as she walked slowly down the stairs.

Too late, she saw Veldt's fingers were moving. Before Miss Weeks could stop him, he wrenched his jacket free of the sword point and grabbed Edmée by the ankle, pulling her down on top of him. She fought for all she was worth to free herself. All she cared about now was preventing this man from killing Miss Weeks, and in that instant, a rage in her, a rage that she hadn't known she possessed, sparked into life. 'This is for you, Mr Hyde,' she said, as she kicked and wriggled her way free of Veldt. She reached for the pistol with a shaking hand and aimed it at Veldt. At that very moment, the front door opened, and there stood a man Edmée did not recognize.

'Quinn,' breathed Veldt, momentarily stopping at the sight of him. Then, seeing Quinn wasn't armed, he rose to his feet and rushed towards Edmée. Quinn pulled her out of the way as the gun went off. Smoke filled the hall, and there was a sound of someone falling to the ground. Miss Weeks called out, 'Edmée!'

When the smoke cleared, Veldt was face down on the floor. Miss Weeks stood there, a look of horror on her face. Her father's sword was sticking out of the middle of his back.

For a while, nobody moved, just stared transfixed at Veldt's motionless body, while a pool of blood began to stain the floor.

'Is he…?' said Miss Weeks.

Quinn bent down. 'Yes,' he said.

'I don't like swearing,' said Miss Weeks. 'It is unnecessary to use rude words. Not pleasant, not pleasant at all.'

'You are not injured?' Quinn asked Edmée.

'No, I stubbed my toe, that is all.'

'You were unbelievably brave,' he said.

'Thank you,' said Edmée. 'But without Miss Weeks, I wouldn't have survived to tell…' She was trembling violently.

Quinn, without thinking about the rights or wrongs of it, put his arms around her.

'It is the shock, that's all,' he said. 'You are safe now. I didn't introduce myself. I am Joseph Quinn, the investigator of Bow Street.'

Edmée said, 'Is Duval here?'

'No, not yet, Lady Harlington; he was delayed.'

'He is not coming,' she said, 'because he knows who I am?'

'Far from it. He should be here later,' said Quinn. 'The weather was bad in London, worse on the outskirts.'

Quinn accompanied the two women over to Miss Weeks's cottage. Once there, he instructed the maid to take care of them. He mounted his horse and rode off to inform the magistrate, Mr Beale.

The village of Witchling, which had been forgotten by time and history, found itself that Tuesday morning jolted back into the realities of the present day. The shocking news travelled fast, and even before the messenger arrived at Muchmore, Lady Harriet was being driven towards the parsonage.

Neither Miss Weeks nor Edmée was aware of any of these comings and goings. Edmée had fallen asleep in a chair and Miss Weeks had covered her with a shawl. It was the maid who answered the many knocks on the front door. Neighbours, who had never shown the slightest interest in the spinster, now came, hungry for news.

When Edmée woke, she pulled the shawl around her and said, 'Where is Lord Harlington?'

'He hasn't come here – not yet,' replied Miss Weeks, who was sitting on a packing case next to her.

Edmée looked at the shawl. 'It is beautiful – the colours in it.'

'It comes from Persia,' said Miss Weeks. 'My father and I travelled there, collecting butterflies. It has the yellow ochre of desert sands, the rose pink of sunsets, the red of passion, and it is my gift to you.'

'No, that is too kind,' said Edmée.

'Every year,' said Miss Weeks, 'I wanted to give you a present to let you know someone cared for you. You see, I saw what Mr Hyde did. I know he murdered my little dog Alfred, so I poisoned him. The world has enough bad men in it. I found the mushrooms on one of my walks and cooked some of my muffins. Nellie Moore asked me what was in them, and I told her about the special ingredient. I saw her take the plate into his study. He was a greedy man; he died after eating them all. The ghost of Alfred told me it was justice.'

Edmée, now wide awake, kissed her on the cheek. 'You saved my life,' she said. 'Not once but twice.'

'But I lost my courage after I poisoned Mr Hyde,' said Miss Weeks. 'I didn't help you as I should have. You see, I expected at any time to be arrested. Anyway, none of it matters. The church committee, in their wisdom, guided by Mrs Beale, have decided to pull down the parsonage, and my house. They are to build something more suitable for a parson and his family. As I most probably will be arrested and sent to gaol or hanged, it is of little matter.'

'No,' said Edmée, 'without you, I would be dead.'

'If not prison, then I suppose the parish workhouse.'

'No,' said Edmée again. 'Whatever happens, you won't end up there. You never married?'

'No.'

'Were you not tempted?'

'I didn't want to be a man's possession.'

'Very wise,' said Edmée. 'I was just that, to two men.'

Miss Weeks looked puzzled. 'I don't know Lord Harlington, but I wouldn't have thought that of him.'

'No,' said Edmée, 'I don't mean Duval. If love is equal on both sides, then neither can possess the other.'

'I never found that man,' said Miss Weeks. 'But it seems you have.'

Edmée held Miss Weeks's hand; both women sat silently and looked into the heart of the small fire.

The afternoon sun was beginning to wane, when there was a knock on the door.

'If that is Mrs Beale come back again, I am going to give her a piece of my mind,' said the maid, opening the front door.

'They are not at home, Mrs B—'

'I am here to see Lady Harlington.'

The maid put her hand to her mouth, and curtsied, 'Yes, my lady.'

Lady Harriet wasn't listening. Through the drawing room doorway, she saw Edmée and almost ran into the room.

'Oh, my darling girl,' she said, putting her arms about her. 'I have come to take you home.'

Then, seeing the packing case, she said, 'Miss Weeks, are you leaving this cottage? May I ask, where are you going?'

'I have been asked to leave by the parish council,' Miss Weeks explained.

'I take it that Mrs Beale is behind this,' said Lady Harriet.

'Yes.'

'There is no question about it. You are to come back with us. I will send William down with a carriage for your boxes and your maid.'

Quinn, who had left the magistrate, two constables and an undertaker at the parsonage, arrived back at Miss Weeks's cottage to witness the happy reunion of Lady Harriet and Edmée. When he entered the small drawing room, Lady Harriet asked, 'Where is Duval? Why is he not with you?'

'The fog must have delayed him,' said Quinn. 'It was thick on the outskirts of London.'

Miss Weeks stood up and said, 'Am I to be arrested?'

'Far from it,' said Quinn. 'You are both to be commended for bravery. Mr Beale, the magistrate, has agreed that statements can be taken tomorrow.'

'You will be joining us at Muchmore,' said Lady Harriet to Quinn.

'Yes, of course,' said Quinn. They all walked out to the carriage. Edmée was helped up to her seat and, once settled, was overcome by a wave of profound tiredness. Miss Weeks sat next to her.

Lady Harriet caught Quinn's arm and whispered something in his ear.

'I don't know,' he said, 'there has been no message.'

*

Later, when it was almost dark, Edmée, Lady Harriet and Quinn arrived back at Muchmore. The grand house had a sombre air to it, seeming to possess the quiet of a funeral.

Lady Harriet was anxious that Edmée should be taken upstairs to bed. Watkins was told to show Miss Weeks to the late Lord Harold's apartment in the Sanctuary to see if it was to her liking.

'I want to talk to you, Lady Harriet,' said Edmée. 'Mr Quinn, would you mind being there? I mean, here,' she said, wobbling slightly. Quinn took her arm and helped her into the drawing room. Lady Harriet ordered brandy and something to eat. 'You look half-starved,' she said, 'and that will never do.'

Edmée sat in a high-backed chair, near a roaring fire. She felt she could fall asleep for all time. The brandy and the food helped. Lady Harriet's face seem to be floating before her. She heard her say, 'I have called Dr Merritt, and he is on his way.'

'I have something to say,' said Edmée. 'I realize, Lady Harriet, that after I say this, you might afterwards ask me to leave, and I would understand it. I just would like to say that, in all innocence, I believed him to be dead. Wait, that's not what I mean… it is, and it isn't… it's just so hard to think when one is so sleepy…'

Lady Harriet interrupted her. 'I think you are going to tell me that you were the marquis's mistress before he married.'

'No,' said Edmée. 'No, no. I was going to tell you I was his lawful wedded wife. In my defence, I believed he had been murdered in the September Massacres – as was my father, a bookbinder by the name of Bernard Simoneau.'

Lady Harriet looked completely composed on hearing this news, almost as if she had expected it. She said, 'I don't think true love can be broken by the chattering of the bon ton. You know, I always suspected something of the sort. I didn't feel it was right to say so. In my humble experience, a man doesn't stumble like the marquis at the sight of an old mistress. But he does at the sight of a long-lost wife.'

Confessions

On Dr Merritt's orders, Edmée was to rest. She fell quickly into a heavy sleep and woke to find the bedchamber in candlelight. Sleepily, she made out Hannah's figure, seated in a chair by the window. Outside, it was raining. She lay there and relished the crispness of the linen sheet and the deliciousness of the soft bed.

'What time is it?' asked Edmée, reluctant to leave the land of sleep.

'Eleven o'clock, your ladyship,' said Hannah.

'I need a bath,' said Edmée.

'Shouldn't you sleep and have a bath in the morning?'

'No,' she said, 'I should get ready.'

Hannah looked baffled. 'Yes, my lady.'

Edmée lay there in the warm water. All she could think was, if she dressed and was waiting for Duval, if she faced the night, it might bring him back. Where was he? Had he disappeared – having found out about the marquis, decided to go abroad again?

In the flickering candlelight, she saw a ghost sitting where Hannah had sat.

'No more proof is needed,' said the ghost. 'I am completely satisfied that all the points in my will have been met.'

'Ashes,' she said, 'all you are is ashes.'

Hannah had brought up a light supper. Edmée ate little. *No*, she thought, *I have survived, we have survived, he will be back*.

'There is a new gown waiting for you, my lady,' said Hannah after she had finished with Edmée's hair. 'Madame Dupont said that it is all the fashion in Paris.'

It was a dusky rose colour and extraordinarily daring, made from the finest, most translucent muslin that clung to the curves of her body.

'I have never seen a dress like it,' Hannah said.

In the glass, Edmée saw a young woman who looked assured of what she wanted, of who she was. And for the first time, Edmée thought, *Yes, this is me; for better or worse, this is me*.

Hannah said, 'You look edible, my lady, like a mouthwatering sweetmeat.'

'I hope you are right,' said Edmée.

'Do you need anything else, my lady?' Hannah asked, after the supper had been cleared away.

'Perhaps something to drink, in case Lord Harlington arrives later. And biscuits.'

'I'll see it's arranged, my lady.'

Edmée jumped when there was a knock at the door.

'Is it his lordship?' she said.

'No,' said Hannah, as a footman entered bringing in two glasses and a bottle of the Viper's best champagne.

'Compliments of Lady Harriet,' he said, hardly able to

take his eyes off his mistress. 'Where would you like it, my lady?'

'Over there.' She pointed to a small side table.

When the footman had gone, Hannah said goodnight, left the room and gently closed the door behind her.

Alone, Edmée went to the dressing table. At the very back was hidden the amount she'd saved from the pin money Duval gave her. She counted out what was needed and put it into a cotton drawstring bag. This she placed next to the champagne, the biscuits and the two glasses, their two crystal rims touching.

She tried to read but couldn't. She wrapped the shawl around her for warmth and waited. She stood up and walked back and forth; she sat down, stood up again and went to the window. It was raining even harder. If Duval was on the road, he might have had an accident… She tried to quieten her racing mind, but the more she thought, the more she convinced herself that Duval would tell her that as their marriage was illegal, she should leave. He would say she had brought him nothing but scandal. She would be blamed for the loss of his estate – all of which she couldn't disagree with.

She was so wrapped up in her thoughts that she was only vaguely aware that a clock somewhere in the house had struck one. She went once more to the window, pulled back the shutter and looked out at the rain. She didn't hear the door open, but felt his presence, and spun round, the shawl falling from her shoulders. There he was, his hair wet. He stood, taking her in, a smile spreading across his face.

'You…' He paused. 'You are the dawn, the light after so much darkness.'

She went to him. He took her in his arms, and everything she was going to say was nearly forgotten.

There were tears in his eyes. 'Forgive me,' he said.

'For what?' she asked. 'It's I who have brought you nothing

but scandal.' She pulled away from him. 'Please, Duval,' she said, 'I must speak. I decided that if I survived Veldt, if I saw you again, I would tell you the truth – no more secrets, no more lies.' She spoke fast, not wanting him to interrupt. 'Do you know why I left after the ball?'

'Yes – that must have taken such courage.'

'It nearly broke me. I would rather have died than let anything befall you. I had no idea what awaited me that night, when Veldt and Carson took me. As days lost their borders with night, my mind became worn by grief at the thought I would never see you again. To me, that was a prison sentence, a living death.

'I was not born to lie, but the more I fell in love with you, the harder the truth became. I told myself there was no need to say anything when all those involved – I assumed – were dead. Ghosts couldn't rise up from the grave, could they? How mistaken was I.

'What a labyrinth is the heart, what a wretched maze. I think you already found me out in some of the lies. You have read my journal, and yet the questions you wanted to ask stayed in your eyes, never finding your sweet tongue to beg the answer with.'

'I know,' said Duval. 'I didn't want anything we had to be questioned, and in that, I am also guilty. Do you know where you were taken?'

'No, I don't remember how I got out of the maze. I woke up in a carriage. I stayed in a house, then I was moved again – how long? All time was lost to me. Veldt found out about the bride stone – that is how I persuaded him to come to Witchling.'

'You are very brave, my dove.'

'I have not yet told you the hardest part. This you might find impossible to forgive. I know Arabella thought I was one of the marquis's mistresses, if the papers are to be believed

– as she said, one of many before he married. But I was not. I am the wife of the Marquis de Soule. My name was Albertine Edmée Simoneau. My father was a bookbinder…' She was telling him information he already knew, and he was about to tell her that, but then she came to Gilbert Hyde. 'It was my idea to be sold at the wife sale. I thought someone might pay a few shillings for me, enough for me to buy a fare to London and for Gilbert to return to his regiment. All I had to do to escape was say something to Gilbert about a cat.

'When I saw you looking at me in the coffee shop, my face swollen and beaten, my hair cut short, I thought you…' She stopped. 'I thought you would be the last gentleman I would see at the wife sale. I lied when I said I was virgin. I cannot lie anymore. But if you believe me at all, believe this: I never lied about loving you. I love you, that is my whole truth. I didn't know the marquis had escaped to London. I thought his bones were buried. It was a terrible shock for me when your aunt said he was going to be here for the ball.

'I felt I had brought all this misfortune upon myself. You asked me, did it take courage? The answer is yes, but now my courage fails me,' she said, her voice wavering.

He titled her head to look up at him and said softly, 'Can you hear me?'

'Yes.'

'When I arrived back in England and was told of my father's will, I, aware of the folly of it, set off to find a wife. Now, I thank him from the bottom of my heart that he set me such a challenge, but the truth is, I bought you to save my estate.

'In La Force, I was left for nearly thirty days in solitary confinement. When I rejoined the other prisoners, I lived in the shadow of the guillotine, hearing the bell toll of the gaoler's keys, and the barking of their bloodthirsty dogs. I believed every day would be my last. To this day, I don't know who petitioned for my release; no one will tell me. On my return home to Muchmore, I was bewildered for a time, dazzled by freedom – a fool who didn't know what he wanted, until I nearly lost you. After we were married, instead of getting to know you, as I should have, I went to London, slept with a madam I knew of old, and allowed Arabella Gosling to flirt with me. I was a fool. Please forgive me, my dove.'

'There is nothing to forgive,' said Edmée. 'I thought I was going to die when I miscarried the baby, and then I heard your voice – you brought me back to life.'

'I don't know what I would have done if I had lost you,' he said, taking her into his arms. 'What shocks me is that you were married at twelve to the marquis... and at fourteen...'

'You knew that already? How...?'

'I called on the marquis – I saw your portrait. I know he refuses to grant you a divorce, because he told me. He's convinced you will return to him.'

She shook her head.

'I never told you that, when I am with you,' said Duval, 'I have everything, and more, that I ever wanted.'

'But I have lost you the estate, and that feels unforgivable,' she said.

'You didn't. I would have won the case against Carson because of the note that he sent you.'

'...What do you mean you *would have* won the case?' she asked.

'I *would have* won the case because Carson is no more. Veldt murdered Carson. That's why I was delayed. Quinn had already left – I had to identify the body.'

He kissed her, a kiss filled with passion, and she nearly forgot what she wanted to say. 'Wait, wait,' she said, 'before you undo me further, will you have a glass of champagne?'

'Thank you,' he said, letting her go. He saw she was shaking as she poured and handed him a glass. 'Are you going to tell me, after all, that you are leaving me for the marquis?'

'No! Heavens, that would be hell.'

'I'm relieved to hear it.'

She went back to the table and picked up the drawstring bag.

'This is the most important thing.'

She took a deep breath and closed her eyes.

'I have never been in love before, never known its power. My life is your life. It is one life. It is ours to be lived. I saved up your generous pin money, and in here is ten guineas. I hope it might be enough to buy a husband, though, of course, in law, and the eyes of the Church, I am still married. I know that could be a stumbling block.'

'I see no reason why that should bother me in the slightest,' said Duval.

'You don't?'

'After what we have lived through, do you really think I care about a social scandal? No. And if the marquis won't grant you a divorce, we will live like Lord Sutton and Mrs Dent.' He kissed her. 'We will relish every day we are alive, and I will love you until the end of all time. Ten guineas is a fair price. I willingly accept your offer.'

'Are you sure, *mon cheri*?'

'Yes, oh yes, my dove, I am sure.'

'You can always say something about the—'

He kissed the words from her. 'You have bought my soul, my heart, my body and my mind,' he said, looking deep into her grey-green eyes. 'You have bought yourself a ten-guinea husband. And no,' he said, lifting her off her feet and taking her to bed, 'I do not wish to say anything about the cat.'

Epilogue

The year 1800

Mrs Beale and her daughter were staying at the Hôtel de Londres, in Ostend. Jocasta had been visiting her husband, Colonel Fitzwilliam, who was on short leave before he returned to his regiment. Mrs Beale had insisted on joining her daughter, claiming that only *she* knew how to be clearly understood in any language, despite the fact that her French extended only as far as speaking English with an atrocious French accent. The waiter had given up trying to understand what Mrs Beale had to say and walked away.

'They are dreadfully rude people,' Mrs Beale announced loudly. 'They have no manners, no manners at all. In addition to impertinence, I have been subjected to frightfully greasy food and lumpy beds. Not that your husband seems at all concerned about the suffering I have had to endure.'

'Mother,' said Jocasta, who had sworn to herself this would be the last time she would ever let her mother interfere in her life again. She was on the cusp of saying exactly that when an elegant couple, impeccably dressed, entered the restaurant and were promptly given a table. The man was strikingly handsome and the woman with him could only be described as dazzling.

Jocasta remarked, 'I do believe that is Lord Harlington.'

Mrs Beale, adjusting her pince-nez, put the newspaper down and exclaimed, 'It is indeed Lord Harlington. I see he was sensible enough to find himself a new wife.'

'Please, Mother, keep your voice down,' said Jocasta. She looked again. 'No, you are wrong, I am sure that is Lady Harlington.'

'You mean the Marquise de Soule.' The pince-nez fell from Mrs Beale's face. 'So, it is her! If they're going back to Suffolk, I can assure them they will not be welcomed in Witchling society; the Church will want nothing to do with them.'

Jocasta wasn't listening. She studied the couple, rather wishing that her marriage had been even half as exciting or romantic as that of Edmée and Lord Harlington. Hers, on the other hand, had been a great disappointment. As her mother had pointed out in one of her more brutal observations, 'Colonel Fitzwilliam seems more taken with his horse than he does with you, my dear.'

She wished she could have said, 'You're wrong,' but in this instance, her mother wasn't, and it was with a feeling of great sadness that Jocasta looked at Lord Harlington and Edmée and thought, *If only my husband paid me that much attention.*

Mrs Beale and her daughter weren't the only ones observing the couple with keen interest.

Lord Harlington gave his order to the waiter in French, then turned back to Edmée, both seemingly unaware of the intense curiosity their presence provoked among the English travellers, not least because the morning papers had reported that the Marquis de Soule was dead. It was said that the marquis had died of a broken heart – looking at Edmée, it wasn't hard to imagine that might well have been the case.

'There's Colonel Fitzwilliam,' said Jocasta, relieved, and waved at her husband.

'Put your hand down; don't make such a spectacle of yourself,' said Mrs Beale.

The colonel, instead of walking straight to their table, stopped first to have a word with Lord Harlington. Eventually, he came over to where his wife and mother-in-law were seated and ordered, in French, two hot chocolates and a brandy.

'What were you doing talking to Lord Harlington and that trollop of his?' Mrs Beale inquired disdainfully.

She, unlike her daughter, had never encountered the arctic side of Colonel Fitzwilliam – until now. His words made her shrink back in her seat. 'Lord Harlington is one of the bravest men I have ever known; England owes him a great debt of gratitude. I was sent to Paris, madam, at the time of the Terror, to bring back vital information for Lord Grenville, the Foreign Secretary. I was arrested and found myself in La Force prison. I shared a cell with Lord Harlington, who volunteered to change places with me. I was freed, and he was tortured and spent a long time in prison waiting to be guillotined, until finally he was released. But unlike many men, he has never demanded any recognition for the sacrifice he made.'

With that, Colonel Fitzwilliam stood up and abruptly excused himself without waiting for his brandy.

'Where are you going?' said Mrs Beale. Colonel Fitzwilliam didn't answer and even forgot to say goodbye to his tearful wife. He walked away, his boots clicking on the wooden floor, a cold blast of air let in as he left the dining room. Only then did Jocasta notice that Lord Harlington and his wife were gone.

Duval and Edmée's arrival back at Muchmore was cause for the greatest of celebrations. Lady Harriet couldn't have been more delighted to see them. She couldn't remember Duval ever looking as content or happy as he did now. And as for Edmée, she was, in Lady Harriet's estimation, lovelier than she had ever been.

There was a lot the travellers had to tell and a lot more besides that they kept to themselves. There would be time enough to tell their stories in the years to come. Instead, they preferred to listen to all that had happened on the estate while they were away. Both were pleased to see that Miss Weeks had been the best of companions for Lady Harriet; Lady Harriet had absolutely no desire to let her go and live in a cottage on the estate. She said firmly that they had spent quite long enough living on their own; there was no need for it to go on indefinitely. 'No,' agreed Miss Weeks. Never had two women been better suited in knowing how to entertain the other. Miss Weeks added, 'It's to do with having a good sense of humour.'

Duval had kept in touch with Quinn, who was now married to Fleur and had two children. They lived just off Bloomsbury Square, and that year, they had welcomed the birth of a little boy, who they had christened Duval – *after all*, Quinn wrote, *Edmée is now three, and with a sister with that name, there was only one name for our son.*

Arabella's divorce had come through that year and she had found herself an Italian count younger than her by five years who owned a palazzo on the grand canal in Venice. As for her daughter, Fanny, she was sent to boarding school and near forgotten. Mr Gosling and his actress were married two days before the birth of their second son.

The news of the marquis's death had been well reported. Much had been made of his jewellery collection, and the incredible sums of money he had left to the Catholic Church and to the various charities supporting the émigré communities. The marquis's death meant that, at last, Duval and Edmée could make their union legal. The service took place on a Thursday at Muchmore with hardly any fuss, though Duval had asked Mr Gutteridge if he would like to attend the wedding. Lunch was served and extra pay was given to all the servants. After Mr Guttridge had left, Lady Harriet said, 'Well, at last we can settle down to living now,' which amused Edmée, as she had no idea what else they could possibly be doing.

They had barely been married a week when a parcel arrived one morning addressed to Lady Harlington.

Duval was due to meet with neighbouring landlords, but there was something about the parcel that made him stop.

Edmée looked up at him. 'It is from the Marquis de Soule's lawyer. I think I will open this later,' she said.

'Do you want me to read the letter?' Duval asked.

'Very well, yes, I do, though I am sure it is all going to be full of blame.'

Edmée studied Duval's face as he unwrapped the parcel and read the letter inside.

'Is it?' she winced.

'No,' he said. 'His solicitor has written that the marquis's will was read, and this parcel contains what he has left you. Along with this note.'

'Will you read it to me?' she said.

'*My dear Lady Harlington—*' Duval began.

'Wait,' said Edmée, 'he has addressed me as that? Can I see his writing?' She took no more than a glance. 'Yes, it is indeed his.'

'Shall I continue?' said Duval.

Edmée nodded.

My dear Lady Harlington, I was a flea that lived in a lioness's fur. I hadn't your courage, my failing. Will you forgive me?

'Is there more?' she asked.

'No,' said Duval, 'but there is the parcel.'

She opened it, and inside, there was a jewellery box. There could be no mistaking what was inside. The Eye of Envy.

She closed the box. 'I don't want this stone – it is cursed,' she said. Duval took it from her, opened the box again and studied it for a while.

He said, 'The emerald is believed to be the gemstone of the goddess Venus, said to bring good fortune and luck to its owner, to fend off danger, and to give protection against unfaithful lovers. Emeralds are known as a stone of intuition, of second sight and wisdom. They represent a deep and everlasting love. It is the softest and most precious of all gemstones. Tell me if I am not describing you, my love?' he said.

She rested her head on his shoulder.

'I would say this bride stone has found its way back to its rightful owner.'

Acknowledgements

NOVELS ARE hard to write. This one has been a bugger, but the strange thing about it is the characters never left me and have been willing to change and grow with every new version.

It is difficult when you lose your original editor. Rosie de Courcy retired before the book was finished. Usually that is a disaster of mega proportions and unfortunately it has happened to me more than once. But this time it was completely different. Six months later, the novel having been left dormant, the wonderful, and I don't say it lightly, brilliant Sophie Whitehead took over and pulled and pushed this novel, and me, into shape. With perseverance I rewrote most of it and I am eternally grateful for all her hard work and her many patient phone calls. I have also been very fortunate to have Katrina Harvey as my copy-editor.

A novel is not just down to one person. Though it starts out that way, I believe good writing needs a good editor who is prepared go into the novel and extract all those bits that you as an author might have found fascinating but bring the pace of the story to a halt. When written and edited, a team of people – cover designer, publicity, distribution, and many more – help get this book out to you.

A huge thank you to Catherine Clarke, my agent, who I would be lost without. I would also like to thank Jackie Bateman who helped me at the beginning of this book, and on the four previous versions.

I read my work out loud and I have to say a big thank you, with a mighty hug, to my sister in Melbourne, Lucy Gardner, who has patiently listened to four versions of this story, me reading in the evenings while she cycled to work in the mornings. Her suggestions and many questions helped shape the story. I also want to thank Lesley Lim, again for reading and listening, and Ali Caprio the same. Thank you to Jessie Price for the beautiful cover.

The London Library deserves a mention. It is a magical place to go and I always find books on the period of history I am writing about. The French Revolution never ceases to fascinate me, and I have over the years accumulated a small library of my own on the subject.

My reference for the wife sale came from Samuel Pyeatt Menefee's book *Wives for Sale*. To divorce a wife was beyond the pocket of most ordinary men, so the simplest thing to do was to sell her – a wife being chattel, no different from a cow or a sheep. It was illegal and it went against state and church. The last wife sale in England took place in Smithfield Market in the 1930s. It makes me feel grateful that we now have civil partnerships.

I spend a lot of my time alone in my room looking out at a wall. I have a painting that I rather like hanging above my computer. Every now and then, when wall and book defeat me, I trundle off with my laptop to Graze on Grand in St Leonards-on-Sea for a glass of pink fizz and to write with a different view.

Sparrow is my teacup Yorkie, my best-beloved one-eyed

wonder. In the morning she sleeps until 12:30, when she makes her appearance, looking as if she has walked through a bush backwards, her fur all standing up. That is the signal that she needs to take me out for a walk. She has kept me company while writing and has shown me East Sussex.

Finally, thank you to you, my reader. I hope you enjoyed this book.

I am delighted to write these words.

The End.

1 January 2025

About the Author

SALLY GARDNER gained a first-class degree at a leading London art college and became a successful theatre costume designer before illustrating and writing books. Her debut novel, *I, Coriander*, won the Nestlé Gold Award, and she is also a Costa and Carnegie prize-winner. Her books have been translated all over the world and have sold over three million copies.

Find Sally online at sallygardner.co.uk,
or on Twitter @TheSallyGardner.